Stefanie London is a *USA Today* bestselling author of contemporary romance and domestic suspense.

Her books have been called 'genuinely entertaining and memorable' by Booklist, and her writing praised as 'elegant, descriptive and delectable' by *RT Magazine*.

Originally from Australia, she now lives in Toronto with her very own hero and is doing her best to travel the world. She frequently indulges her passions for lipstick, good coffee, books and anything zombie related.

STEFANIE LONDON

THE VOW

avon.

Published by AVON
A division of HarperCollins*Publishers* Ltd
1 London Bridge Street
London SE1 9GF

www.harpercollins.co.uk

HarperCollins*Publishers*
Macken House, 39/40 Mayor Street Upper
Dublin 1, D01 C9W8, Ireland

A Paperback Original 2025
1
First published in Great Britain by HarperCollins*Publishers* 2025

A catalogue copy of this book is available from the British Library.

ISBN: 978-0-00-868830-1

Set in Birka by HarperCollins*Publishers* India

Printed and bound in the UK using 100% Renewable
Electricity at CPI Group (UK) Ltd

This book contains FSC™ certified paper and other controlled sources to ensure responsible forest management.

For more information visit: www.harpercollins.co.uk/green

To Sami, for a sibling relationship so strong and lovely it would never make for a good book.

Prologue

Sofia

As my hand settles on the doorknob an ominous feeling drifts through me, like the shadow from a cloud passing overhead. It's quiet. *Too* quiet. There should be something – footsteps, rustling. A sign of life. I press my ear to the door, straining to listen. But there's nothing.

'Shit.' I bounce impatiently on my toes, nerves gathering like a tight fist in my stomach. 'This can't be happening.'

I glance around to see if anyone has followed me, but the building is still. There's no one about. Outside even the rain seems to have ceased splattering the windows. It's almost as if the earth is holding its breath. Waiting. On the horizon past the lighthouse, clouds – real ones this time – gather in a thick cluster, blackened and heavy. Is the storm headed for us? Or will it drift right on by? It's hard to tell.

I gently ease down the handle, trying to be as quiet as possible. It's pitch-black inside the room and I feel like I'm stepping into someone's deepest, darkest secret.

There's so much to keep hidden.

'Hello?' I whisper.

The only answer is a deep, aching silence.

As I step forward my toe catches on something and I tumble into the darkened room, hands flying out to grab hold of something. Anything. I find purchase on a piece of furniture, jamming my hip against the sharp edge of what is probably a filing cabinet and wincing as the door swings shut behind me, plunging me into utter blackness. My phone clatters to the floor, making a loud noise.

'Fuck.' My hands are shaking. I can't see a thing.

There are no windows in this room. With the power out, my phone's torch is the only way I could possibly see anything. I'm frozen to the spot.

Panic courses through me like a drug and my breath comes faster, my imagination sketching monsters into the darkness. Memories. For a moment I wonder, breathless, if this is a trap. I shuffle forward, hands outstretched, until I find the wall.

'Hey?' My voice rises from a stage whisper to a hoarse plea. 'Are you in here?'

I shouldn't be here. I should have just left on my own. Saved myself.

How did it all go so wrong?

This was supposed to be a joyous occasion. A celebration. Tomorrow Ellie is due to walk down the aisle, looking every bit the rising starlet. The next Margot Robbie, according to the internet. Another gorgeous, sporty blonde Aussie to feed to the American masses. We're all here to witness it.

But everything has gone wrong.

I take another step and my foot shoots forwards, gliding on something slick. My grip on the wall isn't enough to keep me upright and I lurch, my back knee bending in a half split and slamming into the ground.

I gasp, clamping my eyes shut as white flashes of pain burst behind my shuttered lids.

It takes a moment to get out of the position, sliding my front leg back around and putting my weight on my uninjured knee, the other one pulsing with pain. My fingertips come away from the ground wet. I *still* can't see anything. My eyes are trying to adjust, but it's like a black hole in here. Gingerly, I rock back onto my toes and try to stand, uncertain on the wet ground with my impractically thin heels.

Suddenly there's a surge and a buzzing and the sound of electronic products beeping as the power comes back on.

I wish it hadn't.

A pool of red spills across the floor, a violent scarlet nightmare, and a body is crumpled at my feet. There's so much blood I can't tell where it has come from exactly, but it coats the front of the body, as well as my feet and my knees from where I fell, and I clamp a hand over my mouth without thinking to stifle a primal cry of horror. The metallic taste makes my stomach lurch, acid burning a trail up the back of my throat, and I throw my hand to one side, coughing and wiping my mouth on my other arm.

'Oh my God . . .'

The eyes are heavy-lidded, lips parted, and from the chin up nothing is out of place, not a hair nor an eyelash. They could be sleeping. Peaceful. Ready for a new day. I crouch down, panic crawling up my spine as I scan for signs of life. Movement of their chest. The twitch of a finger.

There's nothing.

Yet it isn't the poor person in front of me that has me taking a step back, the icy clutches of fear wrapped tightly around my throat.

It's the item lying next to the body – my Swarovski pen, covered in blood, the crystals weakly attempting to catch the light. My name is engraved on one side of the barrel, although it's impossible to see that now. The letters have been drowned out. Washed away. Now I notice where the blood is coming from. It's a small, round wound at the base of the neck. Blood oozes out.

'I'm sorry.' My lip trembles. 'I'm so sorry.'

It's just like the anonymous text message said: *You like vows, Sofia? Here's one for you: I vow to make you pay for what you did.*

I hadn't wanted to believe it was true. That someone was capable of this. That someone knew what really happened that day. But they do. And they're here. There are forty people on the grounds right now – thirty guests and ten staff.

And one of them is after payback.

SUNDAY

Chapter One

2024

Sofia

'Just watch the . . .' I press a fingertip to my temple and cringe as two men in black almost decapitate a swan ice sculpture as they carry a massive floral centrepiece through the vineyard's reception area. 'You break it, you bought it!'

One of the men mutters something sharp under his breath and the other chuckles as they continue on with the behemoth arrangement towards the bridal table. I cannot afford a headless swan. This wedding has been scheduled down to the minute, and there is zero – *zero!* – room for error.

Obviously, I have advised the bride that the centrepiece was too large for the table, but she has a very 'go big or go home' kind of attitude. It was evident during our first meeting when she could barely lift her hand due to the great honking diamond on her finger. Five *outrageous* carats. Putting my perfectionistic tendencies to one side, part of me is more than a little pleased that they're going to be picking native foliage out of their duck á l'orange tonight, because I love being proven right.

Fact is, I know weddings.

This past year alone I've planned weddings for a federal politician, a current affairs presenter, a Michelin-star chef, three current professional-level athletes – two footy players and a tennis player – and a former Olympian. I'm a semi-regular feature on the morning telly where I teach the public how best to splurge and save on their big day (tip: don't waste money on a pricey dessert buffet, just get a cake that people will remember). Not to mention I've been happily married to my soul mate for three blissful years.

See? I know weddings.

'Sofia?'

I snap to attention. 'Yes?'

The vineyard's event manager, Will, is standing in front of me. He's wearing a navy three-piece suit that's a work of art and Italian loafers without socks.

'What the fuck is with that centrepiece?' he says, keeping his voice low.

I catch a waft of his cologne – Sauvage, if I were to guess, with a hint of the expensive salon hair gel that keeps his artfully highlighted hair in place. Seriously, his hairdresser is a genius. It's a good thing Will married the guy, because a wizard like that is worth their weight in gold.

I stifle an amused smile at the look of disgust on his face. 'What about it?'

'They're going to have to trek through the bloody bush to find their entrees.' He tosses his hands into the air, a gold chain bracelet sliding down his wrist to hide beneath the cuff of his suit jacket as if wanting to escape this conversation.

'You know as well as I do that the bride won't actually eat today,' I reply, fluttering my fingers dismissively. 'Don't be ridiculous.'

Now it's his turn to stifle a smile. He folds his arms across his chest and leans in, gleeful. 'Probably for the best. That dress is going to show *everything*.'

'Right?' I lean closer, matching him. 'When she sent me the picture I had to stop myself from asking if she accidentally went to Agent Provocateur instead of a bridal boutique. It's obscene. She won't be able to wear underwear and unless she has a Brazilian right before the ceremony, the entire guest list is going to see her pubes.'

Will lets out a bark of a laugh and startles the guy carrying the next lot of table centrepieces into the room. 'Most wedding planners have a stick up their arse but you, my dear, are *fun*.'

My dirty little secret is that I dial up my persona to eleven for Will's benefit. Rule number one of being a successful wedding planner: you are not – I repeat *not!* – yourself. You are whatever the bride and the groom and the other key players need you to be in order for the wedding to go off without a hitch. Because *that* is what's most important. The perfect outcome. Not this 'be authentically yourself' Millennial #girlboss bullshit. And if getting people to do what I want was an elite sport, I'd be the Ian Thorpe of it – multi gold medallist in charming people into submission.

And making Will laugh now means he won't snark at my highly sensitive bride when she gets snippy about some silly little detail. One time he fabricated a 'double booking' when a bride pissed him off during a tasting – so I know he has a vindictive streak. Therefore, I need Will to be happy and I need my bride to be calm if today is going to go according to my perfect plan. If that means I need to lower myself to making an inappropriate joke at the expense of her pubic hair, so be it.

Call me a bitch, but I get shit done. Besides, what she doesn't know won't hurt her.

And speaking of getting people to do what I want . . .

'I'm glad you find me fun, Will.' I paste on my most winning smile. 'Because I need a favour.'

He heaves a dramatic sigh and rolls his hand around, granting permission for me to make the request.

'A bottle of the Shiraz Reserve from last year.' I hold up a hand as he begins to protest, my beloved Swarovski pen – rose gold and capped with glittering crystals, gifted to me by my parents when I signed my first ever wedding client – winks in the light. I've just finished making a manual adjustment to the night's run sheet. Old-school, I know, but there's nothing as satisfying as the scratch of pen over paper. 'I know you said it wasn't available for the menu, but surely you can spare one itty-bitty bottle for your favourite wedding planner. You know this place is the first one I recommend to my clients *and* I gave you the spotlight of all spotlights in that *Vogue Australia* article.'

He taps his foot and tuts. That's a good sign. Will doesn't give anything up easily, especially not a bottle of wine that cost as much as a designer handbag and is coveted by anyone who knows anything about wine.

'What do you even want with it?' he asks, turning his nose up. 'I've seen what you drink.'

Apparently enjoying the odd glass of merlot was a federal crime in these parts. It wasn't like I was drinking box wine or, God forbid, Yellow Tail. And while I might have grown up on the wrong side of the tracks, I certainly didn't stay there.

'It's not for me,' I say, upping the wattage on my smile. 'It's my father-in-law's sixtieth birthday next month.'

'I'll see what I can do,' Will replies with a sigh.

'You're a gem.'

'You'll owe me one. And I don't mean more referrals, because I can't keep up with those as it is. Although I wouldn't have said no if you'd brought me Ellie McLeod's wedding – I'm a little hurt you didn't think of us.'

Ellie McLeod is my best friend. Has been ever since we were kids. She's also now a legit A-list Hollywood celebrity.

'Ellie picked the venue, not me,' I reply, holding my hands up. 'I had no say in it, otherwise I would absolutely have suggested you guys.'

'*Where* could possibly be better than here?' Will looks affronted. 'Unless you're going to Bora Bora or something.'

We're not. In fact, we're going to the strangest possible place for a wedding . . .

An isolated lighthouse and crumbling groundskeeper accommodations in a place called Cape Turmoil. So romantic ... not. If she wasn't my best friend, I would have declined the job.

'We're staying local-ish,' I say cryptically. 'But I can't tell you where. It's top secret, sorry. Client's orders.'

I might have hurt my chances of getting a bottle of that wine, but there's only one circumstance in all the world where getting the outcome is second to being 'authentically me' and that's when it comes to Ellie. She's as close to me as the sister I once had but lost. She knows me better than my husband, Rob. Better than anyone.

And she's kept my darkest secret for years – I owe her my freedom. My life.

So Ellie comes first, no matter what.

'I forgive you this time. But I'll come knocking when the opportunity presents itself.' Will wriggles his fingers at me and then turns on the heel of a perfectly polished loafer.

I hope the wine is an acceptable gift, because my husband's family comes from a world that might as well be a solar system – or five! – from where I grew up. My in-laws totally think I married Rob for his money.

I didn't.

I married him because I fell inexplicably and illogically in love. But in their eyes I am, and always will be, little Sofia Concetta Quadrini from Lalor North, granddaughter of Italian immigrants who 'stole jobs from the real Australians', who went to a shitty public school and who sports a tacky tramp stamp on her lower back, proving how low-rent I really am.

Doesn't matter that I'm almost thirty and can stand on my own two feet – financially and otherwise. Doesn't matter that I make more money than my husband. Doesn't matter that I bend over backwards to make Rob happy. I bend over forwards whenever he asks, too. Because I love him and he loves me.

None of it matters to them.

But if there's one thing Rob's family underestimates about me, it's the lengths I will go to have the life I want. The lengths I *have* gone to. When I want something, I take it. Am I proud of what I've done? Not necessarily. But I understand what it's like to lose something precious and have no way of getting it back. To have joy and love ripped permanently from your hands. To be reduced to ash and bone and tears.

I'd rather get on with living my life and make the best of things.

By any means necessary.

When I pull my car into our street later that evening, I'm utterly exhausted.

The hardest part of my day is usually managing the people involved in the wedding. Today, the mother of the bride was trying to make last-minute changes behind her daughter's back and the bride herself had a complete meltdown because the tablecloths had some tiny hint of yellow – detectable only by her – that apparently clashed with her wedding dress.

Like I don't know the difference between cream and eggshell. I'm not an amateur.

A headache gathers steam, like an elastic band tightening around my head. I'm desperate to snuggle up on the couch and unwind because first thing in the morning, Ellie and I and our other friend, Rose, are heading to Cape Turmoil for Ellie's wedding. We're going early so we can spend time together, since our girls' trips are so few and far between these days.

But I haven't even thought about what to pack. It's going to be a long night making sure I have everything I need, with every contingency covered while ensuring I look my best.

As my house comes into view, I have a familiar little twinge of disbelief that I live here. Elwood is not a suburb I ever thought would be within my reach. Not in my wildest dreams. Dreams that weren't far-reaching enough to sketch out the large white rendered home with expansive windows and a garden landscaped by someone who now has a home reno show.

It's a far – *far* – cry from the house I grew up in, where the crowning adornments were two concrete lions guarding the cracked driveway and a print of *The Last Supper* hanging proudly in the front room. I wish my dad was still alive to see this place. He'd be so proud of the Italian marble we used in the foyer.

I pull into the garage, park the car and head through the door that leads directly into the house. Inside, I'm hit with a wave of sensation. The scent of rich beef and tomato sauce made with roasted garlic, onion, a touch of red wine, and herbs from the little garden that Rob tends to as if it were his child. No doubt the kitchen island will be dusted with flour from where he's made the pasta from scratch just the way Nonna taught him to.

Unlike his family, Rob has always taken an interest in my culture.

'That you, Sof?' comes the voice from the kitchen.

'Nah, I'm a burglar.'

His chuckle sends a shot of warmth through me. Rob's laugh is the thing that attracted me first – even before his vibrant blue eyes, which look so much like jewels that people often ask if they're contact lenses. It was the sound of him laughing at something, standing behind me so I couldn't see him, that cracked open the tender insides of my chest in a way no one had done before. How could anyone who laughed like that ever be a bad person?

I dump my bag on the floor and wander into the kitchen.

'Something smells incredible. I'm *starving*. The bride today was so high-maintenance that I didn't even get a chance to eat. I've been subsisting on Mentos all day.'

Rob stands at the stove, a large blue Le Creuset enamelled cast-iron pot sitting over a mild flame while he wades a wooden spoon through its contents. He's wearing a pair of dark jeans and a white Henley that shows off strong arms, over which is thrown a red apron with a floral trim that my nonna sewed for him.

He loves that bloody thing. Wears it proudly. It puts a smile on my face every time I see it because I remember my mother cringing when Nonna handed it to him, asking why she put flowers on an apron meant for a man. But Rob had bundled her into a hug, tears in his eyes, and told her it was the nicest present anyone had ever given him.

It's a legit miracle Rob didn't turn into an arsehole given the parents who raised him.

He reaches out and pulls me to him, arms encircling me, and I sag against his chest. Exhaustion fights against my need to perk up so I can complete my packing. Before I even have to open my mouth to ask, he reaches one hand out and jabs the power button for the espresso machine.

'Double?' he asks and I nod, resting my head against his chest and letting out a breath. 'How was the wedding?'

'Exactly what you'd expect,' I reply, pulling away and shooting my husband a knowing look. 'The bride wanted to make sure her wedding was bigger, better and shinier than her sister's wedding.'

'Ah, so the important things in life.' Rob shakes his head and his long, slim fingers handle the machine and my favourite porcelain espresso cup with care. 'I don't know how you can stand it.'

'Weddings?'

'More the fact that they aren't what weddings *should* be about.' He hits the button for a double shot and rich, dark liquid drips into the espresso cup. 'It's meant to be a celebration of two people sharing their lives, not about which bride and groom has the biggest cake and the most exclusive venue.'

Sometimes Rob forgets where he comes from. That these weddings are from *his* world, not mine. My parents got married in my grandparents' backyard, with the veggie patch in the background of the photos. Mum made her bouquet with flowers from the next-door neighbour's front yard, and my father wore a second-hand blue velvet disco suit that was at least a decade out of fashion. They danced *la tarantella* and cut a homemade ricotta cake and were happier than two people could ever hope to be. But it was a modest affair, like most things in my parents' lives.

Thinking about my dad causes a wave of sadness to wash over me. It kicks up the sediment of grief in my mind, like a wave disturbing the ocean floor. Grief for *all* the people our family has lost. The list is too long. But Rob doesn't seem to notice as he barrels on.

'Don't you ever want to work some normal weddings?'

he asks, handing the espresso cup to me and knocking out the coffee puck into the little bin we keep for compost. 'Where people are getting married because they love each other and not because they're trying to show off?'

'There's no money in that,' I say with a shrug. 'It's the showing-off part that makes people want to hire me.'

Most weddings I plan are designed for spreads in *New Idea* and for inducing gasps on social media and for making life seem larger and grander than it really is. It's not really about capturing the spirit of marriage. Because I know the truth.

No wedding could *ever* capture what it means to be married.

Besides, weddings are supposed to be fantasies. It's all about the one perfect day where people get to feel special and extraordinary. And for that one day people swallow their pride and sweep their troubles under a rug and they stuff the family skeletons back into their closets, all for a belief in happily-ever-afters. That's how it's supposed to be. Although unfortunately, every now and then, one of those skeletons refuses to stay in the closet. *Those* ones . . . well, that's the closest a wedding will ever get to revealing what marriage is truly about.

Keeping secrets. Hiding away the truth of who you are and what you've done, so your spouse can still sleep beside you at night.

Or maybe that's just me.

'I'm going upstairs to have a shower,' I say, leaning in to peck him on the cheek.

'I'll miss you.' He catches my chin with one hand and directs my kiss away from his cheek towards his mouth.

His lips are hungry, his tongue probing. I press against him, my body humming with desire.

I'd better pack quickly, so we can have some husband-and-wife time tonight before I collapse in a heap.

'It's not long,' I murmur against his lips. Rob is going to be joining us for the rehearsal dinner, the night before the wedding. 'Only one night.'

'Any time away from you is too long.'

'Sap,' I tease, pulling away.

'Go on, wash the stink of overindulgence off you. Dinner's almost ready.' He grins and turns back to the food, totally and utterly in his element.

I sip my coffee and thumb my phone as I head up to the bedroom. Fifty-three unread emails. Ugh. Because we're always busy executing weddings on weekends, my administrative assistant, Tiffani, doesn't manage the inbox on Saturdays and Sundays, so the emails always pile up. One catches my attention, a new Google review for my business.

I open it and follow the link. One star.

I blink, stalled in the doorway to my bedroom. One star? What the fuck . . . ?

> *I would never hire Sofia Quadrini for ANYTHING. She ruined what was supposed to be an incredibly special day for my husband and I, and no amount of money could ever compensate for that. Because of her, my father couldn't attend our wedding. Don't believe all these rave reviews. I'm sure she pays for them. It wouldn't be the first time she's done something unethical. That's the kind of person she is. Avoid at all costs.*

I'm shellshocked. For a full minute I stand there staring, unblinking, my brain scrambling to make sense of this vicious and false account of my services. The name on the review is Tegan Marshal.

The thing is . . . I've never planned a wedding for someone named Tegan.

MONDAY

Chapter Two

Ellie

Aussies going for gold! Ellie McLeod dazzles in Dior and Cate Blanchett is magnificent in Mugler.

Best-dressed beauties: Stone, Ferrera, Nyong'o, and McLeod top all the lists.

Watch this face: insiders say Ellie McLeod is on her way to stratospheric superstardom.

I lie curled up in my bed, cradling my phone as I scroll through the news. I know, I know, I know. Googling yourself is a bad idea. At best, it's vain. At worst, it's a recipe for self-loathing. Trust me, I don't exactly go looking for the dark, shady corners of the internet where people have something nasty to say. Although I suppose these days, nastiness isn't relegated to the corners, lurking in places like Reddit, 4chan, IMDb reviews and the comments section on YouTube, but rather everywhere, like a cancer that has spread beyond its original source.

The weeks after the Oscars is the one time I allow myself to google 'Ellie McLeod' without guilt. Especially when I know my stylist nailed it. Looking at pictures of myself on the red carpet almost feels like trying to piece together fragments of a dream. The night comes in flickers – camera flashes, stopping and posing, stopping and posing. Waving. Meeting people I've looked up to since I was a little girl gaping open-mouthed at movies on a TV smaller than most of today's computer screens. Cheering when I know the name of someone nominated. Jumping up if a friend or respected colleague wins their category.

Hoping I don't do something stupid and get turned into a meme.

Getting turned into a meme is *the worst*.

And sure there are a few fashion reports who say dressing in gold is tacky or obvious or even bad luck. *Please*. Like a little old statue is going to know what I wear. But for now, thankfully, the internet has been singing my praises and I'm letting my people-pleasing arse soak it all up. Gold star for me . . . no pun intended.

Besides, why shouldn't I relish the praise? I slogged my guts out the first few years I was in Hollywood, waiting tables by day and tending bar by night, squeezing in auditions between the two. Letting sleazy directors leer at my tits while I did the soul-destroying work of playing Sorority Hot Girl #3 or Sexy Jane Doe #2 on an episode of some short-lived *Law and Order* spin-off. I didn't know I was expected to be pretty while dead, but apparently that's a thing. I had a director demand one time that I 'be dead more attractively' while I was lying on the ground, smothered in fake blood and makeup bruises.

So why shouldn't I enjoy the little moments on the hard climb to the top?

My phone pings. It's a text from my fiancé.

MITCH: *Counting down until I see you. No delays for the flight so far, so we're looking good. I'll keep you posted xx*

I smile and send him a picture of me blowing a kiss, making sure the angle gets a good shot of my cleavage to show him what he's missing. I wish he were here now. But Mitch has his priorities. He's a professional golfer. Truthfully, for a long time I didn't even think golf should be considered a sport. To me athletes run and swim and lift heavy things, while he takes a nice walk in a park and stares at the grass before gently hitting a small ball into a hole. And it's not exactly hard yakka riding around in a little powered cart, now is it?

I would *never* say that in front of him.

Given the granddaddy of golf tournaments – the Masters – is coming up in a few months, he likes to play some of the smaller PGA tournaments beforehand to make sure everything is fine-tuned. I'd begged him to skip this one and come to Australia early. I haven't seen him in weeks and the last time we caught up we didn't even have sex because it was the night before a competition started. Like, seriously! We had *one* night together where our schedules let us be in the same place and his head was totally in the game.

What thirty-year-old guy has a fiancée raring to go and *isn't* jumping to take advantage of the situation?

A trickle of worry meanders down my spine. He isn't getting bored already, is he? We're not even married yet. Not for two more days. He can't have lost interest yet.

I hop out of bed and glance at myself in the long mirror propped against the wall, cringing at the dark circles under my eyes. I'll be thirty next month. That's almost ancient by Hollywood standards. In another five years I'll be stuck with 'mother' roles, rather than being a leading lady. Time's ticking. I have to hit my peak, stat. As soon as the wedding is done, I'm flying back to LA to start shooting a new movie. A big one with loads of potential!

But right now I have to finish packing and head to Sofia's house so we can start our road trip to the wedding venue.

I wander downstairs to make myself a green juice in the hopes it might help me shake the swirling cacophony of worries in my head. Making my juice always puts me in a good mood. Sofia thinks I've bought into 'Big Kale' but I swear drinking those things makes a *real* difference.

As I'm coming down the stairs, I hear a noise. 'Mum, is that you?'

'In the kitchen, darl.'

I find her standing by the stools that line the island, putting something into her handbag. There's a stack of mail sitting in a haphazard pile on the marble countertop, all the envelopes ripped open, leaving jagged little pieces of paper everywhere. She always opens my mail. I know Sofia and Rose find it weird – both her opening the mail and the fact that I haven't taken the time to switch to electronic bills – but if she didn't collect them and stick them right on the fridge, they probably wouldn't get paid. I'm useless, like that, when it comes to the mundane stuff. It just slips out of my brain.

'I wasn't expecting to see you this morning,' I say, leaning in to give her a peck on the cheek.

Mum is dressed in a perfectly matching Lululemon outfit – skin-tight leggings and a zip-up top with long sleeves despite the warmth. She's been obsessed with sun-protection for as long as I can remember, always fearful of getting spots and discolouration on her pale skin. She used to slather me in so much SPF when I was young that the other kids called me Casper.

I'm pretty sure she's been getting Botox too, because she looks much younger than her impending fifty-ninth birthday would suggest. Even more than I remember.

'I stopped by on the way home from the supermarket to make sure you're packed and ready to go,' she says.

That's fair enough. I am notoriously last minute with . . . well, everything. It gives Mitch hives when we travel together.

'Morgan came past last night to make sure I was all set,' I reply. Morgan is my assistant and she's the only reason I ever make my flights. In fact, she'd come around last night, looked utterly disgusted at my packing 'technique' – aka tossing everything in haphazardly without thought to wrinkles or order – and had swiftly repacked my suitcase. She'd also steamed my wedding dress and rehung it in the garment bag. Bless her.

'Thank goodness,' Mum says with a cheeky smile. 'Otherwise who knows what state I would have found you in this morning.'

'Love you too, Mum.' I roll my eyes.

'Oh, and your mail is here. Your phone bill is overdue – this was a reminder, so make sure you don't forget it. And it looks like you haven't checked the mailbox since you've been back,' she admonishes, gesturing to the pile. 'I tossed the advertising rubbish. You need to get Morgan to spray the letterbox, too. The bugs have taken over.'

Supporting her assertion – both that I leave my mail too long and that there were bugs in the letterbox – the envelopes are textured and riddled with holes. I mean, to be fair, I've only been back in Australia for a few days so the bugs must have been there prior to that. But there's no sense arguing. Mum knows best.

And I hate conflict, so I keep my mouth shut.

'I'll pop this here so you don't forget,' Mum says with a nod, using a magnet to hold the phone bill reminder to the fridge. I'll ask Morgan to take care of it when she arrives. Maybe I need to formally add 'bill management' to her job description.

'Thanks, Mum,' I say, leafing through the remainder of the mail. There's a credit card statement, my new Medicare card, a toll invoice and something from the government. Nothing interesting, which is why I always end up leaving them sitting there too long. I just can't seem to force myself to do things that are boring.

Don't ask me the last time I ironed something.

'Almost ready to go to Sofia's?' Mum asks. 'I can drive you.'

'That's okay. I need to have breakfast first and then Morgan has offered to take me – she has a lash appointment close by.'

Mum nods. She seems . . . flat.

I know the wedding is weighing on her.

Mum thinks all marriages are doomed because her own failed in a spectacular fashion. But the truth is, she and my dad were never meant to be together. They only got married because she accidentally fell pregnant with me and Gran was a strict Catholic who wouldn't stand for her daughter giving birth out of wedlock. They were never happy as a couple. Mum has high expectations and spends money like water and my dad is the kind of bloke who thinks a man should control everything. They used to scream at each other all the time. The days the credit card bills came were always the worst.

It's why I hate conflict.

When Dad eventually left us, Mum lost the plot. It was a hard time. I had to go live with Sofia's family when I was in year eight, because Mum would forget to buy groceries and refuse to take me to school, saying she couldn't get out of bed. The Quadrini family took good care of me. So I don't share Mum's view that all marriages are doomed, because Sofia's parents were the most in-love people I'd ever seen. And Sofia and Rob are just like them.

I want Mitch and I to be happy like that, too.

'Are you okay, Mum?' I ask as I head over to the fridge to pull out the ingredients for my green juice.

'Of course – my baby girl is getting married. I'm over the moon.' She smiles.

Lies, lies, lies. All of it.

'I just have a lot on my mind, you know. It's hard work being the mother of the bride.' She nods. 'Finding the perfect outfit and getting my hair touched up and nails and makeup and shapewear. Oh, the shapewear! I need to get to David Jones tomorrow. I want some of those Kardashian things that are supposed to flatten your tummy.'

She pats her non-existent stomach. When it comes to

Mum, the more she speaks the harder she's trying to hide her feelings. I know she's not happy about the wedding.

'Are you sure, Mum?' I ask, peering at her closely. 'You can tell me.'

'Are *you* sure, darling? It's never too late to change your mind.'

I knew this was coming. We've had this conversation several times now – marriage is a risk, a fool's errand. Men want to take me away from her. From my home. What if I forget all about her? Who will she have then? She'll be alone in the world.

I'm toying with a hangnail on the side of my thumb and I bring it up to my mouth to chew. Only Mum's sharp look makes me drop my hand back down – nail biting is a disgusting habit. I don't know why I do it. Any time there's friction with people I love, it's like I have this compulsion to bite at myself. To make myself bleed.

But I can't have ragged hands for my wedding. That would be unbecoming.

'I love Mitch,' I say. 'I'm not going to change my mind.'

She looks at me, her mouth opening like she wants to say something. But eventually she just nods, averting her eyes. 'Well, don't forget about your dear old mum then, eh? Once you're a married lady, I mean. Don't forget about me.'

'As if I would forget about you!' I tsk. 'Don't be silly.'

I can tell my words don't soothe her, but she's going to drop it.

Nothing I say seems to ease her fears.

'Oh, and Ellie darling. I had a favour to ask,' she adds.

I don't respond as I pry the kale leaves from their thick,

fibrous stalks. She's going to ask for more money. I can feel it in my bones. The requests are increasing in frequency. When my career started taking off, she asked for reasonable things like a new fan belt for her car. Instead of fixing that old rust bucket, I just bought her a new one. She was my mother, after all, and she'd spent a good chunk of her life driving me around for school and auditions.

I owed her that much, at the very least.

Then it was a 'loan' to pay an unexpectedly high electricity bill. I told her not to worry about paying me back. Then her landlord increased her rent and I'd just signed my first big box-office deal, so I bought her a house in a better neighbourhood and hired someone to help her decorate.

That was last year.

But the requests keep coming. Flights to Paris with her sister, a holiday to some exclusive resort in Thailand, a Chanel handbag that she just *had* to have, a monthly stipend to cover 'maintenance' like pedicures and manicures and getting her hair done. Then the car wasn't driving 'smoothly' enough. She wanted an upgrade. And she wanted to remodel the bathrooms and kitchen in her new house. Then she wanted a boob job, just like I'd had. Why should I get all the fun?

Sofia keeps telling me I need to set boundaries. But what can I say? She's my mother and I love her. She worked hard for years so I didn't have to miss out on school trips and acting classes. I'd never have made it this far without her.

I owe her everything.

'Ellie?' she asks, tentative.

It occurs to me that I haven't responded yet, too lost in

my own mounting worry about our relationship and her spending habits. I continue to tear the leaves off the kale stalks. 'Yeah, sorry. Big night last night. What do you need?'

'Do you think Joe would be able to take me out to Geelong next weekend? Bernadine is having her sixtieth at some yacht club out there and it's a bit of a drive, especially at night on the way back. You know my eyesight isn't what it used to be.'

My shoulders almost sag in relief. 'Of course. Just text him and make sure he's free. He can bill my account.'

'Thanks, darling.' She's next to me suddenly, hand on my shoulder and the waft of her perfume – still the same one she wore when I was a little girl – comforts me. At least *that* hasn't changed. She kisses my cheek and I feel like an absolute arsehole for making assumptions about her intentions.

Is it really *so* bad that she wants me to support her after all the years she supported me? It's not like money is a problem anymore. I mean, I still have bills and being part of Hollywood is expensive. And there's a lot of pressure to be perfect. To look perfect.

But last year I had more success than ever before and it's all because of Mum. An excited flutter in my gut tells me I'm going to do even better this year. I'm almost itching to get the wedding over with so I can start shooting the project that is going to push me a couple of rungs up the ladder of silver-screen success. *Heartland*. It's big. *Big* big. An Oscar-bait all-female production – female director, female screenwriter, female lead actress (that's me) and a story based on a woman who defied the odds. I salivated when I first saw the script.

This could be my ticket to a little gold statue and then I won't have to worry about anything ever again.

'I love you, sweetie. I'm so very proud of you.' She squeezes me and we stand there, in the quiet kitchen, just the two of us like it's been the vast majority of my life. I lean my head against hers for a moment. I'm shunted back into the past, wearing my checkered school uniform dress and crying on her shoulder when the girls were mean to me at school. She was always there for me and now I need to be here for her. 'Make sure you don't forget about your poor mother once you have a husband.'

'Don't be ridiculous,' I reassure her. 'I love Mitch, but being married to him takes nothing away from our relationship. You'll always be my mum.'

'And you'll always be my little possum – no matter how famous you get.' She straightens herself up and has a little shake as though trying to let go of something. 'Okay, I'll leave you to finish getting ready. What time is Morgan coming past?'

I glance at the clock hanging on the wall. 'Any minute now.'

'Say hi to the girls for me. I can't wait to see them all grown up. It's been so long!'

'I will.'

'Good.' Mum nods, blond ponytail bobbing. 'I'll see you tomorrow evening for the rehearsal dinner.'

She breezes out of the house, leaving a pink cloud of scent behind her.

I continue to prep my juice, stripping down the leaves, dancing all the while to get my blood pumping. Energy skitters through me as I chop the cucumber, peel the orange and dice up some of the ginger and whiz it all up with coconut water.

I'm dancing around to 'Toxic' by Britney Spears as I hear the front door go. My assistant, Morgan, appears a moment later, her eyes crinkled in amusement. 'Those are some *moves*. You practising for the first dance?'

Her sunshine blond hair is pulled back into a messy bun, though half of it seems to have fallen out around her face and down against her neck – a sign that she's been up a while. The girl is a certified workaholic. She's skipped wearing her contact lenses on account of having her lash extensions refilled today and now a chunky pair of black frames have slid halfway down her nose. They make her look studious and capable, older than her twenty-three years.

I snort. 'Yeah, like Mitch would let me have "Toxic" for the first dance.'

'Going with "Genie in a Bottle" then?'

I grin. 'You know all my favourites.'

'I love the y2k revival. And I'm your number-one fan, remember? It's my job to know *everything* about you.' Morgan winks. 'Like, the fact that you definitely forgot to pack your pill last night even though I reminded you, like, three times.'

'Shit!' I bound off towards my ensuite bathroom because I have, indeed, forgotten to pack my contraceptive pill. And there are no pharmacies close by in butt-fuck nowhere coastal Victoria, where I'm getting married. The last thing I need is an unwanted wedding-night *oopsie*.

'You're welcome,' she calls after me.

'Seriously, I have no idea what I would do without you,' I

say as I return, pill sleeve in hand. I tuck it into the interior pocket of my weekend bag, which sits – stuffed to the brim – by the front door.

'You didn't try the dress on again, did you?' Her eyes narrow at me.

I got a lecture last night because I keep trying it on and putting wrinkles in the delicate satin. But I'm just so excited about getting married, I can't help myself. I was that kid who always sneaked a peek at her Chrissy presents, leaving little telltale tears in the wrapping paper around the strips of sticky tape. Willpower is not my thing.

But this time, I'd heeded her lecture.

'I left it alone,' I reply proudly. 'I didn't even open the zip after you closed it back up last night.'

'Good. I'll bring the steamer anyway,' she says, lifting the garment bag delicately off the doorway it's currently hanging from, handling it with as much care as if it were made entirely of priceless diamonds.

I mean, it's Monique Lhuillier, so it's not far off.

'I'm sure Sof will have all that stuff.' I take a long pull on my juice, already feeling the healthy ingredients perking me up. 'She's a pro.'

'Doesn't hurt to have two people trying to cover all the bases,' Morgan says sagely. 'That way nothing will slip through the cracks.'

'True.' I nod. 'I'm lucky to be surrounded by such organised people. I couldn't do this on my own.'

In fact, I'm pretty sure if it wasn't for Sofia and Morgan, I probably would have suggested that Mitch and I elope. Weddings are *so* much work. And boring work, too. Like decisions and budgets and silly unimportant details like what shade of white goes with my dress. Who cares? It all looks the same to me. It's just lucky that my best friend is a genius with weddings and I have an assistant who's always ready to get her hands dirty with whatever I need. Add to that a fiancé who loves me wholeheartedly despite my flaws, and I'm pretty much the luckiest woman alive.

Some days, when I remember what I have done, I don't think I deserve it.

Chapter Three

Rose

My hair is still damp when my husband shouts my name from the front of the house. It's time to go and . . . I'm a mess. I want nothing more than to shrug on a cosy pair of pyjamas and crawl into bed with a glass of red wine and a guilty pleasure book. I know I should be excited. Getting to stay at some accommodation that belongs to a famous Hollywood director and hanging out with my closest friends *is* exciting. We don't see each other often enough these days.

But if I'm being honest, I'm okay with not seeing them *all* the time. I'm not sure my ego could handle it, to be honest. Ellie was on the cover of *Sports Illustrated* last year, for crying out loud! And Sofia has her blossoming wedding planning career with a regular column in *Vogue Australia* and appearances on *The Morning Show*.

Meanwhile, I'm a mum.

I'm the only one of the three of us who went down the traditional life path of settling down to raise a family. It's the life I want. The life I've wanted desperately since I was a little girl making my dolls shack up together. At least, that's what I tell myself.

Truth is, when I was young I had another dream. A dream that I was fighting tooth and nail for . . . a dream that turned to dust in my hands.

And while *I* know what an important job it is to raise a small human – I adore my son and love being his whole world – I'd be lying if I said I didn't feel a little insignificant next to my friends who are 'doing something' with their lives. Sometimes I wonder if they think I've fallen short of my potential. I could have been an Olympian. I could have been . . . more.

On the bed my phone lights up with yet another message. The family group chat is blowing up.

DAD: You make us so proud, my darling girl. Congratulations. You deserve it.

MUM: What an honour. When do we get to see you on the TV again??

AUNTIE LINH: Did you call the family back home? They'll be thrilled.

UNCLE TIM: I wonder if the guy at the pub will give me a free beer because I'm related to an Aussie legend. Worked when you won gold! Great job, Lily. We're proud of you.

I swallow back a wave of blistering, caustic emotion. Jealousy. It's the ugliest one of all, and when it comes to my twin sister I can't help but let it boil over. I'll leave it until tomorrow before I respond, even though I know the whole family will judge me for it. Especially her. They assume I should be ready at all times to pick up the phone because what could *I* possibly have to keep me busy? Just my boring, ordinary life.

Not like Lily, multi gold medallist. Now official torch bearer for Australia in the next Olympics. My twin sister. The golden child who has the dream I once clutched tightly in my fist as her everyday reality.

'Rose!' Malachi calls. 'Get that lovely arse out here. It's time to go.'

I've put on skinny jeans – the ones with a ton of stretch since they're the only non-maternity jeans that fit right now – and I've thrown a loose, flowing blouse over the top to hide my stomach. According to TikTok, skinny jeans are totally out of fashion. Cheugy, I think they called it. Twenty-nine and I'm already behind the times. But these are literally the only pants with a waistband I can stand if I'm expected to sit and eat. I stuff my feet into a pair of flats and grab my handbag and phone from the bed, feeling frumpy and dissatisfied.

'Old age is a blessing not everybody receives,' Mum said on her fifty-fifth birthday a few months back, beaming over a cake stuffed full of blazing candles. Easy for her to say, she's fitter than most thirty-somethings from the three different types of sports she plays. 'And competition keeps me young.'

Welcome to the theme of my childhood. Unfortunately, when there's a winner, there's also a loser.

'Coming!' I yell back, tossing my phone into my bag without reading the messages that continue to light up the screen.

'There you are.' Malachi beams as I finally make it out of the bedroom and into the living room. 'I was starting to think we'd need to send the search party.'

He's dropping me off at Sofia's – since she's driving our

little group to Cape Turmoil – and then he's off to work for the day. That means we need someone to look after our son, Isaac, until he gets home. Usually Mum and Dad would be happy to take him, but they're off on a hiking trip with friends.

'Sorry, I was running a bit behind,' I mumble.

He's standing with our babysitter, Ash, who holds my little boy, bouncing him gently in her arms while she looks up adoringly at my husband. I can't blame her. Malachi has women looking at him wherever he goes. He's tall, broad and strong, with smooth dark brown skin, a brilliant smile and eyes that are so deep and piercing it feels like he can look into your soul. The sexy British accent doesn't hurt, either. Some days I wonder how I got so lucky.

And if I'll *stay* lucky.

I instinctively squeeze my eyes shut and rub at my temple to block out the image of the woman wearing a skimpy string bikini I'd found on his phone last month. All sun-bleached blond hair and naturally perky tits and abs so tight you could bounce a tennis ball off them. The very opposite to my soft, lumpy post-partum body. It's almost like he was trying to find someone diametrically opposed to me.

It's nothing, Rose. Just a dirty picture on the internet. Why are you making a mountain out of a molehill, love? You know you're my number one.

'Thanks for coming, Ash,' I say, forcing a smile. 'Let me give my little man a kiss goodbye.'

She dutifully holds Isaac out, whose stocky arms immediately shoot towards me. His grabbing hands are puffy and dimpled and I smile, cradling him to my chest and sticking my lips to his head so I can breathe him in. I know that milky baby scent is long gone by now – he's six months next week – but there's still something about the scent of him that fills me with a warm, humming sensation.

Your life might not be 'exciting' but it's meaningful. That has to count for something.

'Are you going to be good for Ash today?' I run my fingers over his head, touching the dark curls blossoming there. He's got his father's hair – though Malachi shaves his curls right down – as well as his long, luscious eyelashes and full lips. There's a hint of my Chinese heritage – on Mum's side – in the low bridge and softly rounded tip of Issac's nose. But he's got my smile. It's a little gummy, but it's wide and genuine and my baby boy smiles readily. 'There's a bottle prepared for his next feed in half an hour, and the formula is on the bench. He's been fussing a bit during feeds lately. You've got our numbers, right? Both of them?'

'Yes, Mrs Harris.' Ash nods, smiling patiently.

'And you know to call triple 0 if there's an emergency, right?' I ask.

Ash's expression shows some confusion. 'Well, yeah. Of course.'

'It's just I read an article that said young people watch so much American TV some of them dial 911 instead and . . .' I shake my head. 'Never mind. Okay, there's money for pizza on the kitchen bench in case Malachi is home from work late this evening. You can keep the change.'

Malachi leans in and places a hand gently on my hip. 'I told her, Rose. We've covered everything.'

I swallow, nodding and still holding my little boy. Isaac gurgles in my arms, squirming and looking back around at

Ash, then to Malachi. His thick eyelashes touch innocently as he blinks, taking in his surroundings. I don't want to let him go. This is my first time being away from him overnight. It hurts, like I'm breaking some tether between us.

'We should get going,' Malachi says, nudging me. 'Otherwise I'll be late.'

Ash holds out her hands and I hesitate.

She's nineteen, technically an adult, and she has the day off from university. She's a good student, responsible. We've had her over twice before to babysit for shorter periods, like when Malachi took me out for my birthday to a nice restaurant down the road. We were only gone a few hours and I'd had my phone on the table the whole time, checking it every few minutes, terrified something would happen.

I don't think I even tasted the food. And yes, I killed the romantic buzz.

Since then, he hasn't pushed for another date night. On one hand, it's a relief. On the other, I'm worried he secretly thinks I'm being ridiculous. Frankly, I'm not sure I'd blame him for feeling that way. When the invite came to spend a night with the girls ahead of the wedding, it was only my deeply entrenched FOMO that had me agreeing to leave Isaac. I couldn't stand the thought of Sofia and Ellie getting to hang out without me.

'Is everything okay?' Ash asks. Her delicate eyebrows knit with concern in a way that makes me want to lash out at her.

She's far too young, too pretty. She's got small perky boobs and a waist that dips inward where mine puffs out. The woman across the street, Almeida, made a comment the other day how she'd never let a young girl like Ash into the home. Too risky.

'You know what men are like,' she'd said, rolling her eyes.

But Malachi *isn't* like that. I'm sure of it. He's a wonderful father and husband, a caring brother to his siblings and a doting son to both his parents and mine. It's why I'm so terrified of losing him, because I know I've hit the jackpot. But why can't I seem to get my head together when it comes to letting him touch me? I know I'm pushing him away.

That's probably why he's looking at pictures of half-naked women online. I know he's . . . taking care of his own needs right now.

What if he decides to let Ash take care of his needs tonight?

'Rose.' Malachi's voice pulls me out of my thoughts and I reluctantly hand Isaac over to Ash. His flat little nose wrinkles in confusion and his head swings back to me. Oh dear, the waterworks are coming. 'Let's go.'

Malachi ushers me out of the house as the wailing starts, knowing the longer I listen to those pained cries the higher the chance that I'll bail on the whole thing. He's right.

I'm tense the entire trip over to Sofia and Rob's place, and when we pull up Malachi lets out a long, low whistle. He hasn't been here before. Usually, when we catch up as couples, it's at a restaurant halfway between our homes.

'It's a right fucking palace, innit?'

Normally when he says 'innit' it makes me laugh, but not tonight. I feel strangely wound up about this trip. Strangely on edge.

I'm toying with my phone, having kept it in my hands the entire journey from Narre Warren North to Elwood.

There are some big homes where we live – but they're definitely more of the mass-produced kind. In fact, Sofia made a joke one time about all the 'McMansions' in our area, saying if she'd had to stumble home drunk during her university days she would surely have gone to the wrong house, because they all look the same.

Well, not everyone can afford a custom architecturally designed palace in one of the most expensive suburbs in the state.

'Must be compensating for something.' Malachi winks at me and I feel a familiar flutter low in my belly as I look at my husband.

It's been far too long since we had sex. My body has become a source of discomfort and shame lately and I don't know how to fix it. To think at one time it used to be a temple of performance. Now there are marks, scars, bits that haven't gone back to where they used to be. I haven't dared try to put on bathers, much less a bikini, and I haven't felt at all like me since before I got pregnant.

Malachi has been gloriously patient. I love him more than anything. I really need to show him that with more than words . . . soon.

'Be nice,' I warn, swatting at his leg playfully. 'And yes, they're probably compensating for something.'

'Would you rather that? A giant house and a husband with a small dick?' He shoots me a mischievous look and I roll my eyes. I know he's just saying this to make me laugh. Despite having a humble job working in warehousing for a white goods company, I doubt there's ever been a day where my delightfully confident husband felt less than worthy. 'You *would*, wouldn't you?'

I laugh. 'Stop it.'

For a moment the banter makes me forget about the dirty photo, but then the image pops back into my head like a fly that won't stop pestering me. I want to swat it away, but it keeps coming back, drawn to my sweat and my scent, uncaring of my mounting frustration. I swallow. I can't let it get to me, because if I even exude a hint of annoyance towards Malachi then Sofia will catch on like an airport drug detection dog sniffing out someone's party stash.

And I hate looking like a fool around her.

We park our car on the street and head to the door, Malachi carrying my small suitcase and me with a large tote bag filled to the brim with snacks and wine and some card games and a book. I'm not really sure what amenities this place is going to have, so I've packed a little bit of everything.

'Are you sure you're okay to bring all of Isaac's stuff?' The boys are coming tomorrow, and I've already packed everything that Isaac might need. It's more luggage than Malachi and I will both take.

But babies need a lot of stuff! There are nappies, extra changes of clothes for when he makes a mess, bottles and baby formula, and books and toys and blankets and medicine and—

'Do you mean am I capable of transferring the already-packed bags from our bedroom to the boot of a car?' Malachi asks drily. I can't tell if he's annoyed or just teasing me.

'Don't be like that.' I frown. 'I just want to make sure this all goes smoothly. It's our first time away with Isaac and I would have liked to be there for when you leave, but Sofia was insistent we girls go early and—'

'You're spiralling,' he says gently.

I have a tendency to do that sometimes. Frequently. More frequently since I became a mum. It's like bringing a baby into the world has heightened my ability to see all the things that could possibly go wrong in any given situation. I was born that way – a stress head, people have called me. But now it's even worse.

'Everything will be fine, Rose. I promise.' He looks me in the eyes and I feel my heart rate start to slow. Malachi has that effect on people. He's funny, relaxed, charming. It puts people at ease. 'And if something is forgotten, Isaac will be okay. There are plenty of babies who survive with a lot less than what he has.'

I suck in a breath and nod as I push the doorbell. He's right. Everything will be okay.

There are footsteps inside and suddenly the door swings open. It's Sofia. She scoops both Malachi and I up in one tight group hug and makes a little squealing noise that feels like it might burst my eardrum. I know Malachi will have to stop himself rolling his eyes – he thinks Sofia is a bit fake.

'It's been *forever!*' she says, pulling back.

This is one of those aspects of being in a group of girlfriends I always secretly loved, even though I feel like that would be pretty cringe to admit out loud. You know that thing, when girls run screaming towards one another on the first day of school as if they didn't have a sleepover just the week prior. They're all air-kisses and high-pitched noises and colour and praise.

I like it.

It's nice to be included. To be missed. To be one of the girls.

'Is Isaac off with Grandma and Grandpa today?' Sofia asks.

'Nah, they're away at the moment. We've got a babysitter today.' I shift on the spot, tugging at the hem of my blousy top. 'One of the neighbour's girls. She's very responsible.'

'Oh that's good. I was worried you might not make it.' She smiles.

I'm not sure Malachi catches the little barb under her words, but I do. I missed her birthday party last month. I just couldn't leave Isaac. He'd had a rough night and a rougher day to follow, and he'd cried so much he made himself throw up. I'd sent a hurried text, very last minute, lying and saying the sitter cancelled.

I think she knew I'd fibbed. She doesn't understand what it's like, since she's never had – nor wanted – kids of her own. When they're so little, you're their whole world. Their safety net. Their protector. It's not easy to leave them behind . . . and for what? A party full of hoity-toity Elwood types with their fancy cars who would probably look down their nose at my unfashionable outfit and Malachi's blue-collar job.

But still, Sofia can hold a grudge about stuff like that. It's easier to lie.

'Ellie's already here.' Sofia gestures. 'Let's get this party started.'

'I'll leave you ladies to it.' Malachi leans down and gives me a kiss on the cheek. 'I've got to get to work.'

As I see Malachi out and close the door, Ellie materialises from somewhere inside the house.

'Rose!'

For a moment I barely recognise her. Long blond hair tumbles down her back in effortless loose curls. That can't *all* be her real hair, can it? Her skin is perfectly clear, limbs slender and long – the awkward gangiliness of her youth morphed into statuesque elegance – and her other 'flaws' have magically been taken care of. The ears that earned her horrible nicknames like Dumbo and Dobby in high school have been delicately pinned back, her formerly surfboard-flat chest enhanced with a convincing set of C-cups a few years back and her cheekbones are so sharp I wonder if she had that buccal fat removal procedure I read about online.

Or maybe it's just a good contour stick at work. I'll have to ask for some tips.

She rushes over with the energy of someone who works out regularly and sucks down a litre of green juice every morning. When she envelops me in a great big hug, I am eye level with her boobs because of our significant height difference. I'm not short, by any means, but Ellie is taller than most of the men I know.

'Are you trying to make me motorboat you?' I squeeze her back.

'Gotta get my money's worth.' She winks. 'It's *so* good to see you. It's been way too long! You look fabulous.'

I don't. I'm exhausted and it shows, but I don't want anyone to see my raw, frayed edges. 'Mum says this top makes me look like a peasant.'

Ellie snorts. 'You know I love your mum. But a fashionista she is not.'

'And you . . .' I take a step back, holding her hand and making her twirl, which she does with a smile on her face. 'Hollywood looks good on you.'

'I'm glad you think so, because I feel like the pace has aged me a decade.' She laughs.

'Try having a baby,' I quip and out of the corner of my eye I'm sure I catch Sofia shaking her head. Or maybe I'm just being paranoid.

'Let's get everything into the car,' Sofia says. There are bags piled up by the door that leads to the garage and I roll my suitcase forward. Ellie has a Gucci overnight bag slung over one shoulder. I wonder if she got it for free.

That stuff happens when you're famous, right?

'Do you start shooting right away when you get back after the wedding?' I ask as we filter into the enormous garage where a big, shiny four-wheel-drive Mercedes sits. It's black and so clean I could do my makeup in the reflection off the paint. 'I know you were really excited about this next project.'

'I am!' Ellie nods enthusiastically. She shifts her position frequently, switching from putting her weight on one side and then the other side. Tapping her foot. She's a bundle of energy, like always. 'It's such a different experience working with a female director. I have more input, more say. It's a really collaborative experience. And if I have to get my tits out, there's a reason for it, you know?'

I wonder how her fiancé – soon to be husband – copes seeing her body naked on screen and knowing there's probably a load of teenage boys wanking off to her. Ellie hasn't done *loads* of nudity, but it seems to be a staple for young, gorgeous actresses earlier in their careers. Her second year working in LA she did a *Game of Thrones*-esque fantasy mini-series, where they had her butt naked wearing nothing but a gold harness and a merkin. She said it was horribly uncomfortable, the way the director leered at her. But what could she say? When that was the only job on offer, she had to take it.

And it had ultimately led to better things.

'What else has she done?' I ask, hefting my bags into the back where there's space. If I thought I'd gone overboard with the snacks, then Sofia has packed an express supermarket!

'She's done a few art-house movies, an Austen adaptation and she did that series with the BBC about the MI6 agent who goes rogue after her daughter is killed. God, what was it called?' She snaps her fingers. 'It was really bloody good.'

I try not to cringe. I know exactly which one she's talking about, because I couldn't get through the first episode. Ever since I became a mother, anything with harm coming to a child makes me feel ill.

Thinking of that makes my hand twitch and I want to reach for my phone to make sure Ash hasn't tried to call or text. I try to inconspicuously reach for the zip on my bag and drag it open enough to slip my hand inside. Ellie is talking like she does – a million miles a minute – and if she notices me sneaking a look down at my phone she doesn't mention it.

There are no calls or texts from Ash, thankfully. But there *is* a text on the screen. My blood runs cold. It's from a name I'd hoped never to see again.

JAMIE: Hi Rose, I heard that your sister has been

announced as torch bearer. That's great news. The paper wants me to do a piece on it and the editor won't sign it off unless we cover some of the history. Any chance you'd be open to providing a quote? I'll give you a call later. It would be great to get a bit of a 'where are they now' comment. Might be a good chance to show the world you're doing well and that you've moved on.

Moved on? How would anyone think it was possible to move on from a scandal that took place in front of the entire world and ripped everything I'd ever worked for to shreds? To move on from a family shame so deep that my own mother has banned anyone from mentioning it in her house? A shame so deep she told me that if I let *60 Minutes* interview me, like they desperately wanted to, that I would be cast out of the family?

No one moves on from something like that.

Chapter Four

2013

Sofia

We're sitting on the brick wall before school starts, the three of us – me, Ellie and Rose. It's the last week of term one and things are already – *already!* – going to shit. How has it happened so quickly? Every day I think about how I can't wait to get out of this place and on to bigger and better things. I know the others feel the same. We talk about it a lot.

'Why do you think they haven't invented time machines yet?' Ellie asks out of the blue, almost as if she's reading my thoughts. Her feet swing, the heels of her black school shoes bumping against the brick wall in a rhythmic staccato. One of her laces is undone and her blond hair is pulled back into a loose plait, the sides carefully styled to hide her ears because the girls in the popular group always call her 'Dumbo'.

I happen to like Ellie's ears. I think they're cute.

But if they're not picking on her ears, they're calling

her 'stretch' or 'Lurch' or 'man hands'. Personally I think Ellie looks like a model and her hands aren't even *that* big. The girls at school are just jealous that she's going to be a famous actress one day and Ellie is too soft to stick up for herself. Lucky she has me to do it for her. I'll put all those bitches – every single one of them – in their place.

'Having a time machine would be *so* cool,' Ellie adds with a sigh. 'We could get out of here right now.'

'Time travel violates the second law of thermodynamics,' Rose replies. She stinks like chlorine, even though she always washes her hair after swimming practice. It's like the chemicals have seeped deep into her skin so that she'll always smell of the pool. 'Who would even sign up to test it? What if you went into the time machine and someone got the calculations wrong and boom! You've been popped like a grape.'

Ellie wrinkles her nose. 'I never thought about that.'

'Besides, where would you go? Back to a time when women had to wear corsets and couldn't own property? No thanks.'

'She'd go to the future, dummy.' I roll my eyes. 'Not the past.'

'Oh.' Rose nods, her cheeks reddening. 'Yeah, that would be cool, I guess.'

Ellie shoots me a warning look over the top of Rose's head. She doesn't like it when I say anything mean to Rose, because Rose is, quote, 'sensitive'. She's even cried at school before. Literally in the classroom! That's basically the social kiss of death unless you *really* have something to cry about like your grandpa or grandma dying or your parents getting divorced or something. *I* have things to cry about.

Real, sad, fucked-up things. But I'm not a cry-baby like her. It was so stupid, too. She cried because her sister beat her at some swim meet and their mum made a big deal about it. Gimme a break.

That's *nothing*.

I got a C+ on my English Lit assignment last week and now my *entire* plan for the year has been ruined. You see, I was going to be the school dux. That's a special title given to the highest ranked student in the graduating class and it's a sure-fire way to get a scholarship for uni *and* fulfil the promise I made to my parents. How am I supposed to make up for everything that's happened if I don't graduate top of my class?

It's non-negotiable. I *must* get that spot.

And all last year I didn't get a single grade below an A. But now my English Lit teacher has it in for me. A C+? Seriously? Like, is he an idiot or something? Apparently I 'misinterpreted' the themes of *Tess of the d'Urbervilles*. Bullshit. I know full well what the main theme is: Thomas Hardy hated women. Period.

Still, I didn't cry. There's no point getting sad about it. I'd rather get mad instead. Being mad is more productive.

'Why are you glaring at me?' Rose asks, with a crinkle between her eyebrows, her lips pouting. I swear, sometimes I think she's scared of me. 'What did I say?'

'She's not angry with you. She's thinking about her C+ again,' Ellie says, frowning.

See, this is why everyone needs a best friend. They just *know* you. They know what you're thinking, what makes you happy or sad, and you don't even have to say a thing.

'I just can't believe it.' I push off the wall and land with an ungraceful thud, the hem of my blue and white checked school uniform dress flying up for a moment before falling back down. 'How is it possible that I went all last year without a single bad result and now I fail in term one! My life is *over*.'

'Technically if you were failing you would have got a failing grade, not a C+,' Ellie says.

Bless her, but she's not the best student so she really doesn't understand. In her books, a C is normal. Anyway, her mum only cares that Ellie stays skinny and pretty so she can become the next Miss Australia or something. She doesn't understand the pressure I'm under.

I'm out here trying to make my parents happy again. Trying to make them proud. Trying to make them see that I'm still alive.

'You know what my mum and dad are like. Anything less than an A might as well be an F.' I huff dramatically in the hopes of bolstering my point.

The plan is simple. I have to get perfect grades, so I can get an ATAR of at least 95 – which means I'm in the top five per cent of the state's graduating class. Then I can study law at the best university in Victoria and then I can become a lawyer and then I can *marry* a lawyer and be rich and take care of my parents when they're old.

This is the Italian way.

Ellie's an Aussie, so she doesn't quite get it. If anything, Rose is more likely to understand. Her mum is Chinese and the Chinese and Italians have a lot in common when it comes to family and expectations. Like how they expect their kids to study hard and get perfect grades. None of that 'follow your dreams' BS here. And like how they expect their kids to make the most of the sacrifices the previous generations made in coming to another country. Her mum puts so much pressure on Rose and her twin sister Lily, both when it comes to sports *and* when it comes to school. In fact, Lily is probably my main rival for dux.

She's smarter than Rose, but Rose is the better swimmer.

In any case, my grades aren't only about becoming a lawyer and taking care of my parents. It's penance, in a way. I gotta make things right. I have to . . . fill the gap in our family.

My sister's face flashes in my mind for a second – big brown eyes sparkling, dainty fingers, her long, brown hair glowing like silk, a crinkle forming in her nose when she laughs.

Formed in her nose when she *laughed*. Past tense.

In the image in my mind she's not laughing anymore. Her eyes are closed. She's on her back, face up to the sky. Her skin looks funny – she's wearing too much makeup. There are little marks they've tried to cover up. And her hair is styled to one side, covering the side of her head where . . .

Whenever I try to think about what happened my brain shuts down. It's like there's a little spark and a fritz and then . . .

Nothing.

I shake myself. What matters now is that I fix – *properly* fix – this problem. Because if I can't be the best in the whole school, then I've failed my parents. I've failed Daniella.

I may as well be dead, like she is.

Rose gasps suddenly. 'What if they take back their promise to help you out with a car?'

I turn eighteen next month and my dad said he'll match whatever I can save for a car – it'll be a beater, since we can't afford more. But it will be mine.

I stick my hand into my pocket and feel for the key chain nestled inside. Last year, on my seventeenth birthday, Daniella gave me a Swarovski keyring with my initials engraved on it. We both love shiny things. It didn't come in the official packaging, so I suspect it's either fake or 'fell off the back of a truck' but I don't care. It's beautiful. The silver bar is filled with crystals that look all different colours in the light. She told me that when I'm old enough to drive, I'll have a fancy key chain ready to go with my car. It was the most thoughtful present anyone has ever given me.

And the last present I ever got from my sister.

'They can't do that.' Ellie shook her head.

'Why not? If I don't uphold my end of the bargain and get good grades like I promised, maybe I won't make it to university at all and then what? I'll be stuck working at Muffin Break forever.'

Now *that* was a sad prospect. As it was I couldn't wait to tell my boss I was quitting one day, because she always gave me crappy shifts and made me do the gross jobs like walking through the grimy hallway to the rubbish bins. Not to mention all the grumpy older women customers who complained if their coffee was too hot or too cold. I even had one lady complain that there were too many sultanas in her sultana muffin. Like, sorry we gave you extra value?

'Nobody deserves to work at Muffin Break forever.' Rose shudders.

'Maybe a C+ doesn't have to be a C+,' Ellie says lifting one shoulder and smirking in a way that looks both mysterious and worldly.

Sometimes I can tell when she's practising emotions for drama class.

'What does *that* mean?' I exchange a look with Rose who shrugs like she's as clueless as I am.

It's a first. I'm not usually out of the loop.

'Meet me here after school.' Ellie jumps off the wall and dusts her backside free of twigs and leaves and crushed gumnut pieces. 'I'll introduce you to someone.'

I shake my head. 'What are you talking about?'

Ellie looks pleased to have an idea up her sleeve. 'You know that girl in my homeroom, Michelle?'

'Smelly Shelly Smith?' Rose wrinkles her nose and I think about reminding her that she doesn't smell so hot herself, but I hold my tongue for Ellie's sake.

'She *doesn't* smell.' Ellie rolls her eyes. 'And she hates being called Shelly. But she's super smart with computers and stuff, if you know what I mean.'

I don't really, but I would trust Ellie with my life. And if she has any idea of how I can fix this mess with my grades, then I'm all ears.

I'll do anything – literally anything – to make my parents happy.

After the final bell rings, I head to the brick wall to meet Ellie. Rose is there too, even though this doesn't really have anything to do with her. I spot her sister, Lily, standing close by with her own group of friends. Lily hangs out with the geek crowd – the ones in the anime club, who all want to get into designing video games or making robots.

'Ready?' I shift my backpack from one shoulder to the other. 'Where are we meeting Smell—uh, I mean Michelle?'

Ellie shoots me a look. 'Don't you call her that. She's going to help you . . . hopefully. You should be nice.'

'But *how* can she help?' Rose asks, looking confused. Her long, black hair hangs in a tidy plait over one shoulder, a blue ribbon matching the colour of the checks on our uniform dress dangling from the end.

Ellie shrugs cryptically. 'You'll see.'

It's not like her to be so secretive. I'm intrigued, though.

The school is rapidly emptying out. Students pour out of the gates like water rushing over a waterfall and the air is filled with chatter and the sound of honking horns from the nearby main road, which is clogged with school pick-up traffic.

We make our way back into the building like salmon swimming upstream, bumping shoulders and bags against the kids desperate to get outside into the sunshine.

'Where are we meeting her?' I ask again.

'Computer labs,' Ellie replies.

The three of us traipse towards the labs, which are a dark, musty set of rooms at the back of the school building. I've always thought the IT teacher, Mr Fyffe, was like a mole. He's got pale skin and beady eyes and he's short and kind of squat, and he never seems to care what his students are doing. How he's still employed is kind of a mystery.

Mr Fyffe looks up as we walk into the computer labs, but as soon as he realises we're not here for him, he drops his head back down to his phone. There are three students in the room and writing on the blackboard says 'computer club: 3.30–4.30 p.m.' Two boys huddle over a computer down the back and Michelle sits away from them, on the far side next to the windows.

Her hair is curly and short, like a boy's, and her skin is light brown and freckle-dusted. She has a large nose that hooks at the end and a mole clings to the point of her chin. It's a bad spot for a mole, since it has a witchy vibe. She's got earbuds in and the white cords dangle from her ears, down into the neck of her checkered school dress. She's working on a computer. It sits in pieces on the desk and she has a little can of something that she sprays inside the case, sending dust bunnies skittering out onto the desk.

I can hear the sound of bass-thumping coming out of her earbuds, and we get almost all the way to her desk before she realises we're approaching. Startled, she rips the earbuds out by their cords. 'Yeah?'

'Hi, Michelle.' Ellie smiles but Michelle doesn't smile back.

I can't blame her for being wary of people. I've never been popular – too much of a book-smart nerd for that – but I'm not an outcast like Michelle. One day the popular girls were chanting 'Smelly Shelly is a dyke' during English class, and the teacher had to fetch the principal. Ellie told them to shut up and mind their own business, and then they'd turned on her. Bitches.

I thought about slipping a laxative into one of those energy drink things they're always guzzling instead of eating actual food. But Ellie said that wasn't kind.

No shit Sherlock. Why should we be kind to bullies?

'What do you want?' Michelle asks, her eyes darting from Ellie to me and Rose, and back again.

'I uh . . . well, rather, *we* were hoping you might be able to help us.' Ellie knots her hands together and gives a furtive glance around the room. 'With some . . . school stuff.'

Rose looks at me with a confused expression and I shrug. But the words have such meaning to them that I'm sure Michelle must know what she's talking about, even if Rose and I don't. I glance back to where Mr Fyffe is at the front of the room, feet propped up on his desk, totally engrossed in whatever is on his phone. The boys behind us are laughing and talking loudly. They're not paying any attention to us at all.

'Like, grades and things,' she adds, her voice low. 'I heard you can do that.'

Michelle nods. 'Basic homework is $40 per subject, essays are $75 and research projects are $150. But I don't do Literature, since I don't have time to read the books. Basic English only, and anything else. You supply the textbooks. I guarantee an A on everything except Specialist Maths. That's not my forte.'

I look on incredulously and Rose's mouth drops open. I have literally never been in the market to buy homework since I'm smart enough to do it myself. Usually. How did Ellie even find out about this? Has she bought Michelle's services before? I doubt it. The girl doesn't care about her grades enough to fork out for someone to do her homework.

'If you were getting A's in every subject, you'd be on the advanced track,' I say. 'And you're not.'

The 'advanced track' is a program the school is trialling to keep high-performing students working hard by giving them access to things like special study rooms, canteen vouchers and other perks. Having more students succeed academically brings up the average, which means attracting better students in the future and getting more funding.

I'm in the program, obviously. Lily is in there, too. Rose

has been trying to get in ever since last year, but her grades are just slightly off the requirement. I've *never once* seen Michelle in the study rooms or noticed her name on any of the program's material.

'Of course I'm not,' she replies, rolling her eyes like I'm an idiot. 'The school isn't exactly going to look at a basic B-grade student to be supplying consistently A-grade work to other students, now are they?'

'That's smart, actually.' Rose bobs her head, looking impressed. 'So you purposefully hand in stuff you know is wrong?'

'*Strategically* wrong.' Michelle folds her arms across her chest. 'Now, what do you need? The schedule is starting to fill up, so if you want in for this term then I need to know now.'

'Uh, actually, we had a different kind of request.' Ellie wrings her hands. 'It's about a grade that's already been logged in the system.'

The penny drops. I now know what Ellie thinks Michelle can do for me. God, if I could just pay her to go into the school's computer system and change the grade so my average doesn't tank . . . that would solve everything!

'I heard you know how to uh . . . make adjustments,' Ellie finishes.

'Ah.' Michelle's eyes sparkle with interest and I feel shame flush through my system. If only my bloody English Lit teacher wasn't an arsehole. I don't deserve to be here, making this request like some deadbeat who can't do their own homework. But I've got no other options. 'That's going to cost you a lot more than $150.'

'I'll pay,' I say. 'So long as you can fix it.'

'Just what I love, a desperate customer.' Michelle leans back in her chair and thinks for a moment, nodding slowly. Ellie glances at me, anticipating that I'm likely to react to being called desperate. But she's right. I *am* desperate. 'Five hundred.'

I try not to blink. Five hundred dollars is *so* much money. It's a huge chunk of what I have saved up to put towards a car. But what's the point of even having wheels if you're not going anywhere in life? Besides, if I tell my parents I flunked out on an assignment, then they might not be willing to chip in the extra I'll need to actually buy the car anyway.

And the most important thing isn't really the car. It's not disappointing my parents. It's making them stop wishing that I had died instead of Daniella.

'Four hundred,' I counter.

Michelle simply shakes her head. 'The way I see it, you're going to make that money back as soon as you get to university with your perfect grades. Five hundred is a bargain.'

She's got me in a corner – I need her more than she needs me. It's not a position I like to be in. But I have no bargaining chips, no leverage.

I need this.

'Fine,' I reply through gritted teeth. 'Five hundred.'

Michelle reaches out her hand. 'Then we have ourselves a deal.'

Chapter Five

2024

Sofia

The drive to the wedding venue is four and a half hours of highways and country roads, nothing but blue sky and cotton-ball sheep as far as the eye can see. We're so bloody far west we might as well be in South Australia! Ellie stopped pointing out the farm animals about an hour in. The first hundred sheep and horses are exciting. The next thousand, not so much.

Although there was a paddock of llamas – or were they alpacas? – which was a nice change of pace.

Boring bitumen and brown grass scenery aside, being with these two is just like old times – stereo cranked, singing early Lady Gaga at the top of our lungs, windows down, air whipping our hair around our faces. It reminds me of being sixteen again, dancing around my bedroom with Ellie and Rose, using a hairbrush as a microphone and reading copies of *Cleo* and *Cosmopolitan* that we'd snuck from my sister's room, giggling over the sex tips even though none of us had done it yet.

It was the best year of my life.

It was the time *before*.

Before my sister's life was stolen from us. Before my mother turned into the shell of the woman she is now. Before all my dreams were sucked bone-dry with tragedy.

Before I did the unthinkable.

'At the roundabout, take the third exit,' the GPS instructs as we approach, slowing behind a small line of cars.

'Are we almost there?' Ellie is glued to the window, despite the fact that we can't see the beach or anything of interest yet.

'We're close,' I say, glancing sideways at her and laughing. 'You're like a little kid! Are we there yet? Are we there yet?'

She twists around in her seat, where she's sitting cross-legged like a genie. Thank goodness I'm not driving a manual, because her knee bumps against the centre console. 'Excuse me for being thrilled at the idea of being away with you ladies.'

'And getting married,' I point out.

'And getting married.' She lets out a cry of happiness and then, in true impulsive Ellie fashion, she winds down the window and sticks her head out and screams, 'I'm getting fucking married!'

A hearty laugh bubbles up in my throat and I shake my head. 'You're ridiculous.'

I sense movement in the back seat of the car, and Rose's head suddenly pops in between me and Ellie. She must have unbuckled her seatbelt to be able to lean so far forward. 'What's going on? I hate sitting in the back by myself! I can't hear what you're talking about over the music.'

Typical Rose. Her FOMO is out of control sometimes.

I roll my eyes and Ellie shoots me a sharp look. I can practically hear her admonishment: *don't be a bitch, Sof.*

I pull the car up to the entrance of the roundabout, pausing until there's a break in traffic, and then I plant my foot down to dart into a gap. I sense Rose falling backwards against the seat behind me with a loud *oof* and I shoot her a look in the rear-view mirror.

'Seatbelts on at all times,' I say, curving around the big, sweeping line of the roundabout and exiting onto the last highway before our destination. 'Safety first.'

'Lead foot,' she shoots back, but I hear the click of her seatbelt nonetheless.

Ellie, always determined to keep the peace, twists around to talk to Rose through the gap in the seats. Her long blond hair tickles my bare arm. 'I'm *so* happy you guys are here with me for this. I couldn't imagine getting married without you and I've missed you both so much these last few years.'

'I've missed you too, El,' I say.

'Me too,' Rose echoes from the back.

'This week is going to rock!' She squeals and turns the radio up, almost bursting my eardrums with vintage Katy Perry. Rose sings from the back, totally off-key and I can't help but join in.

Because the fact is, I haven't felt it up until now. Excitement.

You'd think I would have. A chance to be away on some secluded, private beach for a few days while I help my best mate down the aisle *should* have me beaming with joy. Not to mention having a Hollywood celeb on my business portfolio is a big deal! It could help give me access to even more prestigious clients. But the truth is . . . I've kind of been dreading it. Not seeing Ellie, of course. But the rest of it. Being around Rose, who always seems to get under my skin no matter how hard I try to resist it. Spending time with Ellie's soon-to-be-husband, who, frankly, is about as much fun as a cereal box. Dealing with Ellie's mum . . . God, don't even get me started on that woman. And missing Rob, even if it's only for one night.

And now, to add to this pile of prickly little burrs, a fake one-star review for my business. Ugh!

I grit my back teeth and tighten my grip on the steering wheel. I'd tossed and turned all bloody night thinking about 'Tegan' and the review. I'd wanted to do some investigating, but I spent last night packing for the trip and then Rob had grabbed me from behind and . . .

Well, that was the rest of the night done.

'What's wrong?' Ellie asks, her attention drawn to me suddenly like a cadaver dog sniffing out a body.

'Nothing.'

'You stopped having fun.' She frowns, her blue eyes scanning me like lasers, as she brings her hand to her mouth. As soon as I spot her starting to chew on a nail, I slap her hand away.

'I'm concentrating on the road, El,' I say. As if to illustrate my point, I flick my indicator and move around a car that's travelling too slow for the right-hand lane. 'If I don't get you to the venue in one piece, then Mitch is going to be pissed, isn't he?'

She settles back into her seat, her eyes still on me. It's been so long since Ellie and I spent an extended period together that I'd forgotten what she's like. She picks up on everything. Every little detail, every little twitch, every little thing you want to hide. She knows it's there and it worries her.

I have to be careful what I show.

'In five hundred metres, take the exit to . . .' The GPS pauses. 'Cape Turmoil Road.'

Cape Turmoil. What a fucking perfect name.

I'm not exactly sure what I was expecting this place to be. Even still, I'm surprised.

We see the lighthouse before the grounds, like a tall white finger pointing indignantly up to the sky. Accusatory.

When we started our drive from Melbourne the sky was a vibrant, piercing blue, but it's darkened now, like a flame has licked across it, charring sections. Heavy clouds cluster, silvery with rain, and several seagulls swoop about, their cries slicing through the air. We've been checking the weather report obsessively and the wedding day is supposed to be clear, at least so far. I know Ellie has her heart set on an outdoor wedding, overlooking the private beach that curves along this section of the coast. I agree, it would make for incredible photos. But, like anyone who gets married in Victoria, we have an indoor backup plan.

I *always* have a backup plan.

'It's so . . . quiet,' Rose says from the back seat.

She's not wrong. This place is a little eerie. Definitely not the kind of wedding venue I'm used to, like wineries with lush green backdrops, specialty venues with incredible landscapes and twinkle-light canopies, or stately luxury hotels and high-end beach resorts.

Not . . . a weird, isolated lighthouse owned by some quirky movie director.

But Ellie had her heart set on it. The director is a kind of an 'if you know, you know' eccentric genius who's been nominated for several Oscars for his off-beat artsy films, one of which pulled Ellie out of obscurity. No little gold statue for her, yet. But she's getting close.

Apparently this director guy grew up out here because his father worked as the lighthouse keeper, and when he got rich and famous he decided to buy the cottage his family once occupied. There are five cottages in total and he slowly bought them all up – one article I read insinuated some heavy-handed tactics might have been involved – and now they've been turned into something of a rich-person retreat.

Ellie told me that Ryan Reynolds and Blake Lively stayed here once.

A winding dirt road undulates through long grass up a slight incline. In the rear-view mirror I see a trail of dust behind us, obscuring the view from where we've come and erasing the past. A shudder ripples down my spine.

Why are you being so fucking weird? You sound like Rose.

We eventually approach a long white gate that cuts the road off. I stop the car and Ellie jumps out, punching a code into an electronic lock. A second later, the gate sweeps open, granting us access.

'Dom said to meet him by the event space,' Ellie says, as she climbs back into the car. 'Go past the first cottage and turn left towards the lighthouse. There's a big white building that kind of looks like a barn, but the walls are entirely glass.'

We roll past one of the cottages. It's a Georgian-style sandstone cottage, with white and blue trim. Nothing fancy from the outside, but as I curve around a sweeping offshoot from the main road, I see a beautiful glass sunroom addition at the back, which overlooks the lighthouse and the ocean. Colourful flowers are planted in abundance around a small, paved outdoor area with a table and chairs, and what looks like a hammock strung between two trees.

I feel my shoulders drop. Okay, I have to admit it's quite pretty here. Not nearly as creepy as the old pictures I'd found online, which were evidently from *before* Ellie's director friend cleaned the place up.

'Oh wow, what a view!' Rose exclaims from the back.

As we drive up a smaller dirt road towards the lighthouse, another structure comes into the view. The 'glasshouse', which is exactly as described, is perched on the cliff face. You can see right through it to the shimmering, roiling ocean on the other side.

'It's even better than I'd hoped,' Ellie breathes. She's pressed to the passenger-side window like a small child approaching a fairground or a theme park. 'Mitch is going to love it here.'

There's a large four-wheel drive with darkly tinted windows waiting, and as I pull up beside it, a man gets out. He's *huge*. Towering. It's not just his almost-impossible height, but the breadth of his shoulders and chest. His body looks like an oversized barrel and everything else about him is sized to match – hands like dinner plates, tree-trunk legs and a broad mouth that looks like it could devour a steak whole. His dark hair is wiry and streaked with salt, the frizzy strands sticking out in all directions like he's stuck a finger into an electrical socket.

He's dressed in mud-smeared gumboots and a riding coat with a storm cape in dark brown oilskin that looks worn and softened with age. There are cuts and scrapes on his hands. If I had no idea who he was, I would have assumed him to be a groundskeeper. Not a multi-millionaire director.

Ellie is unbuckling her seatbelt before I've even got the

car in park and she flies out, racing towards the guy with her arms open. He scoops her up into a big bear hug. Rose and I get out of the car and hang back, allowing Ellie her moment. We're immediately hit with a strong wind coming off the water, it whips my hair around my face.

'Dom, these are my *bestest* friends in the whole world. This is Sof,' she says, gesturing grandly to me. 'And this is Rose.'

'Ah, Sofia, you're planning the wedding.' He nods. 'You've been dealing with my property manager, Nikoleta.'

'That's right. It's nice to meet you.' I swipe my hair out of my face and walk forward, sticking out my hand. It's engulfed in his grip, making me feel like a child for a moment. I can tell he's strong enough that he could easily crush my hand to dust, but his handshake is surprisingly gentle, like he's very conscious of his size and power. 'This is a stunning property you have here.'

'Absolutely gorgeous.' Not one to be left out, Rose is at my side in a flash, sticking her own hand forward.

'It's been my dream ever since I was a boy to own this place of such important memories,' he says. 'All the cottages here are made from sandstone quarried from local cliff faces. The flora is native and all the art featured in the buildings has come from local artists. The staff we employ here have all grown up in this area too, and they cook with ingredients sourced from nearby farms and businesses. I wanted to keep this place as true to its heritage as possible.'

'Nikoleta said you've had quite a few weddings here,' I say. 'It's such a unique venue.'

Dom nods. 'A few times a year, yes. But I only rent it out to people I know personally. You won't find us listed on Airbnb or anything like that.'

Doesn't exactly seem like the most fiscally smart business model, but I get the impression this isn't so much a business as it is a passion project. Dom makes his money in Hollywood, not here.

'Thank you so much for letting me have my wedding here,' Ellie says, her eyes sparkling. The wind has loosened strands of her blond hair from her ponytail and they flutter around her face.

A drop of water lands on my cheek, and another on my nose. It's starting to rain.

'Let's just hope the weather holds up.' Rose lets out a nervous laugh. 'Nothing like rain on your wedding day to make things difficult.'

I see Ellie frown and shoot Rose a sharp look. She shrugs, as if confused. Honest to God, sometimes I wish I could tape Rose's mouth shut. She has no idea how her worries bring the mood down for everyone else. I don't want Ellie to feel stressed about her big day. Whatever happens – rain, hail, or bloody tornado! – I'm going to do my best to make sure she feels like the special person she is and that her wedding is everything she wants it to be.

'You three head inside The Glass House and I'll have Nikoleta come to meet you for the tour. I'm so gutted I won't be here for the wedding. I've got to be in Prague tomorrow to start work on a new project and there was nothing we could do to budge the filming dates. We're running tight as it is. I'm sorry, my girl.'

'That's okay, Dom. You know I understand,' Ellie replies.

Dom pulls Ellie in for another hug and kisses the top of her head. He seems sweet. I can see why she likes him so much. 'Have a beautiful wedding, my darling girl. Your bloke is lucky to have you.'

He waves with one of his dinner-plate hands and heads towards the lighthouse. The ground is a little damp – likely it's been raining on and off all day – and I see it squelch with each heavy-booted step.

I look down at the chic little black Italian designer loafers I'd worn because they're comfortable to drive in and scrunch up my nose. Looks like I'll be giving them a clean later. I hope the ground dries out. Even though we're only in the first part of autumn and it *is* still warm, we do get these clustered rainy days. More droplets splatter my bare arm and there's a small grumble up above as the wind continues to whip around.

Unfortunately with Ellie's film commitments and Mitch's hectic competition schedule, there was limited flexibility for choosing a wedding date – hence why we missed the summer weather *and* why they're getting married on a Wednesday. So now all we can do is pray for a clear day.

'Come on,' I say to the others. 'Let's get inside before the heavens open up.'

We wait in the glass-fronted building for a good fifteen minutes before Nikoleta arrives. It gives me time to check the place out. It's minimally appointed – a stunning long table cut from a single piece of wood dotted with stools, tightly woven rattan rugs and modern yet warm lighting. It's sparse. No OTT wedding bling here. When I started dealing with Nikoleta I was told they never – *never!* – change the space for weddings. No decorations, no rearranging the furniture. Nada.

I mean, when you look through the glass I can see why

they haven't cluttered the space with attention-grabbing things. The view of the cape stretches out like a great blue mouth from our vantage point up on the clifftop. The water is slate-like today and the white-capped waves thrash at the rocks below. For a moment, I have the urge to leave the room and walk right to the edge, to feel the rush of death calling me. To hear my sister's voice.

Tears prick my eyes.

Why did she have to go out that night? Why didn't she tell anyone what was going on?

The creaking of my door is enough to make me stir. It's still dark outside, inky blackness cut through by a high, full moon. Ribbons of pale yellowed light streak in through the slatted blinds, creating stripes across the foot of my bed. Groggily, I roll over. I know it's Daniella before my eyes adjust to the darkness. It's the smell of her – strawberry shampoo and vanilla body lotion.

'Dani?'

'Shhh.' She creeps inside and closes the door behind her.

'What are you doing?'

'My nice top got mixed up with your laundry. Go back to sleep.' She pads over, leans down to kiss me on the forehead. I hear jangling, like car keys.

But I'm so tired. I had a big test at school and I stayed up late cramming last night, so at her soothing voice and the calming press of her hand at my shoulder, I feel sleep tugging me back to dreamland.

'I love you,' she whispers.

'I love you, too.'

I don't know how long she stays looking for her top, but suddenly she's gone and the buttery yellow stripes of moonlight have turned to a dusty lilac haze. There's a thumping on the front door. I groan and pull a pillow over my head, catching sight of the alarm clock next to my bed. It's five fifty-three in the morning.

Who the bloody hell is at the door at this hour? It's inhumane!

I hear noise in the hallway as someone shuffles past my room, grumbling angrily. It's Mum. I hope she gives them a good telling-off, whoever they are.

I'm almost back in the clutches of sleep when I hear a wail that is unlike any sound I've ever heard before. Mum! It's like her soul is being ripped out through her throat. I've never gotten out of bed so fast in my life, but I'm in the hallway before I even know what's happening, still in my pyjamas as I run towards the front of the house.

Mum is on the floor, on her knees, and two police officers stand in the doorway, grim-faced. I know in my heart of hearts that I will never see my sister again.

'Sof?'

I jump when a hand lands on my shoulder. It's Ellie.

'Sorry.' I shake myself. 'I uh . . . I get real into the zone on the job.'

Her blond eyebrows crinkle like she's not quite sure whether to believe me. But knowing Ellie, she won't make me feel bad even if she knows I'm telling a white lie to save face. 'The pictures are going to be incredible.'

'I mean, you're in them so of course they will be.' I nudge her with my elbow.

I catch Rose looking at us and she immediately scuttles over, her long dark hair swishing around her shoulders. 'What are you guys talking about?'

I grit my teeth. I hardly ever get to see Ellie anymore

these days and it would be nice to have a moment alone with her, just to . . . talk. To catch up. But every time she's home, she never wants anyone to feel left out and so it's always the three of us. I miss the time when Ellie lived temporarily at my house, where we would giggle until our eyes watered, just the two of us. She's like a sister to me.

The only one I have left.

At that moment, Nikoleta walks through the door. I've only talked to her over the phone, but her appearance matches her voice so perfectly there could have been no doubt in my mind who she was.

'Dom said you were all in here. Let's go.' There are no smiles, no greeting, no welcome.

Like Dom, she's big. Tall and broad-shouldered with a presence that could be intimidating if not for the stooped shoulders that make it seem like she's carrying the weight of the world. I assume they're related. She has the same wiry, salt-streaked black hair, but whereas he was warm, she is cool. Remote. Like him, she's also dressed in practical attire. Another oilskin jacket over jeans tucked into gumboots.

'We call this The Glass House, and this is where the wedding reception will be. Tomorrow night the rehearsal dinner will be in here, as well as breakfast the morning after the wedding. The rest of the time you may make use of the kitchens in your individual cottages. The cottages have been stocked with the items you requested in advance.' She runs through the items as if checking things off a list, without emotion or enthusiasm. 'Follow me outside and I will show you the directions to your cottages.'

As Nikoleta turns to exit The Glass House, I see Rose frowning. She's always a little weird around people who aren't outwardly effusive and often jumps to the conclusion that they don't like her, even if she hasn't done anything wrong.

We all head outside and cluster by the door. Thankfully, it's only spitting and we don't get too wet.

'Here is a map of the grounds,' Nikoleta says, handing a piece of paper to Ellie. Rose and I lean over one side each to peer at it.

There are five cottages plus The Glass House and a utility building where I assume the kitchen is housed along with perhaps staff accommodation. It's marked 'private'.

'This is the cottage reserved for the bride and groom.' Nikoleta jabs at the paper, indicating the cottage marked with the number one. 'You two are in this one.'

Sorting the accommodation for the wedding had taken a lot of mental gymnastics and back and forth with Ellie. She and Mitch obviously need a cottage to themselves because nobody wants to listen to someone consummating their marriage!

Mitch's family are staying in cottage number two. Rose and I and our husbands plus my assistant, Tiffani, who's helping out with the wedding so I can actually enjoy myself for at least part of the day, are sharing cottage number three. Ellie's mum is going to be staying in cottage number four with Ellie's Auntie Pat and Ellie's assistant, Morgan.

The last cottage houses Mitch's best mates, which still leaves quite a few people without somewhere to sleep. We've booked out two nearby bed and breakfast spots as well as private coaches to ferry people from the venue safely back after the wedding, to ease Ellie's guilt that not everyone got offered a bed on site.

Destination weddings always come with extra logistics,

but it's nothing that a few cups of coffee and a spreadsheet can't handle! And as I've said a thousand times before – I know weddings.

Nothing will ruffle me.

'The only rules for the property, other than treating it with respect, are that you are to stay away from this building at all times,' Nikoleta says, pointing to the spot on the map marked private. 'And do not go south of The Glass House past dusk. It gets very dark out here and there are no set paths or lighting around the cliff. If it's a cloudy night, the visibility is next to nothing and it's dangerous. Someone could easily slip over the edge.'

Ellie, Rose and I exchange glances. A blackened night, a dangerous cliff edge and a wedding with bottomless champagne seems like a recipe for disaster. I'll be sure to make an announcement at the wedding, because the last thing I need is some drunk arsehole plunging to their death and ruining everything.

'Don't worry,' Rose says with a firm nod of her head. 'We won't do anything wrong. We're not those kind of . . .'

She trails off because it's a lie.

We are *very much* those kind of people.

Chapter Six

Ellie

Two hours after arriving we're settled in the cottage that Sofia and Rose are sharing. It's a gorgeous building – two bedrooms, a bathroom with one of those deep claw-footed tubs and another with a rainforest shower. Despite the plain, heritage style outside, the inside is sleekly modern and beautifully decorated. I'm standing in the main living area, admiring a large painting, which depicts the lighthouse at dawn.

We've got all the lights on because it is properly chucking it down outside. Rain thrashes against the windows and the big glass door that leads to a little courtyard out the back of the cottage, where the flowers shudder in the wind. Water runs in rivulets across the glass, leaving streaks and snaking tears behind. Autumn can be like this – boiling hot one minute and then storming the next. It's fine, if we get all the rain over with now, then we can have sunshine for my wedding day.

Please!

We need music. I skip across the cottage to grab my

phone and pop it into one of those speaker dock thingies and a few minutes later, some bouncy pop music plays. Not too loud, since Sofia is on her laptop. The girl never stops working, I swear.

Rose is in the kitchen cutting up fruit and vegetable sticks and pouring chips into bowls and setting some homemade Anzac biscuits onto a plate so we can have a 'grazing spread'. I'm bloody starving since all I've had so far today was my breakfast juice and a handful of Arnott's red snakes during the drive.

'You guys are *not* going to believe this,' Sofia says. She's sitting on a white bouclé couch looking like a model in a luxury furniture advertisement. Her shiny dark chocolate hair hangs over one shoulder and stark, black-framed glasses are perched on her nose. Très chic! She's changed into a pair of flowing silk pants and a matching tunic top in a burnt sienna colour. A gold padlock bracelet hangs delicately on one wrist.

'Someone has left me a totally *fake* one-star review on Google.' She taps at her keyboard a little harder than strictly necessary. 'I've never even done a wedding for someone named Tegan. Yet right here is a review saying that I botched Tegan's wedding.'

'How strange.' Rose begins to pick up the platters, trying to pile them on her arms like a waitress. She'd rather struggle to carry it all than ask for help. But I catch her in time and rush over to assist so she doesn't drop anything.

'It's the strangest thing.' Sofia shakes her head. 'I wondered if maybe they got me mixed up with someone else, but they literally refer to me by name in the review.'

'Can you ask Google to take it down?' I suggest as we place the platters on a sleek marble coffee table.

She snorts. 'Yeah right. They don't give a shit that someone is defaming me online.'

'Trust me, I know a thing or two about that,' I reply, reaching for a handful of grapes and sitting genie style on the couch next to Sofia.

Being in the public eye certainly has its perks – like having access to this stunning property for the week as a wedding gift from Dom – but it also has massive downsides. Nasty critiques of your work and unfair criticism about things that are out of your control, lewd comments from random men, people thinking you owe them something because they paid to see your movie. There are whole websites dedicated to trying to figure out what plastic surgery I've had – just my ears and my boobs, if you must know. A wise older actress told me once 'don't fuck up your face, because that's one thing you can't un-fuck.' I've listened to that.

Truthfully, if I had the choice today I probably wouldn't have gotten my boobs done. That happened only a year into me living in Hollywood. Mum said it would help me get roles and she was insistent the loan would pay itself off, so I relented.

'I can't for the life of me figure out why someone would do this,' Sofia says, shaking her head and glaring at her computer.

'People write all kinds of shit on the internet,' Rose says with a shrug as she plops down on one of the solo armchairs that looks puffy but is actually quite firm. She shifts, trying to get comfortable. 'Doesn't matter if it's true or not.'

There's a note of bitterness in her voice. Now that I think about it, all three of us have been in the public eye in some way. Me with my acting, Sofia with her celebrity-endorsed business and Rose with . . .

Well, the demise of her swimming career.

Truthfully, she's had it worst of the three of us. Because a bad review for Sofia and I hasn't really changed anything. We're still working. Still heading towards our goals. But Rose gave up everything. The public's scrutiny ground her confidence down to dust so she went into hiding and hasn't come back out. She could have been an Olympian. An Aussie legend, like her sister. Now, she's just like anyone else on the street. It has to sting.

'They used my name. My *actual* full name. That doesn't feel like a case of mistaken identity.' She lets out a frustrated huff and snaps her laptop shut, putting it onto a side table as though she can't stand the sight of it any longer.

She's going to be seething over this for a while. Sofia takes her business *very* seriously; it's a big part of the reason I asked her if she would organise my wedding. Not because she's my friend but because I trust Sofia more than anyone to stay true to her word.

Most people are flaky, I've come to realise. They're quick with 'yeah, sure!' or 'absolutely!' when what they really mean is 'no' and it's simply a matter of time before the real answer comes out. But not her. When she says she'll do something, she does it. She's reliable, like that. Her word is as good as if it were carved into stone.

As the conversation moves on, it feels like there's a strange undercurrent of tension in our little group. She keeps glancing at her laptop and I notice that Rose's phone screen lights up with a call that she cancels immediately, her face white as a sheet. Outside the storm rolls on, battering the cottage as if wanting to keep us trapped inside.

I give myself a little shake. I'm being silly. This strange feeling I'm picking up on is nothing but pre-wedding jitters. Everything is going to be fine.

At five p.m. we decide to separate so we can unpack and settle in, because I know we'll stay up late talking and catching up after dinner tonight. I can't wait! But for now Rose is getting antsy about calling home to check on Isaac, and Sofia needs to touch base with Tiffani about tomorrow. Both Tiffani and Morgan are due to arrive in the morning to help with preparations before the larger group starts trickling in in the afternoon.

I leave them in their cottage and dash across the rain-slicked, muddy grounds, head down against the roaring wind. My ponytail whips with force and my white sneakers end up splattered and dirty in only a few steps. When I make it to the cottage I skid on the wet pavers, arms windmilling as I struggle to find my balance. My momentum is stopped suddenly when I catch myself on a potted tree, my hand grasping one tough branch. I hiss as I feel a sting on my palm.

'Try not to accidentally kill yourself before the wedding,' I admonish myself as I tread gingerly towards the front door. 'You bloody klutz.'

Inside, the cottage sits in darkness and I fumble around for a light, finding a lamp and switching it on. For a second I stand here, looking down at my palm. There's dirt and some flakes of bark sticking to me and a tiny scrape. A small drop of blood beads and I smear it away. Something deep in my brain twitches – a memory. A tiny droplet of blood. A bright red speck, like a rogue splatter of paint against pale skin.

It was so small. How could something so small signal something *so* bad?

I sway, reaching out for the lamp to steady myself. Why do I still think about that day, all these years later? It's done. We moved on. We made a promise to forget. To bury. To never speak of it again. Yet the memory is like a buoy inside me, trying desperately to push back to the top of my consciousness no matter how hard I beat it down.

'Stop it,' I hiss. 'Stop thinking about it.'

What happened eleven years ago . . . it's in the past. That's where it belongs.

Shaking my head, I wander into the kitchen and make myself an iced matcha as motivation to unpack my stuff. Just as I'm pouring the milk in and giving it a stir with a reusable straw, my mobile phone buzzes. It's my agent, Rashida.

'Hey you.' I sip my drink as I head towards the bedroom, phone pressed to my ear. 'What's up? It must be like . . .'

I try to do the time conversion in my head.

'After midnight,' I finish. 'Why are you calling so late? If it's to wish me well for the wedding, you're early. Wedding isn't for two more days.'

There's a pause on the other end of the line that flicks on my anxiety like a light switch. Rashida is the kind of person who has a lot to say and not much time to say it, so she talks a mile a minute. I like that about her. She gets shit done. With her, silence is suspicious.

‘Hello?’ I know the connection hasn’t dropped, because I hear her let out a sigh. Something ice cold slithers down the back of my spine.

‘Are you somewhere where we can talk privately?’ she asks.

‘Just you and me, if you want to whisper sweet nothings into my ear.’ I let out a nervous laugh.

‘You’re off the film,’ she says bluntly.

I must have misheard. ‘What?’

‘*Heartland*, you’re off.’ She lets out a breath. ‘I’m sorry.’

Just like that. There’s no beating around the bush with Rashida. Everything is a Band-Aid being ripped from the skin. But this? I never saw it coming.

‘Why?’ I shake my head. ‘I spoke with the team last week and Fanny said she was excited for us to get started.’

Fanny is the director – she’s a powerhouse. Fifty-something, takes no bullshit, has vision like nobody I’ve ever met. I was foaming at the mouth to work with her.

‘They—’ Rashida breaks off and I’m stumped. It’s not like her to struggle for words.

What could *possibly* have changed in a week?

‘What’s going on?’ My voice rises in pitch as the panic really sets in. Something is wrong.

‘They’ve got photos, Ellie. Of you and Antoine Auclair.’

The glass slips from my hand and hurtles towards the floor, hitting the tile with a loud crack and shattering. Dark green liquid splatters all over the crisp white marble tile, like blood gushing out of a wound, shards of glass glinting in the lamp light, pieces of crystal swimming in an oozing, toxic ocean.

I can only stare.

'Ellie? Fuck. I thought you said that was over a long time ago.'

'It was! *Five* years ago,' I croak. 'And we kept it quiet.'

As the shock starts to fade, it gives way to crackling, burbling, frantic panic. I feel it skitter up the back of my throat and wrap its fingers around my windpipe. This can't be happening.

Antoine bloody Auclair. Oscar-winning director. A man twenty years my senior. I met him at a Hollywood party and was utterly starstruck – he'd directed some of my favourite movies. I'd only been in the US for a year and I was struggling to get a foothold in the industry. He was charming, oh so French, and when he invited me out for dinner, we talked long into the night about film and the industry and our hopes and dreams. He confessed he and his wife had split up. I went back to his hotel room that night and it was magical.

When he asked that we keep things on the down low because they hadn't announced their split yet, I was a bloody idiot who didn't see what a giant flashing red flag that was. Stupidly, I believed him and we dated for six months, him flying me back and forth between my place in LA and his apartment in Paris. It wasn't until Antoine's wife turned up one night to the 'love nest' she apparently had only *just* found out about, screaming that she knew he was having an affair while I hid in the bathroom, that the truth of the situation fully dawned on me.

I'd been played. Antoine and his wife were *not* separated. I hadn't signed on to take part in the downfall of another woman's marriage, so I was furious. After she left I told

Antoine never to call me again. Mercifully, he never told his wife – or anyone else – my name. He kept my identity a secret. We haven't spoken since.

That was just over five years ago.

What's that got to do with the movie, you ask? Well, turns out Fanny and Mrs Auclair are BFFs back from their Harvard days. And *Heartland* is a movie about a woman who leaves her philandering husband to start one of the greatest art movements of the twentieth century.

Yeah, my 'affair' is a problem.

'Then why are these photos popping up now?' Rashida asks. I can easily imagine her pacing in her corner office, Los Angeles glittering outside.

'I didn't even know there *were* photos of us! I had no idea Antoine was still with his wife at the time, okay? I swear. How am *I* the one paying for a man lying out of his arse? My only crime here is being an idiot, not a homewrecker. How did they even get these photos?'

My hands are shaking. The sensation is spreading through me like a virus. My whole body trembles. I grip the island, not daring to take a step in case I bring my foot down on glass.

'I don't know, Ellie. One of Fanny's assistants called me just now and she wasn't forthcoming. Sounds like there's no mistaking what's going on in the pictures, though.' Rashida lets out a rush of air. 'Fanny was livid, apparently.'

'Shit.' God, I hope the photos aren't of me naked. You never know with the bloody paparazzi, they sneak around everywhere.

'There's more.'

I press my free hand to my temple, feeling woozy from the stress. 'What else?'

'Apparently the photos have made it to the media.'

'Are you fucking kidding me?' If I'd thought my heart was hammering before then it really is now. The panic of losing a job turns to thick, sticky acid in my stomach. This is so much worse than getting kicked off a single movie. 'Fanny passed them on?'

'I don't think she would stoop that low. Besides, it'll be bad press for the movie and you know she hates drama. I don't know how the photos started circulating. But it's not good.'

'I *know* that,' I bite out.

Antoine helped me to get a part in my first big movie – the one that really got me on the radar of Hollywood higher-ups. He put in a call, made a personal recommendation and boom! Suddenly I'd scored a supporting role in a major film. It's not exactly a secret in the industry that lots of people get their start through personal contacts, even if it's not something we list on our Wikipedia pages. But it won't take long before people are talking loudly enough that it might very well be.

She slept her way to the top. Whore.

Doesn't she have any self-respect? Trying to jump the queue by opening her legs for another woman's husband.

Do you think it was a #MeToo thing? Maybe he forced her.

Antoine is going to come out swinging to protect himself. And the fact is, it *was* consensual . . . well, except for my role in him having an affair. *That* I didn't consent to. But I said yes to the sex. And Antoine agreed to make introductions for me because he thought I had talent. Not because I slept with him.

Not that anyone will care, because the facts don't make for clickable headlines.

'This could ruin me.' I sound like a scared little girl who's about to have everything she loves set on fire. 'I'm finally starting to break through.'

'We won't let it ruin you. But I don't think anything we will say will get you back on *Heartland*.'

'I need to call—'

'I've got one of the girls on the phone with your publicist already. We're going to try to get ahead of this as best we can. Between us, we'll have a statement drafted and ready to go ASAP. I'll touch base with the other directors and casting people we've been talking to recently to smooth things over in the morning.'

For a moment I can't see. Tears have flooded my eyes and my stomach is an ocean. Nausea churns like a whirlpool inside me and I sink to the floor, bowing my head to try to stop it. This is a certified fucking disaster. Everything could crumble. All I've worked for. All that might be in my future.

But who would do this? Not a single soul knew about Antoine. I didn't tell *anybody* because I was so ashamed. Ashamed for being a fool. Ashamed for not seeing the signs. Ashamed for hurting Antoine's wife. But if I try to think about it logically for a moment – not easy, with panic whipping a tornado in my head – why would the paparazzi have waited five years to make use of these photos? It doesn't make sense. It's almost like someone was waiting for the right moment to strike.

Maybe this is karma. I thought we'd gotten away with something terrible . . .

That one little drop of blood.

But what if karma has come to collect?

Chapter Seven

Rose

Three missed calls – one from Mum, one from my sister, Lily, and one that I dread even more than the other two. Jamie bloody Hazlehurst. Sports reporter for the *Herald Sun*. Jamie is the go-to writer for the Olympics, Commonwealth Games, World Cup (cricket and soccer), F1, tennis, surfing, golf . . . you name it. How do I know all this? Well, let's just say that we were previously acquainted.

There's one voicemail on my phone, and I already know who it's from before I punch in the passcode to access my messages.

Rose, this is Jamie Hazlehurst from the Herald Sun. *I sent you a text earlier and mentioned I'd give you a call. I'd really like to speak with . . .*

Delete.

I throw the phone down on the bed and stare at it, biting my lip. Why won't they leave me alone? I don't want to talk about it anymore. It was painful enough living through the whole world inspecting me like a cell under a microscope the first time. Why do I have to relive it every time Lily reaches another milestone in her career?

My stomach roils. God, if a year could go by without it being shoved in my face that she's the golden child and I'm the family fuck-up that would be great. Just one bloody year where *I* was winning at . . . something.

But what? What will you ever do now that could be better than what she's achieved?

I've been dreading this all day, ever since Lily's torch-bearer status was announced this morning. Deep down I knew it was going to drag everything to the surface again, because the whole 'covering the history' bit . . . that's me. *I'm* the history.

I let out a breath and look around the cottage's bedroom, trying to calm down. The walls are a soft blue that's so pale it could trick you into thinking it's merely the sky being reflected on white paint. There's a queen bed, with soft rumpled linen bedding that feels charming and homely, but also somehow luxurious. They've even supplied a small white cot, for when Malachi arrives with Isaac, and in the corner of it sits a knitted bunny with a blue waistcoat. A large window overlooks the crumbling coastline, with the lighthouse off to one side.

It's exquisite. Every detail is thoughtfully appointed, and yet nothing feels contrived or overdone. That's *real* luxury – the kind of stuff that belongs to people who have so much money they don't want you to know about it on first glance.

The last time Malachi and I got away was for our 'babymoon' at Lakes Entrance, staying in a cheap little B & B that smelled of mildew and had spiders hiding behind the couch. We made the most of it – but being here now is a sharp reminder of how different our lives have turned out.

Sofia and Ellie fell on the right side of successful, and I didn't.

As if knowing the exact moment to pour salt into my wound, Lily's name pops up on my screen. Again. She *never* leaves a voice message, she'll just keep calling until you give in and answer the phone. That's how she's done everything in her life – brute force. But it's probably easier to get this over with, than to put up with her calling every hour.

I sigh when I see it's a video call. I slide my thumb across the screen.

'Hey,' I say without much enthusiasm. 'What's up?'

Her image blurs for a second, turning her face pixelated. The reception seems inconsistent out here.

'Can you hear me?' I ask, moving around the room to see if I can get another bar to show up.

Her dark hair hangs over her shoulders, longer than it used to be when we were young and she cut it short to differentiate herself from me. Now she doesn't need to do that. Nobody mixes us up anymore.

'Barely.' Her image blurs again. 'You're already there?'

'Yep.'

Lily is joining us tomorrow for the rehearsal dinner. Funnily enough, she and Ellie didn't hang out in high school. Their friendship only started up after they were both at the Logie awards one year – Ellie was nominated for Most Outstanding Supporting Actress and Lily was part of the cast for a documentary on Australian swimming nominated for the Factual Program category. They'd hung out, gone to the afterparty together and formed a friendship that hadn't been there before. I'd be lying if I said I wasn't jealous – Lily has always wanted anything that I had.

'I can't chat long. I've promised Ellie I'd help her set up some stuff,' I say, hoping the little white lie isn't too obvious. 'What do you need?'

'It's just a quick one. Jamie Hazlehurst called,' she says. 'The paper is doing a big profile on me. Front page and everything. They've got a photographer coming around tomorrow to take the pictures.'

Bitter jealousy coats the inside of my mouth, like sticky, stinging tree sap. 'Congratulations on the torch-bearer thing, by the way.'

'Took you long enough to say it,' she says. Even with the intermittently blurry image on my phone, I can sense her judging me. Or is she hurt? It's hard to tell.

'What do you want from me, Lily?' My voice doesn't have even a hint of fight. I don't have the energy for it.

'It might be nice to feel like my sister was happy for my achievements one time,' she replies with a hollow laugh. 'Whenever something good happens to me, you're just sitting there being sour about it.'

My twin wants a bloody parade thrown for her every time she does something. But what do I get? Nothing.

'I'm not sour.' But even as I say the words, I'm aware the tone of my protest only bolsters her point. In my defence, we spent our entire lives being pitted against one another. Direct competition. A perfect, even comparison.

Apples for apples.

It's hard not to feel bitter that she won and I lost in the game of life. But even as I think those words a pang of shame rings through me. I *didn't* lose. I simply ended up with a different kind of gold. I have my husband, my son. A roof over my head. Friends. There are so many with less and I know I need to spend more time being grateful for what I have rather than focusing on what I don't.

But even as my therapist's words echo in my head – my mind flickers to the dirty picture on Malachi's phone. Can't I even go two seconds without focusing on the negatives? Maybe Sofia is right about me. I can be a real downer.

On the other end of the phone Lily sighs. I get the sense she's too tired to fight as well. We're turning thirty in a few months and it's been three decades of doing battle – board games, swimming, school. It's even noted in the 'baby book' that Mum diligently updated which of us walked first, spoke first, could read first. Maybe it's time we laid down our swords and went about our lives separately, not worrying what the other one is doing.

'Jamie mentioned he's going to get in touch with you as well.' There's a wariness to Lily's voice. 'The editor wants to cover what happened . . .'

The past comes back to me in flashes, water droplets sliding down my body as I exit the pool in my racing suit, muscles aching in the best way. I have a bounce in my step as I suck in the chlorine-scented air. Excitement jitters like a live wire in my tummy. Anticipation. Expectation. Desire. Everything is going my way. I'm at my peak. At my strongest.

I'm going to win. I feel invincible.

But then my phone is ringing, the trill cutting through the sound of thongs and slides slapping against heels and water splashing over the edge of the pool and people chattering nearby. Someone laughs and the sound bounces off the high glass ceiling. I answer. The voice on the other end of the line, tight as a wire, sends sickly intuition rippling through me like water disturbed by fluttering kicks.

Rose, it's bad news. Something prohibited has been found in your sample.

Time shunts forward. Cameras flash and microphones are thrust in my face as I try to duck, storming towards the big, old, imposing building. It stares down at me, judgement made before I've even had a chance to plead my innocence. I'm climbing the steps so fast it takes my breath away, tears stinging my eyes. Dad's hand grips my arm vice-like. He leaves a bruise – not because he wants to, but because he refuses to let go, to let me be whisked away from him by the hungry, angry crowd.

Rising swim star Rose Henderson-Lee suspended for taking banned substance.

Doping scandal rocks Aussie swim team – Henderson-Lee caught cheating?

Twins torn apart – one takes gold in youth championship and the other sits on the sidelines.

Furosemide.

It's a diuretic. I'd never even heard of it. But it's on the World Anti-Doping Agency's list of prohibited substances because it can be used by athletes to mask the presence of performance-enhancing drugs in urine tests. It's mostly used to mask steroids, but it can also excrete water for rapid weight loss in sports where being under a certain weight provides an advantage. The latter wasn't relevant to me. They thought it was steroids I was trying to hide.

'Rose?' Lily's voice yanks me back to the calm blue and white room. Outside, the rain has slowed to a bare patter and a gull cries out. 'Are you listening?'

I shake my head, trying to push the fog of the past away. 'Jamie called . . .'

'Yeah, that's what I said. He called about my interview and mentioned he was going to get in touch with you as well.' Her expression is hard to read, her eyes like dark brown pools of nothingness. 'I said you wouldn't be giving a statement.'

My back teeth clamp together as if magnetised. Even though I had no intention of allowing Jamie Hazlehurst to drag me back into the past, Lily's assumption that she can muzzle me is like a fire poker straight into my arse cheek. Suddenly, I want to act. To speak up.

'Funny, I don't remember having that discussion with you,' I reply coldly.

'Oh come *on*, Rose. You don't want to talk about it and we both know it,' she says.

The background shifts behind her. She's at my parents' place, in the spare room. I can tell because there are clear plastic tubs of red and gold decorations stacked against one wall. Chinese New Year was in February and Mum takes pride in decking the house out. We have a fortune sign that we hang upside down on the front window, red paper lanterns that Dad strings from the veranda out back, and lucky knots on the walls.

When I was a kid, it was always an exciting affair – making sticky rice balls with Mum, going into the city to watch the dancing dragons at Southbank and getting a fistful of precious hóngbāo red envelopes. Now that I'm married, however, that last part is over. It's Isaac's turn to take part in the tradition.

For a moment, I'm hit by a wave of sadness that Lily and I never relished doing those things together. It's why I've been staunch about not having a second child. I don't want Isaac to have that experience.

'You know what it would do to Mum and Dad if you gave an interview,' she adds.

I do.

The matter of my disgrace is a forbidden topic in their presence. In their house. We're breaking a cardinal rule even talking about it right now where Mum might walk in and overhear. There was a time where she barely spoke to me after it all happened. Dad was the one who took me to court, who shielded me from reporters, who stood by my side. Mum . . . she was too ashamed to come out in public. To this day, I don't know whether it was because she didn't believe me or because she couldn't handle the negative attention.

But I don't like being told what to do, especially not by Lily.

'You just don't want me casting a shadow over your success,' I say bitterly.

'Rose, I know you like to think you're always the victim but not everything is about you.' Her lips purse. 'This is supposed to be about *me*. I earned this the hard way.'

The implication is clear – she *still* doesn't believe me. After all these years. After a decade of me proclaiming my innocence. My own sister thinks I tried to cheat. That I needed drugs to beat her. Of *course* she thinks that – Lily's ego is bigger than Uluru.

If only Sofia could witness this. She's always held a grudge against me because I have my sister and she doesn't. She thinks I take this relationship for granted. That I'm ungrateful. Wasting a precious opportunity.

She'd give anything to have Daniella back and I . . . well, there are days where I wish I was an only child.

'I never took that drug,' I say through gritted teeth.

No matter how many times I say it, people don't believe me. They think the pressure to win got too much. That I couldn't rely on my talent to take me all the way. That I was desperate. That last part might be true. But I'm not a liar *or* a cheat.

Some people speculate my coach coaxed me into it. Not long after the doping scandal, he quit coaching altogether and moved overseas. Sofia and Ellie always found it suspicious. But I think I ruined his career as well as my own. Simple as that. The stench of a scandal like this never fully leaves you, even when you protest until you're hoarse and broken.

'The whole world knows you took that drug, otherwise you wouldn't have been found guilty.' There's a pity in her eyes. I don't like it. She thinks I'm less than her. Lower than her. 'I started to get faster than you and you couldn't take it.'

I hate to admit it, but there is truth in her words.

I'd always been faster than Lily, but she started to catch me the year after high school. She got herself a different performance coach and suddenly her head was in a different place. She was like a greyhound, bolting along after a rabbit. She started to accelerate in a way that terrified me. Because we'd always had our thing – I was the better swimmer and she was the better student. If I got an A, Lily got an A+. If I got ninety-eight per cent on a maths test, she got one hundred per cent. But I had more medals. I knew Lily had always wanted to go to university and study medicine, more than she wanted to swim.

But it changed that year. Suddenly she was better than me at *everything*.

I remember googling things late at night: natural performance enhancers that weren't on the banned list, exercises to increase speed and agility, success mindset meditations. Anything I could think of to stop her getting past me.

But nothing worked. She kept getting better and better. By the time we turned nineteen I'd started to see the writing on the wall – that Lily was going to get gold one day. And I would get silver. It made me cry in the middle of the night. Coming second was . . . it was torture. Especially coming second to her. So close and yet so far. The praise she would be showered in while I would get nothing.

In my family, second might as well be last.

I'll admit, I *did* get desperate.

'The past is in the past,' she says, shrugging. 'If you can't own up to it – if you *never* do own up to it – that's ultimately your choice. What I *do* care about is not having our family name dragged through the mud again by you getting all chatty with a reporter. If you can't do it for me, then do it for Mum and Dad. It's not fair on them. You know what happened to Mum last time.'

How could I forget? She didn't look me in the eye for years. It wasn't until I got pregnant that we started to patch things up, because she wanted to be involved in her grandson's life.

'If I want to talk, I'll talk,' I say, my face set into grim determination. 'Maybe it'll be good to tell the world that I'm doing just fine without swimming.'

I'm being contrary for the sake of it. It's not mature, I know. It's not the high road or the 'be the bigger person' thing to do. But right now I'm feeling raw and vulnerable and I want, for once in my bloody life, for someone to care about how *I* feel. And not to treat me like I'm just some annoying hanger-on. A pathetic footnote.

Lily looks at me for a long, hard minute, not saying anything. Eventually she shakes her head, disappointment flooding through the screen. 'You would always do anything to have the spotlight.'

It's not true. Not anymore. I don't want the spotlight anymore.

Because it shines too bright. It's a torch hunting for hidden things. Lies, half-truths, omissions, secrets. Anything the media can use to generate clicks. My career was the carcass thrown to the public for consumption. My life, their dartboard. My secrets, their treasure.

'Sorry, Lily, I have to go. I'll see you tomorrow.' I hang up before she can say anything else.

Dropping down onto the bed, I rub at my temple with my free hand. I can feel the tension building there, like a balloon being slowly blown up inside my head. It pushes on everything, making the space feel tight. Full. Should I talk to Jamie? Or should I be a good daughter and keep my mouth shut, letting myself fade back into obscurity once more?

Sometimes I wish I had that time machine we talked about back in high school – only I wouldn't go forward into the future like Ellie wanted to. No. I would go back into the past and fix my mistakes. Make better choices. Be a better version of myself. And I'm not talking about the doping scandal.

Because the biggest secret in my past isn't anything to do with drugs.

It's a crime far worse than that.

Chapter Eight

2013

Rose

'What do you mean I can't come?' I bounce on the spot, ashamed that tears are springing to my eyes so readily. I can't believe they're going to leave me out! We're supposed to be a group, but I swear Sofia tries to make it feel like her and Ellie are best friends and I'm just a tack-on. An afterthought. The third wheel.

'We need an alibi, Rose.' Sofia tosses her hands into the air like I'm stupid for not understanding. 'You have to be here so if anyone asks where we were, then you can say we were all hanging out here together.'

This whole 'hacking the school system to change Sofia's grade' might have been Ellie's idea, but Sofia has truly taken over the role of mastermind. She always does that. In her mind, her ideas are always right and she knows best and blah, blah, blah.

You just wish you were as confident as she is.

I brush aside the thought, because it makes yet more

tears prick my eyes. I can't cry. I can't give her reason to call me a baby.

'It's a really important job,' Ellie says, placing a hand on my arm. 'We couldn't do this without an alibi.'

'Then why do *you* get to go, too?' I hate how my voice really *does* make me sound like a baby. Lily says it all the time.

You always whinge so much, Rose. Wah, wah, wah, everyone should feel sorry for me.

That argument had devolved into me pulling her hair so hard she smacked me across the face. I'd had to rock up at training the following morning with a cut on my cheek from where her nail had made a little gash in my skin.

'Because *I* came up with this whole thing,' Ellie replies, stuffing a baseball cap over her head. It bulges at the back from where she's tied her blond hair into a bun. 'Besides, we can't use my house for the alibi. You know what my mum is like.'

Ellie's mum never leaves us alone when we go to her place. She's always hanging around, wanting to know what we're doing, trying to pretend like she's our friend. And we always have to eat gross things like celery and carrot sticks at her house. They have a 'no sugar' policy. Whereas here, at my place, Mum and Dad are off playing tennis with their friends. They won't be home until late. And Lily is studying for a biology test, so she won't come out of her room for hours.

We can do whatever we want.

'But why do *I* have to be here if no one is going to see us anyway?' I protest. 'Can't I just *say* we were here?'

I catch Sofia rolling her eyes. She does that a lot around

me. But it's not fair! I'm part of this group and I deserve to be part of this plan. Why do I always get the short straw?

'What if your parents come home?' Sofia is changing out of her school uniform and she doesn't bother to turn around when she whips the blue and white checkered dress over her head, revealing a lacy white bra underneath.

Not that she needs it. She's flat as McDonald's hotcakes.

'They *won't* come home. Wednesday night is comp night – they take that very seriously. No way would Mum leave the court early. One time she fell and sprained her wrist really bad, but she wouldn't let Dad take her to the twenty-four-hour clinic until the match was over. She played with one hand.'

'I thought tennis was one-handed anyway?' Ellie says, cocking her head, her mouth falling open in thought.

Sofia snorts and continues getting changed into a pair of black skinny jeans and a skin-tight black T-shirt. 'That's why you always get picked last in PE.'

'I want to come.' I have to stop myself from stamping my foot because that will *really* make me look like a baby. 'It's not fair that I have to stay behind.'

'Life isn't fair, Rose,' Sofia snaps. 'If life was fair then I wouldn't even be doing this in the first place, because my English teacher wouldn't be an arsehole who's trying to ruin my life. If life was fair, Ellie's dad wouldn't have fucked his assistant and you wouldn't have a twin who hates you.'

I don't know that Lily hates me, but she certainly doesn't *like* me. The feeling's mutual. She's the oldest by nine minutes and she acts like I only exist to take things that should be hers. Doesn't help that she's strong, like Mum. She doesn't cry or complain or need to be hugged.

She performs – all day, every day. I, on the other hand, am a needy pain in everyone's arse.

'You're staying here.' Sofia nails me with a look and I see Ellie frowning. She usually tries to stick up for me, but this time she stays quiet. 'End of discussion.'

'You're a bitch,' I mutter.

But the insult slips right off Sofia like water droplets on a lotus leaf. She doesn't care what I think of her. She doesn't really care what anyone thinks – aside from her parents and Ellie. And no matter what I do or how hard I try, I've never been able to break into that inner circle.

'It's for the best,' Ellie says gently, as she scrunches up her school dress and pushes it into a black nylon backpack. I cringe at how creased it's going to be when she takes it out later. 'Besides, if something goes wrong and we get caught . . . then you won't be in trouble.'

This *does* appeal to my rule-following ways. But FOMO is always stronger for me. I *hate* being left out! I bite down on my lip and think about what else I can say to make them change their minds.

'Nothing will go wrong,' Sofia says, straightening up after tying the laces on her black runners. She looks like she's about to burgle Bruce Wayne's mansion. 'Because everyone is going to play their part.'

I think for a moment about threatening to call the school and ruining Sofia's whole plan if they don't let me come along, but something in my intuition tells me this is a bad idea. Sofia's temper runs hotter than the molten core of the earth and, frankly, I don't want to get on her bad side.

She's changed a lot in the last year.

Before, she didn't used to be angry all the time. She was

light-hearted and funny and nice to people, and we . . . we were closer. After her sister died, Sofia became a different person. She got fixated on being the dux of the school, like that would somehow make up for the fact that Daniella was gone. I don't think perfect grades are going to make her parents feel any better about their daughter dying, but I'd never say that out loud. When she gets like this I wish we had the old Sofia back.

'We're going now,' she announces, slinging her backpack over her shoulder and marching out of my bedroom.

'Thanks for helping,' Ellie says, leaning in to give me a hug. 'I know you and Sofia don't see eye to eye all the time, but . . . things have really been hard for her. She needs this.'

I don't say anything back – what's the point? They're not going to listen to me.

I follow them down the hallway. Lily's door is closed, but I can hear the faint pulse of dubstep music floating out from the gap under her door. The sound makes me cringe. It's so . . . aggressive. Jarring. She always listens to that crap when she studies. I hate it.

As Sofia and Ellie leave, I stand in the doorway, watching them go. They hurry down the driveway, past the collection of garden gnomes Dad insists on keeping, despite everyone else in the house thinking they're super cringe. They walk close, arms linked, and jealousy sears through me hot and furious. Ellie might get picked last for PE, but I get picked last for friendship . . . and it hurts.

'Not even your friends can stand to be around you, huh?' Behind me Lily's voice turns up the boiler on my emotions.

I whip around and find her standing at the mouth of

the hallway, leaning against the wall, the white stick of a Chupa Chup dangling out of her mouth.

'Shut up, Lily.' I scowl. 'I'm going with them, I just forgot my keys.'

She looks pointedly down at my bare feet, the lollipop stick bobbing in her mouth as she sucks on it. 'Suuuuure.'

'Why are you such a bitch?' I fold my arms over my chest.

'I'm going to tell Mum you swore at me,' she says and I can't help the worry that flashes over my face, which only makes her laugh. She slaps a hand down on her thigh. 'God, one threat about telling Mum and you turn into a quivering mess.'

'I do not!' I'm aware I sound like I'm about to have a toddler tantrum.

Then I remember that we're supposed to have everyone think we're hanging out at home all evening. Crap! I've screwed up the alibi.

'Uh . . .' My brain whirs as I try to think of how to save things. 'We're just going to the milk bar and then we're coming back. Want anything?'

I'm betting on the fact that she'll say no on account of never wanting anything from me. Because if she asks me to bring back a Big M or something, then I'm done for.

'Nah, unlike you I'm watching my weight for the next meet.' She pats her stomach. 'I'm going to win the one-hundred-metre fly.'

I grit my teeth. 'We'll see about that.'

I stuff my feet into a pair of battered runners from the shoes lined up by the front door and grab the spare keys sitting in a little glass bowl on a console table.

'We'll be back in ten minutes,' I say, hoping I haven't ruined things.

Lily watches me go without saying a word.

*

The walk to school takes forty-five minutes, and the girls have a good head start on me. Bloody Lily. She always has to make me feel like a loser! I *am* part of this group and I won't be left behind.

The creek bubbles quietly as I clomp through the bush, trying to catch up to Ellie and Sofia. I can't tell how far ahead they are, because they're being quiet. Every so often I hear a twig snapping or the scuttle of something underfoot. There are probably *loads* of spiders here. I startle as I feel something brush my leg and I whip my hand down to swipe it away, but it's only a blade of long grass.

Don't go by the creek in summer; there's snakes.

I can hear Dad's warning ringing in my ears as fear winds through me, coiling around my heart like the aforementioned reptile. I want to call out, ask them to slow down and wait for me. But I know it's only going to result in Sofia yelling at me to go home.

I trudge ahead, keys jangling in my pocket. It's just before six-thirty p.m. when the school fence finally comes into view. I feel like I've been picking through the bush forever and I'm sweaty, my legs speckled with dirt and itching like something is crawling over my skin. I try to shake off the feeling.

'There are no spiders on you,' I say softly to myself. 'It's all in your head.'

It would have been easier to catch the bus, but Sofia

figured it was safer to go on foot because they could cut through the park and follow the creek, staying mostly out of sight. They're meeting Michelle at the back of the oval.

We're meeting Michelle at the back of the oval.

It's a good spot to sneak onto school grounds because there's a cut in the chain fence behind the sports equipment shed. It's where kids slip out to wag school. I've never done that. If Mum ever found out I left school in the middle of the day to go shopping – or whatever kids do when they wag – she'd rip me in two.

I suddenly notice how isolated I am. Big gum trees reach up towards the sky, their silvery-green leaves shuddering in the breeze. Something snaps a few metres behind me and I turn to look – but there's nothing there. It's probably an animal. I saw an echidna once, pottering around, lumbering on its stumpy little legs through the fallen leaves and discarded nest-building materials. Sometimes, if you're here early in the morning or later around dusk, you can even spot the kangaroos. They love to hop along the fence and the school is always warning us not to get too close if we see them. The males are huge!

I finally break through the trees near the oval. It looks like Ellie's backpack has gotten stuck on the fence and Sofia is trying to help free her. Thank goodness that slowed them down. I approach and two heads snap in my direction, one surprised and one furious.

'What are you doing here, Rose?' Sofia hisses. She's working to free Ellie's backpack and when she finally gets it loose, the fence falls back into place, sealing me on the outside.

'I didn't want to be left out.' I plant my hands on my

hips, wheezing a little. Everyone expects me to be super fit, but swimming fitness and bush-walking fitness are two *totally* different things. You don't have to scramble over things and worry about spiders and snakes in the pool. 'Gee, you guys move fast.'

'You were supposed to stay back and be our alibi.' Sofia tosses her hands in the air. 'Are you purposely trying to fuck this up?'

I shake my head, defiant. 'No, I'm not.'

'Then are you not able to understand basic instructions?' She glares at me and I say nothing, but I stand my ground.

Ellie comes forward and threads her fingers through the wire. 'You shouldn't be here, Rose.'

'Why not?' I hate that my voice sounds so wobbly.

They think I'll blow this whole thing. Sofia said it once – I'm an open book. An easy target. They probably think I'm going to get nervous and dob them in. Or crack if a teacher questions me. They don't think I can be trusted.

But I can.

'Because this is all risk and no reward for you,' Ellie says imploringly. 'If you get caught and kicked out of school, your parents will go mental. You might not be able to compete in swimming. We could get expelled! If we get caught—'

'We *won't* get caught unless we stand around here arguing,' Sofia says, tugging on Ellie's arm. 'Leave her.'

'I'm coming.' I press on the flap and try to squeeze myself through, fuelled by Sofia's desire to push me away. Something deep inside makes this feel like a make-or-break moment. If I don't come on this adventure, then I'm not really part of this group.

Then I don't really have friends.

Ellie sighs, her gaze swinging from me to Sofia and back again. She decides to side with me, because she pulls on the fence's flap to make more space for me to come through. Soon three of us are standing behind the equipment shed. Sofia looks like she's going to flip, but in the end her desire to solve her problem takes control.

'Come on,' she says, peering around the side of the shed to check that the coast is clear. 'Michelle said to meet her by the goal posts. I think I see her.'

As we emerge, we spot Michelle walking towards us with her arms wrapped around her body. I've noticed that she doesn't *ever* raise her hand in class to answer questions. In fact, she barely speaks at all. The day we went to go see her after school in the computer labs she spoke the most words I've ever heard her say.

She's wearing baggy jeans with sneakers and a white T-shirt with a saggy neckline. It looks like she stole the items from the closet of someone two to three sizes bigger than her.

'You got the money?' Michelle asks as we meet up.

Sofia nods and pulls an envelope from her bag. The paper is bright pink, like it was intended to accompany a birthday card. Michelle opens the envelope and inside is a messy jumble of currency, mostly blue ten-dollar notes and orange twenties. I spy a rogue yellow fifty-dollar note too, as Michelle counts it.

Sofia didn't tell us where she got $500, but I can guess. I know she's been trying to save for a car, but that's slow going when you work in food service. Would she have stolen the rest of it from her parents? I couldn't imagine her doing that, since Sofia lives for her family.

But she seems so desperate lately.

'Let's go.' Michelle pockets the envelope. Maybe that's why her jeans are so big and baggy – don't need a backpack if you have huge pockets. 'We're going to climb in through the computer lab window. I made sure to unlock it and leave it open a crack when I was in class this afternoon, so we can get in.'

'What about security cameras?' I ask, my eyes darting around as we walk. The gravity of the situation – of the *crime* we're about to commit – is starting to sink in. 'There could be some, right? Do you think they have that kind of security? What if—'

'No cameras,' Michelle says with complete confidence. 'They've been talking about putting CCTV in key spots, like the admin office and at the entrance. But there's a group of parents who've been protesting it because of privacy.'

'How do you know all this?' Ellie asks.

'Teachers feel sorry for me, so they let me bend the rules. I go places where other students don't and I hear things.'

Why did the teachers feel sorry for her? I'd heard rumours her dad turned up at the school one time yelling and the police were called. But I never found out why.

We're almost all the way across the oval now and it feels freakishly open out here, like anyone could come out of the building and see us. But the school looks dark inside and there's nothing going on at this hour. Footy practice wrapped up an hour ago – Sofia checked the schedule – and the only other after-school activity was tae kwon do in the gym. But they finished earlier, too.

We make our way to the outside window of the computer lab, which is in a small courtyard area surrounded by the other lab-style classrooms, like the two science labs, woodworking lab and art lab. Calling the latter two 'labs' feels a bit dumb, but I think the school is just trying to sound fancy.

Michelle pulls a screwdriver out of one of her massive pockets and jams it into the corner of the window, using it to lever the sliding window open enough to wrap her hand around the side of it so she can ease it open the rest of the way.

The window is kind of high and I wonder how we're going to get over the ledge. Michelle motions Ellie over. 'Give me a boost.'

Ellie laces her fingers together and squats down, ready for Michelle's foot, which she places there as she steadies her hand on the window's frame. 'Ready?'

'Ready.'

Ellie boosts her up, grunting with effort. They manage to get up high enough for Michelle to hook a leg over the edge of the sill and then she drops down on the other side. A second later I hear the scrape of a chair against the floor.

Sofia strides over and puts her foot into Ellie's hand before I even have a chance to ask who's next. Ellie boosts her up with a bit more ease than she did with Michelle, and Sofia is surprisingly agile as she slides through the open window.

Ellie then turns to me. I walk forward, expecting her to hold out her interlaced hands, but instead she brushes her palms down the front of her jeans. 'Go home, Rose. You don't need to be here putting yourself at risk.'

My heart sinks. She doesn't want me here, either?

'Then why are you here?' I ask, bunching the hem of my

T-shirt in one fist. I feel worthless. Invisible. 'You don't have to put yourself at risk, either.'

'Sofia is like my family,' she says with a shrug. I know there was a time in year eight, after her dad left, when Ellie stayed with Sofia's family. They took her to school every day and she slept in Sofia's bed. I'd been jealous of that – and I think it's how they got so close. 'I owe her.'

'Come *on*,' Sofia says, poking her head out the window. 'What's the hold-up?'

'Last chance to save yourself,' Ellie says. 'You don't have to do this.'

But her words only cement my stubbornness. I *won't* be left out. I won't be second best, like I am at home. I hold my foot up, awaiting her hands, my eyes locked onto hers. With a resigned nod of her head, Ellie holds her hands out and boosts me up.

There's no turning back.

For better or worse, we're all in this together now.

Chapter Nine

2024

Sofia

The evening is surprisingly uneventful. I'd expected the three of us to sit around and get rowdy on champagne playing the silly bridal games I'd planned since Ellie's schedule hasn't allowed time for a hens party. But Ellie seems out of sorts and Rose refuses to put her phone down, constantly looking at photos of her son and checking to see if her husband has called. I'd be lying if I said I wasn't disappointed that we all went to bed before eleven o'clock.

Are we officially old now? What happened to us?

Now it's almost one a.m. and I can't sleep. The bed is comfortable – a Goldilocks perfect mattress with sumptuous Egyptian cotton sheets, fluffy marshmallow pillows and a soft linen doona. I hate feeling the empty space in the bed next to me and I think about calling Rob to see if he's up for a little phone sex. Not as good as the real thing, obviously. My own fingers will *never* compare to what he can do with his tongue. But with the quality of the camera on my phone it could certainly scratch the itch, at least for now.

But if Rose wakes up and hears us I'll never hear the end of it. She's a bit of a prude like that. One time she told me off for making a comment about my sex life when we were all at brunch because it was 'vulgar' to discuss such things in public. According to her, sex shouldn't be discussed at all. I almost wanted to ask her if a stork delivered her baby or if she had to do it the old-fashioned way.

Huffing, I turn onto my back. Then I throw one arm over my eyes. Then I kick the covers off. Why can't I get comfortable?

Groaning, I push myself up into a sitting position and roll my shoulders, trying to release the tension there. I'm sure the reason I can't sleep is because I'm still stewing on that bad review. Am I overreacting? Probably. But thinking about someone purposefully writing a bad review for something I didn't do . . . ooh, it boils my blood.

And not knowing who did it only makes that feeling worse.

I push off the edge of the bed and my bare feet hit the cool floorboards. Maybe a cup of warm water will help get my body into sleep mode. I can't afford to be tired tomorrow, because we've got a lot of work to do and I want to be awake early enough to get a swim in, if the weather permits.

Trying to be as quiet as possible, I pad into the open-plan kitchen and living area of the cottage. It's dark outside, but the distant turning lens of the lighthouse makes the darkness rise and fall like breath. It's almost eerie, how quiet it is. I can hear Rose snoring in her room. She chugs like a freight train! It's a wonder her husband gets any sleep at all.

I don't bother turning on the lights since the glow from

the lighthouse gives my eyes enough to get around. We've left the blinds open. It's not like anyone is going to peer in since it's just us here on the property tonight. Well, and Nikoleta, I assume. But I doubt she's going to be skulking around trying to look in the windows while we sleep.

I hold the kettle under the faucet, looking out the large window that faces the coastline. From here I can see The Glass House, and the lighthouse beyond it. As the light flashes from the lantern room at the top of the lighthouse, the glow reflects across the glass, illuminating it for a moment, then plunging it back into darkness. Thick, dark clouds gather in the sky and the whole effect seems delightfully gothic – like something in a sweeping romance novel with a heroine trapped in a crumbling castle and a love interest who might just be a villain.

I make my drink, flicking off the kettle before it can whistle and wake Rose. For some reason, warm water calms me. It was something my mother used to do when I couldn't sleep as a kid, my perfectionistic tendencies pushing slumber away on a regular basis. As I stand here sipping, looking at the dark mural of a view, I lean against the countertop.

My laptop is sitting where I'd plugged it in to charge earlier. I click the trackpad to bring the screen to life and my business inbox is the first thing I see. There are more than thirty new emails – and more Google reviews.

With a sinking feeling in my stomach, I click on one of the alert emails and follow the link to the review.

> *Sofia Quadrini is the* last *person you want to plan your wedding – she's unprofessional, rude, and defensive. She will never admit when she's wrong. Arguing with her*

caused me so much stress on my wedding day that I was crying in the toilets before I cut my cake with my new husband. She ruined our big day. I have never regretted hiring someone so much – Sally-Anne

It's another name I don't recognise. Another situation that doesn't sound familiar. I have *never* argued with a bride on their wedding day or reduced a client to tears. Ever.

I navigate back to the inbox with a shaking hand and click on another review alert. I'm not surprised to find it's yet *another* one-star review.

Sofia cancelled on us at the last minute, leaving me without any support on my big day! I booked her because of all these great reviews and I was so disappointed. We had to scramble last minute to find someone to take over. You can't trust her! – Marisha

I click on the next email and follow the link. One star again.

I don't know what is happening with Ms Quadrini lately. She came highly recommended by a friend . . . but it was a total disaster! She messed up key details for our wedding's theme, dropped the ball on several big items. Our wedding was only a shadow of what it could have been. Worst of all was that she flirted *with my husband in front of me on the day. Can you believe it? – Lydia*

I couldn't, actually. Because it never happened.

I want to vomit. Why the hell would I do *any* of these things? It would be bad for business. Brides might be difficult, but most of them want the same things: to feel beautiful, supported and to have their day be as drama-free as possible.

That's it. If I do my job properly, they'll barely notice I'm there.

I have *never* cancelled on anyone last minute and I have absolutely never flirted with anyone's husband. Like with Tegan, the names of these brides are unfamiliar – Sally-Anne and Marisha and Lydia.

This isn't an error. The reviews are fake. They're an attack.

The profiles attached to the reviews reveal nothing – though they appear active enough that they don't look fake. Frustrated, I pull up my CRM system and run a search for the name 'Tegan'. The software is custom-designed and it's brilliant – it allows me to track all the nitty-gritty details of a wedding, from the colour palette, links to the client's inspiration boards, likes and dislikes, and the names of all the important people like bridal party members, parents, siblings et cetera. But my search results in nothing.

I repeat the process for Sally-Anne, Lydia and Marisha, but come up similarly empty.

Rob would probably tell me it was nothing more than an internet troll and that I should ignore it. But I can't! Something about these reviews feels . . . personal. I mean, they all mention me by name. Not my business. *Me*.

I close my laptop screen and rub at my eyes, frustrated. Rose has finally stopped snoring. I listen out to hear if she's woken up, perhaps hearing the clink of my mug against the countertop or me tapping at my computer. But her door remains closed. I'm sipping the last of my water when I hear something faint outside. I still, gaze darting to the big glass panels running along the back of the cottage – a modern adjustment to the old building. I squint, trying to see. I can make out the shapes of the outdoor table and chairs, every so often illuminated by the light directed towards us by the lighthouse's Fresnel lens.

There's a blur of shadow by the door. Movement.

The hairs on the back of my neck immediately stand on end and I feel my stomach clench. There's a person out there.

What if someone is looking to break in? Maybe they know the usual clientele Dom has here and they think there's money to be had.

Heart hammering, I quietly shrink back against the kitchen counter and open one of the drawers, searching for something to use for self-defence. There's a set of knives and I wrap my hand around one of the handles, easing it out and letting it fall by my side as I crouch down behind the kitchen cabinets.

There's not much here of value, unless they're planning to make off with the designer furniture. Nobody carries cash anymore, and Rose and I didn't bring our wedding presents with us. We left those for the boys to bring tomorrow. But a criminal might not know that. They might be looking for jewellery or expensive handbags. A dark thought rockets through me – what if they're here for something other than monetary value? Maybe someone knows we're three women here alone. A sick churning sensation makes me sway.

We're totally – *totally* – alone. Totally vulnerable. There's nothing along the winding dirt road leading to this place for kilometres. The nearest town is a thirty-minute car ride away. If we scream, no one will hear us.

I contemplate going to Rose's bedroom to wake her. Two against one is better odds. But what if there's more than one person outside? I tighten my grip on the knife.

Be calm, keep your head on your shoulders. Panicking is the worst thing you can do.

I slowly creep alongside the cabinets until I can peer around the corner into the living area. My heart pounds like a punching fist and I flatten myself against the wooden doors, the handle of one poking into my arm. I strain to listen. Outside, something scrapes along the ground. Or maybe it's shuffling. My irrational mind conjures up the image of a half-decayed zombie with a familiar face.

Expressionless eyes. Mouth open, blood splattered.

Fear turns to rage, even though I know I can't afford to let my fire take over. I do stupid things when I let my emotions run hot. I do life-ending things.

I look out through the glass and swear I see a shadow there, someone reaching for the door handle, but as the lighthouse lens turns, I see that it's just a potted plant, spindly branches capped with leaves rather than arms and hands. A leaf bobs in the breeze, rubbing against the glass.

Have I imagined the whole thing?

I slowly get to my feet, never letting my eyes leave the glass panes. My ears strain, trying to turn silence into information. But it's quiet and I'm alone.

It's all in my head.

Admonishing myself for being paranoid, I walk over to the window and look outside. The calm landscape is spread before me, benign and peaceful. I'm an idiot. One night away from my husband and I turn into a mess. No way am I going to mention this to the girls tomorrow; they'll think I was hitting the wine too hard.

I head back to the kitchen and return the knife to the drawer. The clock tells me it's past one-thirty now, and I really need to get some sleep. Just as I'm about to head back to bed there's a soft knock at the front door and it takes everything in me not to let out a cry. With a shaking hand, I swipe my thumb across the screen of my phone. I'm about to dial triple-0 when a text pops up.

ELLIE: Are you awake? I'm at the front door.

I pad over and look out of the little peephole. Sure enough, it's her. Why am I so on edge right now? I'm making monsters out of nothing. I let out a shaky breath and pull the door open, surprised to find Ellie's face crumpled.

She's definitely been crying. Her eyes are puffy and red-rimmed, and the bags underneath are big enough to carry luggage for a round-the-world cruise. Her skin has a sickly pallor to it and her hair is unbrushed, sticking up in a weird way, like she slept funny. Or tried to.

'Hey, what's going on?' I pull the door open wider. 'Are you okay?'

'It's . . . just . . . I couldn't sleep . . .' She hiccups. 'Oh, Sof . . . everything is turning to shit.'

'What do you mean?'

She lets out a wobbly breath. But she doesn't say anything. It's almost like she's trying to find the right words. Her eyes shift around, not landing on anything in particular. There's a tornado in her head – I can feel it.

'Is it Mitch?' I ask, scanning her face for tells.

'No, no.' She shakes her head. 'It's work. I . . . I got kicked off the movie.'

'*What?*'

She looks up at me with tear-filled eyes. 'This was supposed to be my Oscar. My dream movie. And now it's ruined.'

I reach out and pull her towards me, wrapping my arms around her. She hugs me back, her body shaking with quiet sobs. I pat her back. 'Oh, Ellie. I'm so sorry.'

How many times have we been like this during our lives? When she came to stay with my family, when Daniella died, when Nonno died, when Ellie got her first big Hollywood rejection for a part she desperately wanted. When she got her second, third and fourth rejections and was thinking about giving up. When I had to drop out of university to take care of my mother, who wouldn't get out of bed and refused to eat after Dad passed away. When I had to take a job working at a bridal store to make ends meet and keep the lights on. When a producer told Ellie to lose more weight for a role when she was already hungry all the time. When a mean-spirited film critic said she was wooden and untalented. When I overheard my father-in-law calling me a 'dirty wog' behind my back.

Ellie and I have always found comfort in one another.

'Come inside. I'll make us a cuppa and you can tell me everything,' I say.

I guide her into the cottage and tell her to go sit on the couch. I wonder if she was hovering around outside the front door, trying to work up the nerve to knock. That's probably what I was hearing all along. Just the shuffling footsteps of a friend in need, not the psycho killer I'd sketched with my imagination.

But just as I'm about to close the front door to go tend to Ellie and her tears, I notice something. By The Glass House, with its sheer, reflective walls, there's a shadow. Someone opens the door and slips inside.

TUESDAY

Chapter Ten

Ellie

I wake, disoriented. It's dark from the heavy block-out blinds, but a single thread of sunlight slips past the edge, carving a line down the wall beside the bed. Next to me, Sofia sleeps curled into a ball like she's always done, long brown hair fanned out across the pillow. It reminds me of being a teenager again, when I stayed at her home, sharing her bed every night, feeling comforted by her presence. She never once made me feel like I was intruding. No one in her family did.

I'm sad her mum and nonna aren't coming to the wedding. I'd invited them, of course. But her nonna is frail these days and doesn't leave the house, and her mum finds weddings too sad. Sofia once confessed that she had to beg her mum to come to her own wedding and that she was sure the tears she shed during the ceremony were for Daniella and not her.

Last night Sofia stayed up with me while I cried, holding me, both of us trying to keep quiet so we didn't wake Rose. But eventually she stirred and joined us on the couch, the two of them comforting me while I panicked that my career was over. Sleeping didn't help my anxiety, like it usually does. There's still a feeling of dread in the pit of my stomach. Still a menacing dark cloud in my brain. I tried to call Mitch last night after I got off the phone with Rashida, but he must have already boarded the plane. He's due to land later this morning.

I have to talk to him. I can't let him hear about the Antoine thing from the media.

The vitriol has already started to flood in.

Homewrecker.

Slut.

Disgrace.

The pictures have been splashed across the internet with frightening speed and my DMs are awash with hate mail. The worst of all are the messages about how I'm a bad role model for young girls. Those cut deepest. Fanny has already made a statement that we have 'parted ways' and I will no longer be part of *Heartland*. My entire world has begun to fall apart. I'm like a quilt with the stitching unravelling, the threads popping, popping, popping until I'm left in pieces.

But I can't stop wondering how anyone managed to take these photos or even how they knew to *look* for us in the first place. Antoine and I were covert. If we were at a restaurant, there was no kissing or intimacy so anyone looking at us might assume we were having a business meeting. This wasn't because we were having an affair – or so I thought at the time – but because of my concern about people thinking I was sleeping my way to the top. He'd shared those concerns, because of #MeToo. Not to mention the 'fact' – as I believed at the time – that he and his wife hadn't yet announced their divorce.

But someone found out.

Now three slightly grainy, washed-out photos are circulating. We're standing in a small courtyard, outside a pretty but rather unremarkable apartment building in Paris. It was Antoine's second place – the place where he was supposedly staying during the separation from his wife, but which actually turned out to be a property he'd rented behind her back.

Antoine and I are close, heads bowed. In one photo he has his hand on my arse, clear as day against my fitted black jeans. In the next photo I've turned to him, smiling. And in the third we're kissing, bodies pressed together, and it's unmistakable what's going to happen the second we get inside.

But *who* knew about his secret apartment? Who tipped off the paparazzi to follow us? And why keep it quiet the past five years?

Nobody outside Australia knew who the hell I was back then. I was just another Hollywood hopeful. A mid-twenties blonde who'd done a few years on an Aussie soap opera and was working two jobs to make ends meet, taking whatever bit parts I could get. The best friend, the sister, the sidekick. Unnamed inmate. A background figure. The first chick to get killed off in a B-grade horror movie.

Back then, I was *not* someone worth following. I don't remember ever having someone try to take my picture.

But the person who took these photos *could* have exposed Antoine's affair. He's a successful director. Not a household name – not a Tarantino or a Lucas or a Bay

– but big enough that if they'd wanted to blackmail him I could almost guarantee he would have paid up to keep his secret. The photographer could have made some solid coin. So why wait? Why not cash in as soon as the pictures were taken?

Why sit on them for five bloody years?

It's almost as if whoever took the photos popped them on a hard drive, waiting for me to get famous enough for them to be worth something. Waiting for a time when it would hurt me the most.

But why?

An irrational thought streaks through my brain, a lightning-fast bullet of anxiety that makes me wonder . . .

Is this connected to what happened at school?

I immediately shake it off. Every time something bad happens I wonder if it's karmic retribution. But Hollywood is about as far away from little old Lalor as you could possibly get. I'm being paranoid.

Yet a tiny voice in the back of my mind tells me I have reason to be.

The person who took these photos wanted to hurt *me*, not Antoine. I'm sure of it.

How am I going to explain things to Mitch? The media are presenting these images as current. Like the affair is recent. Active. Because how would they know when it happened? There's no date stamp and someone who follows a person to take 'gotcha' photos is hardly going to be honest.

Aside from the fact that I'm wearing skinny jeans, which I wouldn't be caught dead in now, the photos could have been taken whenever.

'Ellie?' Sofia's eyes are open, sharp. She's watching me like a mama bear. 'Stop that.'

She smacks my hand away from my mouth. I didn't even notice that I was chewing my nails, and now they sting like my brain has caught up to the fact that I'm inflicting pain on myself. The nail is ragged and my cuticle is torn, bloody. You can see the tender underside the nail normally protects.

Morgan is going to kill me.

'Is it pointless to ask if you got any sleep?' Sofia looks concerned.

'I'm fine,' I lie. My eyes are hanging out of my head. They're dry and gritty and my mouth feels like it's stuffed with cotton balls.

She raises an eyebrow. 'Don't bullshit me, McLeod.'

I scrub my hands over my face. 'I'm worried about Mitch . . . the articles make it sound like the affair is recent. But I swear, I didn't even know him back then.'

The wobble in my voice makes her brows crease. 'He'll believe you. He loves you.'

'I guess we'll find out.' I sigh. 'Who knows? Maybe he's been looking for an excuse to run.'

Even saying these words makes my chest clench. The thought of Mitch leaving, even though we've only been together a short time, is anxiety-inducing. I saw what it did to my mum when Dad left. I don't want to end up like that.

Sofia pushes up to a sitting position and grabs my arm, giving me a little shake. 'I don't know why you always talk yourself down like that. You're Ellie fucking McLeod and you're a bloody award-winning actress. You're a legit star and one of the kindest, most generous good-hearted people in the world. He wouldn't be marrying you otherwise. You're a catch.'

I'm not sure about that. Right now, I feel like an idiot who's made all the wrong decisions and is on the fast track to becoming a has-been. Not to mention getting jilted at the altar.

'Don't even try to argue with me,' Sofia says before I can voice those fears aloud. 'This is a blip, okay? In a few days, the internet will have moved on to something else. Look at Kristen Stewart – she's all over the fashion mags now and everyone loves her. They've all forgotten about the time she cheated on Robert Pattinson with that smarmy director.'

I stare at a spot on the doona. There's a smear of blood. The vibrant crimson is almost obscene against the soft creamy linen and it makes an image flash into my mind. A body on the ground, unmoving, eyes rolled back as if looking into the past. Blood dots the corner of their mouth, like a fleck of crimson paint. It's the only colour that remains as their skin seems to turn pale before my eyes. There's no rise and fall in their chest, no twitch in their fingers.

Lifelessness. Nothing.

I suddenly feel like I'm going to vomit.

I push off the bed and stumble forward, towards the ensuite bathroom.

'Ellie?' Sofia is at my side in a moment, steadying me. Her eyes search my face. 'Are you okay? Do you feel sick?'

'I . . .' My breathing is coming fast. Too fast. I can't get the air in.

I squeeze my eyes shut, trying to calm down enough to get a proper breath all the way in, but it's like trying to suck a pebble up a straw. I haven't felt like this in a long time. Not since . . . not since . . .

'Shouldn't we call triple 0?' I can't take my eyes off the body on the floor.

'No,' the girls say. A chorus of denial.

The person on the ground doesn't move. Are they breathing? Are they . . . still alive?

The girls try to herd me away. Hands pulling, mouths whispering, voices pleading. Trying to convince me that it's okay to leave someone in need.

To leave them to suffer.

'We could call anonymously.' I wring my hands together. 'And leave before . . .'

But we didn't leave right then. We didn't run. We should have.

Maybe things would have turned out differently.

My knees buckle and I hit the floor, on all fours, desperately trying to drag in a breath. It's like I'm there. The body just . . .

Not fucking moving.

'Ellie, Jesus. You're scaring me.' Sofia is at my side, a flittering little bird, her arm encircling my shoulders.

My heart is still thundering, so I sit there, allowing it to slow. Allowing Sofia to hold me. My entire life feels like a mess right now – losing this movie, potentially having Mitch think I'm cheating on him, having the whole *world* think I'm a bitch and a slut and God only knows what else . . . it's too much.

'You're okay,' Sofia says, rubbing soothing circles on my back. 'You're not alone. Mitch doesn't hate you. You'll book another movie.'

I finally get a proper breath in. Then another. And another.

'Should I call your mum?' she asks softly.

I shake my head. 'Don't. It'll just stress her out for the drive down here. I'll tell her when she arrives. She'll make it all about her, anyway.'

'Do you want me to see if I can get a lawyer onto things? I might not have graduated, but I still have all those old contacts. We keep in touch.'

'Not yet.' I shake my head. The dark edges start to flare up, but I can't afford to fall apart. 'I can't do anything until Mitch gets here. I need to speak to him first.'

'How about we have a breakfast picnic on the beach?' she suggests gently. 'Go for a swim, try to take your mind off things. Tiff will be arriving before lunch and I think you said Morgan is coming around then, too?'

I nod. I spoke with Morgan last night, since I need her help with managing this situation. She's taken over my emails and social media for now, as well as responding to any local media enquiries. Thank God I have her and Rashida and my publicist to help shield me from the worst of it. Now I can focus on making sure Mitch doesn't think I'm cheating on him.

'That's a good idea.' I nod. 'A breakfast picnic sounds great.'

Within half an hour the three of us are on the beach. Last night's storm is a distant memory with the wide blue sky gleaming like freshly polished aquamarine. A few wispy clouds drift overhead and the ocean sparkles as each gentle, silver-capped wave rolls lazily in like a tongue lapping at the shore. There's a set of wooden plank steps that lead down from the cliff edge to the beach below. We move slowly, gingerly, because the steps seem rickety and they creak and groan under our weight.

Rose grips my arm as we make our way down, carrying towels and tote bags stuffed with bread and fruit and cheese. Sofia even made some coffee and put it in a thermos so we could have a nice hot drink with our breakfast.

I'm trying my hardest to be in the moment. This is supposed to be a special time – my last days a single woman, spending them with the friends I've held dear since childhood. Instead I'm panicking about my career. My reputation. Wondering if my marriage will even go ahead after all.

A sudden surge of anger bubbles up inside me, hot and sticky. I want to kick something.

Fucking Antoine and his lies. Mitch still hasn't answered his phone – the plane landed ten minutes ago. I know this, because I've been watching the flight tracker like a hawk. I texted him to say hi and hope he had a good flight and to ask him to call me. The sad thing, however, is that the real reason I texted was so he knows that *I know* he's landed and he can't avoid me. Jesus. If Sofia knew what I was doing she'd tell me I was acting like Rose and to get my shit together.

But I'm panicking. What if he doesn't believe me? What if he thinks the same as the people sending me hate mail? That I'm a homewrecker. A liar.

'I can't believe Dom has this all to himself,' Sofia says. She's the first one to make it to the bottom, where the white sand meets the last step. She pauses to slide off her brown leather sandals and picks them up, letting them dangle from one fingertip while she scrunches her toes in the sand. 'It's magnificent.'

She's not wrong.

The beach isn't huge, but it's spectacular. A defined section of sand tapers off in both directions. To the right, the beach dissolves into a sheer rock face, and to the left it slowly tapers out in a long point. The only way to get down to this section of the beach is from the stairs we just descended, or perhaps by boat. Otherwise, it's totally secluded. Totally private. It's almost like we could drift out to sea and simply cease to exist.

'What a view!' Sofia says. 'If I had this place, I'd never want to leave.'

She's wearing plunging black bathers with an oversized blue and white striped shirt over the top, the sides flapping open in the breeze. Her olive skin is tanned and her dark brown hair hangs in a loose plait down her back, several strands fluttering down around her face. Over the crook of one arm is a straw bag, the top of the thermos and a French stick poking out.

There aren't many moments in Sofia's life where she looks totally free. Being by the water is one of them.

'Same,' Rose echoes as she continues ahead, lugging a battered Woolies tote that's lumpy with fruit and other snacks.

She, on the other hand, looks overdressed for the beach. Too many layers. She's in jeans with the bottoms cuffed, a paisley print singlet top that swishes around her hips untucked, with a lightweight cardigan over it. It almost looks like she's going to the supermarket or the bank, rather than the beach.

'You going to take that all off and go for a swim?' I ask, giving her a nudge as we walk across the sand, our heels digging into the soft surface and leaving evidence of us behind. 'You're going to boil.'

'It's not *that* hot.' She avoids my eyes.

I wonder if she's ever been back in the water after what happened. I still remember the day I found out – not from Rose, but from the seven o'clock news. I'd been having dinner with Mum, one of the calorie-controlled meals she made for me back then. Low fat. Low carb. Low taste. Bland white fish with a few scant boiled baby potatoes and a mound of steamed vegetables. I'd been pushing a carrot around my plate when Rose's face flashed up on the screen, along with declarations that she'd been caught cheating.

I couldn't believe it. Rose wasn't the kind of person to cheat or take drugs – she was too scared of the consequences. Now, if it was Sofia . . . *that* would be a different story. She had the drive and the ruthlessness to do it. But not Rose. I still remember shaking my head and pointing at the telly, defending her. My mother had simply shrugged and said, *'Everyone fails their moral code eventually, if they get desperate or greedy enough.'* Cynical.

But that was Mum after Dad left – always thinking the worst of everyone.

'You brought your bathers though, right?' I ask.

'It was on the packing list I sent around,' Sofia adds as she comes to a stop, declaring this to be the best spot to sit on the beach. The sun beams down and I feel it seeping into my muscles, trying to loosen me up.

Maybe everything will be okay with Mitch. And with my career eventually. Maybe I'm worrying for nothing.

'I didn't feel like going for a swim today,' Rose says, plonking her bag down on the sand and shaking out a large colourful beach towel.

Sofia looks at me with a raised eyebrow, but I don't say anything. Rose has refused to talk about her trial and the subsequent media attention all these years. I know she was offered a lot of money, too. *Sixty Minutes* wanted to do an exclusive interview – they tried for *years* to get her to talk. But she clammed up tight, as did the rest of her family. Lily went on to have an incredible career, but it was always peppered with comments and questions about Rose. People speculated about whether she'd ever cheated herself, but nothing ever came of it. Lily kept her nose clean and Rose faded into the shadows.

'Well, I want you girls to have fun. So, whatever that means to you, then do that.' I shake out my own towel and lay it down. Then I slip off my crochet beach cover-up to get maximum sun on my skin.

My bikini is one of those strapless, bandeau types that won't leave any unsightly white marks on my shoulders. I wriggle the fabric down my chest to expose as much of myself to the sun as possible without getting my nips out. At least here, I can do it without the fear of any paps watching me.

You didn't think they were watching you five years ago, either.

'That's it, get your tits out, McLeod.' Sofia waggles her eyebrows at me and I laugh. Out of the corner of my eye I see Rose subtly tug her cardigan closed, brows furrowed. 'Got to do it now while we have total privacy. Geez, you could go buck naked here and nobody would see.'

'We're not doing that, are we?' Rose looks mildly horrified.

'Maybe.' Sofia shrugs as she starts setting up the picnic. 'We're all alone here. We can do anything we want.'

For some reason, the statement makes me look over my shoulder, back towards the steps leading up and away from the beach. There's a prickle along my spine, like someone *is* watching us. But as my gaze scans the land around us, there's nothing. Nobody. The stretch of beach is empty, except for us three and a handful of gulls who pad around the firmly packed sand, pecking around and looking for grub. It's totally silent, the soothing *whoosh* of the ocean like a relaxation soundtrack, lulling us. Calming us. Tempting us to forget our trouble and even the existence of the outside world.

Here we are free. We are ourselves. We are delightfully and gloriously alone, revelling in the pure peacefulness only a deserted beach can provide.

That is, until a blood-curdling scream rips through the air.

Chapter Eleven

Rose

The scream sets off something inside me. Maybe it's a mother's instinct. A woman's instinct. Or maybe it's that I'm someone who has been hunted by others.

Prey. A victim. Now, a forgotten footnote.

I take off running towards the stairs, already losing ground to Ellie who's fighting fit from training for her last movie, and Sofia who runs for fun. Their feet kick up plumes of sand with each powerful stride and I feel the spray of the tiny grains against my shins. Beads of moisture gather along my hairline and trickle down my spine as I propel myself forward, bare feet pounding, thongs left behind in the sand. I'm sweltering in my inappropriately warm outfit.

Better than running in a bikini. Nobody needs to see that.

The air is eerily quiet after the scream. Not even the gulls cry, perhaps frightened away by what I can only describe as a sound of absolute fear. Was it human or animal? Sometimes goats sound like a human screaming. But I haven't seen any goats here since we arrived yesterday.

'What do you think that was?' I huff as we reach the stairs. Ellie is already striding up with ease, but Sofia is going slower, stepping carefully.

'No idea,' she replies, turning to look at me over her shoulder. Her dark brows are furrowed. Whatever it is, it's got her spooked too. 'I didn't hear a thud or a big splash . . .'

Oh God, I hadn't even thought of that – the cliff that Nikoleta warned us about. The sheer drop to what could very well be sudden death. Or, at the very least, a lifetime of pain. I push harder, panting as I approach the top of the steps. Ellie is already on the grass above.

'Morgan!' she calls out, still running.

'Morgan?' I try to place the name for a moment and then I remember that she's Ellie's assistant.

Sofia makes it up onto the grass just ahead of me and when I follow behind her I'm surprised that I see . . . nothing. At least, not at first. Three women stand clustered in front of The Glass House – Nikoleta and two younger women in their early-to-mid-twenties, both blond. One natural, one definitely *not*. At first I don't quite understand what made one of them scream. But as I finally make it over to the group, the last to arrive, understanding filters through me like cold droplets of frigid ice water.

The Glass House has been . . . defaced.

Across the transparent walls are big sweeping streaks of something dried and red. At first it looks like someone has swirled paint across the glossy surface – possibly with their hands. Maybe a brush. It's only when I take a step back and look at the wall in its entirety that I realise the swirls are letters. A message.

I know what you did.

On the ground, under the writing is a pile of . . . oh my God. I turn, clamping a hand over my mouth as something sticky and acidic rushes up the back of my throat. I can't stop it. I've never had a strong stomach and my trigger-hair gag reflex has shamed me many times before. When I was pregnant it was constant. So embarrassing. But this . . . this is understandable. Reasonable. Nobody could look at this image and *not* feel this way. I understand the scream now, the rawness of it. The unbridled fear.

I drop to my knees and whatever is left in my stomach from last night comes up, splashing across the grass. I heave, tears streaming out the sides of my eyes, though I'm unsure whether it's just a reaction to the vomiting or if I'm actually crying. There's a hand at my back suddenly. It's Ellie. She doesn't say anything. Nobody does.

A second later there's someone else – the natural blonde, who has her hair pulled back into a messy bun – she's holding out some tissues.

'Thanks, Morgan,' Ellie says.

I take them and try to clean myself up, my stomach still roiling and my mouth tasting of bile and shock. I don't want to turn around. I don't want to see. But everyone is still staring at the sight – at the pile of four or five decapitated seagulls who lie bloodied and discarded at the foot of the message like some grotesque full stop.

'What the actual fuck?' Sofia is shaking, her usual bossy bravado strangely and totally absent. The fake blonde stands next to her, as if huddling close to shield herself from the scene. That must be Tiffani, Sofia's employee who's here to help with the wedding. The younger woman picks at the ends of her frayed blond hair extensions. They reach almost to the top of her bum.

'This is . . . vandalism!' Nikoleta shakes her head, cheeks as red as the message smeared on the glass before us. 'It is a crime!'

Nobody says anything.

Being able to see right out to the ocean through the clear walls of The Glass House makes it feel like the message is floating on top of the water, like a disembodied threat from the beyond. But *someone* must have done this. Someone came here and killed these birds and used their blood to write this message.

'What does this even mean: *I know what you did*?' Tiffani looks up at Sofia, her lips downturned and a groove embedded between the dark brows that hint at her natural hair colour. 'Who is that message for?'

Sofia keeps her face a perfect mask of neutrality. 'I have no idea.'

But I hear the disconnection in her voice. It's the sound of her mind leaving the present and going back eleven years. I'm catapulted there, too. A fateful day that would bind the three of us together, cementing our friendship forever.

Because if someone left the group . . . they might tell the truth about what happened.

*

Instead of having a relaxing morning picnic with my friends, the group splits up. Nikoleta goes to fetch cleaning products to remove the words from the window and, uh . . . dispose of the seagulls. Sofia decides that she and Tiffani should start getting everything set up for the rehearsal dinner tonight, and Ellie claims not to be feeling too well and decides to retire to her cottage for a bit. I notice she's been checking her phone a lot – so I wonder if she might still be trying to get in touch with Mitch.

That leaves me and Morgan.

'Do you want to join me on the beach?' I ask. All I want is to forget about that bloody message and those poor birds. But if I'm alone, my mind will spin like a propeller.

Was the message aimed at Ellie? Or at us? Or maybe it's nothing to do with us at all and someone has beef with Nikoleta and Dom.

Morgan glances back at the retreating group and toys with a strand of honey blond hair that has escaped from a messy bun on top of her head. She's dressed practically – in loose jeans, a baggy T-shirt and worn brown Birkenstocks, a pair of chunky black glasses perched on her nose. I'd always expected a celebrity assistant to be tottering around in high heels and looking like they could have stepped off an *Emily in Paris* set. But if you were to walk by Morgan on the street today, she could easily pass for any other young university student or recent graduate. She could even be Ellie's little sister, just as down-to-earth and unassuming.

'We were about to set up a picnic and there's food waiting down there,' I add. 'It would be a shame for it to go to waste.'

'I'm supposed to be here to help Ellie.' She sucks on the inside of her cheek.

'I think she needs a moment to herself,' I say gently. Last night had been rough, watching her cry and panic about her career and seeing those awful pictures. I know how deeply stressed she is about Mitch believing her.

There was only one picture on Malachi's phone and it's been eating away at me ever since. I almost wish I'd taken a shot of it with my own phone camera, so I could study what he saw in that photo. What he liked. But a quick glance was all I got before he snatched it away. If Mitch thinks those photos of Ellie and the French dude were taken recently . . . I can only imagine how pissed off he must be.

And right before their wedding, too! It couldn't be worse timing.

'You're right. She needs to talk to Mitch, and his plane should have landed by now.'

'Ah, so you know about the photos, then?' We start heading towards the stairs that lead down to the beach.

Morgan looks momentarily unsure. 'Ellie called me yesterday. Even if she didn't, it exploded all over her social media so it wouldn't have taken me long to figure out what happened.'

I forget sometimes that I exist in a bubble. Because of what happened with my own personal scandal, I've never been present anywhere online. No Facebook, no Instagram, no Twitter . . . or whatever the hell Elon Musk is calling it these days. I only heard about TikTok a year ago. I've never even created secret private accounts, because I've always been so scared people would find me and try to violate my privacy all over again. Unless you've been involved in something like that, you have no idea the specific and personal way it hurts. It's like your life has been cut open for the world to see. You're a product. A headline. A punching bag.

No longer human.

'I know she didn't cheat on Mitch,' Morgan says, glancing

over at me as we descend the stairs. The wooden boards feel warm under my bare soles, already absorbing the sun's rays. The strong breeze whips our hair around and flutters the panels of my cardigan. 'Ellie's not like that. She's . . . like a normal person, you know?'

I chuckle. 'Of course she's a normal person. Isn't everyone?'

'Nah, it's different with some celebrities.' She shakes her head, blond strands flicking around her shoulders. 'The fame turns them into something else.'

'How did you get into working for celebrities?' I ask.

'I started out in the music industry,' she replies. 'After high school I worked part time at this bar that did a lot of live gigs. One day we had a solo artist booking and the guy's assistant was sick. So I stepped in to help him and he offered me a job. It kind of went from there.'

'How did you and Ellie come to work together?'

We've hit the sand and we're strolling across the beach, heels sinking and leaving impressions with each step. Morgan smiles, her eyes going faraway for a moment. 'Ellie was in *Neighbours* at the time, but she booked a gig doing a music video.'

'Oh that's right!' I still remember squealing when I saw it on TV. I can't remember the name of the singer – he was some *Australian Idol* finalist – but the film clip had been epic. They'd shot it on the steps of the Sydney Opera House and Ellie had worn this incredible red gown. She'd played the love interest. 'I remember that music video.'

'There was a big party when that song went platinum. Ellie was there and I was sick of working for that other musician. He was a real arsehole. Ellie and I were chatting and we clicked, so I said she should call me if she was ever looking for some help. The rest is history.'

'Serendipity.'

'That's right.' Morgan nods. 'You're the swimmer, right?'

A lump sticks in the back of my throat. It seems no matter how hard I try, I can't escape my past. Is it going to follow me around forever? Will I be on my death bed still croaking out pleas of innocence? Trying to convince people until my last breath that I'm not a cheater and a liar and a fraud?

'Used to be.' I drop down to my knees on the picnic blanket and Morgan follows. 'Not anymore.'

'Ah.' She nods. 'Sorry, I couldn't remember if it was you or your sister who was . . .'

She breaks off and looks down at her hands, crinkling her nose again. She doesn't need to say the rest. I've heard it a thousand times before.

Which twin are you? The decorated Olympian or the one who tried to dope her way to the top?

'My sister Lily is the one who's still swimming,' I say, looking wistfully out to the ocean.

Even though this was not my domain – the vast, roiling waves were always too unpredictable for me – nostalgia always washes over me whenever I look at a body of water. Doesn't matter if it's bracketed by sand or cupped in reflective blue tile, whether it smells of salt and brine or chlorine, there's something about the water that feels like home. I feel my fingers twitch, desire to walk up to the water's edge and run my hands through a wave, feeling the foam tickle my skin and the cool liquid bring my temperature down.

But I can't. Not now, not ever. Part of me wonders if I could even do it anymore, it's been so long. Can a skill atrophy like that? Or will that knowledge be sewn into my muscles forever?

'Sorry,' Morgan mutters, her cheeks tinted pink.

'It's okay,' I reply, a sigh easing out of me. 'You're not the first person to ask that question. Won't be the last, either.'

As if on cue, my phone rings and my heart skitters thinking it might be Malachi. But it's not. It's Jamie Hazlehurst. Again. I cancel the call and a few seconds later a text comes through.

JAMIE: The article is going to be written whether you talk to me or not. Don't you at least want to have your say?

At some point, I'll have to decide whether I defy Lily out of spite or keep quiet to please my family. But right this moment, I have other things to worry about than rehashing the past.

Like the fact that when I called home around five-thirty yesterday to check in on Isaac, there was a strange vibe with Malachi. He'd seemed in a hurry to get off the call. I might not have noticed if we hadn't been on FaceTime, but I could see the tension in his expression. Then there'd been a noise in the background, like something falling off the edge of a countertop. A little tinkle.

When I'd asked what it was, he'd walked out of the kitchen and into the living room, eyes somewhere else. If it was simply Ash finishing up babysitting duties in the background, he would have said so. But he didn't. His response had set off a strange thumping in my chest, like intuition knocking on a door. I'd asked him if someone else was in the house – but he'd said no. Too quickly, I thought. Too readily.

Stop being paranoid, Rose. You're always worrying.

But life had taught me to worry. It had taught me to hone my senses, looking for the little ripples of discontent that signalled bad things were on the way, like the sweeping light of the lighthouse warning boats away from the shore.

My husband wasn't alone last night. I'm sure of it.

Chapter Twelve

Ellie

When Mitch finally answers the phone, I almost go weak at the knees. I've been trying to get in contact with him for what feels like hours, although it's probably only forty minutes or so. I'm totally shaken. Rattled about like a toy in a baby's hand. Something bad is going on and I feel like I'm looking at the answer through textured glass. It's there, but not.

I know what you did.

The words strike fear in my heart, because they can only be referring to one of two things: one thing I categorically didn't do and the other . . .

Nobody knows about it. Because the only people who were there that day made a vow to keep quiet.

'Ellie?' Mitch sounds exhausted. 'Sorry. Getting out of the airport was a nightmare. One of the sniffer dogs was hovering around my bag and I thought they were going to pull me into secondary.'

'You trying to smuggle apples into the country again?'

The first time he came back to Australia with me, he'd

accidentally forgotten a piece of fruit in his carry-on. It was easy for him to do – he'd only landed back in LA from a tournament in Florida the night before and we'd taken off the next day with barely twelve hours for him to freshen himself up and repack his luggage. But Aussie customs is next level. They'll treat a rogue apple rolling around in your carry-on like you've shoved some cocaine up your arse.

Okay, maybe that's a slight exaggeration, but still. They take it seriously.

'Hardy har,' he says without any humour. The knot of emotion in my stomach pulls tighter.

'Where are you now?'

'Driver just picked me up.'

I'm aching with desperation to see him – to see in his eyes that everything is good between us.

There's a knock at the front of the cottage and I'm sure it's Sofia without even needing to check. She hovers whenever I'm stressed.

'How was the flight?' I ask, creeping quietly towards the sliding glass door that leads out to a little sitting area overlooking the lighthouse at the other side of the cottage, while Mitch recounts the irritation of dealing with customs officers and the lines at Tullamarine.

I hook my finger into the handle of the sliding door and drag it open as quietly as I can, listening for sounds at the front of the house. I hear footsteps milling back and forth. If she comes around the side of the house to check in through the glass, she'll see me. You might not think a friend would invade your privacy by peering into your accommodation, but Sof would. When something is wrong, she doesn't pay any mind to boundaries. I understand why – she blames herself for not questioning Daniella that night. Not telling her to stay home. Not intervening. Not being more forceful.

But I can't handle her intensity right now.

So I slip outside and close the door silently behind me. Then I pad across the small, paved area, dodging the table and chairs, and head onto the grassy grounds, scuttling off towards the lighthouse.

The day is warming up, sun beating down through parted clouds that have scattered as if scared away by our drama. I understand how they feel – I, too, would like to disappear.

But I can't. In a mere few hours all my family and friends will start arriving. It feels like the eyes of the world are on me. I guess they are. Everyone is looking, watching, curious to see if my ascension to 'famous person' will end in success or with me being knocked off my perch.

'Sorry I'm complaining about everything,' Mitch finishes. I haven't heard a word he said and guilt strikes me in the chest. Do I even deserve a good guy like him after I slept with another woman's husband?

That wasn't your fault.

But I think about Mrs Auclair – Francine – sometimes. I wonder if she was okay after finding out Antoine was a cheating scumbag. Or did she crumple and fall in a hole like my mother did? Did she cry her eyes out for weeks, eventually turning listless and unable to get out of bed?

They're still together. He must have spun some incredible tale.

Could she *be behind this?*

Then I remember that I'm not listening to Mitch. *Again.* Fuck.

'I've missed you,' I blurt out, cutting him off mid-sentence.

The cottage shrinks behind me as I charge up the path towards the lighthouse, which is bracketed by small white fences. The building itself looms upward, pure white with a red roof like a little baseball cap sitting atop it. There are two small windows on the side – blackened eyes – and a small balcony encircling the top. The salty ocean air is stronger here. I'm right on the high point of the bay and it tosses my hair around my face. I try to smooth it away from my eyes.

I realise then, that Mitch hasn't responded.

'I've missed you,' I say again, that knot pulling tighter, tighter, tighter until it feels like I might never untangle it.

There's a sigh on the other end of the phone. 'We should talk when I get there.'

'We're talking now.'

'Don't you think this is a conversation we should have in person?' he asks and my stomach sinks. I'm too late.

He's seen the photos. Seen the articles. Seen the accusations.

'I'm *not* cheating on you, Mitch. You have to believe me. Those photos were taken years ago.' I feel my voice getting higher with each word, panic tugging at the strings inside of me until it feels like I might faint from the pressure. I raise my hand to my mouth, teeth desperate for blood, but instantly tug it away. I need to stop doing that. 'Long before we met.'

'And they just . . . did nothing with the photos until now?' The disbelief in his voice is like having something rammed into my chest, skewering my heart.

I went over the pictures with a fine-toothed comb before I went to Sofia and Rose's cottage last night, trying to find something – *anything* – to prove when they were taken. But there's nothing. No movie posters or newspapers or billboards or signs. Not me clutching an old model iPhone no longer in my possession or some other obsolete piece of technology to point a finger away from me. After staring at the images until it felt like my eyes would bleed, the only thing I could come up with was the fact I was wearing skinny jeans.

But I know telling my fiancé the photos must be old 'because skinny jeans are, like, *so* five years ago' won't have the intended impact.

'Mitch, I can't explain why this is happening,' I say as I slowly approach the lighthouse. I'm now in its shadow and the air feels cooler, eerie, like I've stepped into a dark place where the sunlight has been sucked out. The lighthouse is automated these days, Dom told me. Left alone to do its one job. No longer tended to and cared for by a human. I shiver and wrap my free arm around me, keeping my phone cradled to my ear. 'All I can do is promise you with my whole heart that I have never been unfaithful. My dad did that to my mum and it nearly killed her. I would *never* cheat.'

It's why Mrs Auclair pops into my head whenever I'm having a down day and want to pile on in order to wallow in my misery. I hurt her, even if I didn't intend it. I hate knowing that. It feels like a slap in the face to my mother. And while it's hard to say I regret meeting Antoine, because the connections he helped me forge in Hollywood are probably the reason I made it to the big time, I sure as shit regret sleeping with him.

If you knew he was married you would never *have slept with him. Stop beating yourself up.*

'The whole thing just seems so . . .' Mitch breaks off in a curse. 'Ellie, I'd rather be doing this where I can see your face. And I don't mean on a screen. This isn't a conversation for a phone call.'

I blink, trying to fight back the tears that blur my vision. I don't want to seem weak. Or guilty. But my gut churns and the sensation is so violent it makes me sway on my feet. Having this conflict with him . . . it makes me feel ill. I'm so untethered that if a strong gust of wind came off the ocean it might knock me over the edge and wash me out to sea.

'Mitch, please believe me.' My voice trembles. 'I love you.'

The pause on the other end of the line is agonising. In the space between our words, my heart judders in my chest, overworked and underfed. Why is this happening right now? Right at the moment where he could walk away and leave me here to be humiliated. Leave me here alone. Leave me here discarded and unloved and rejected, just like Mum was.

'I swear, I'm telling the truth,' I croak.

I count the beats in the silence – one, two, three, four . . .

'I love you too, Ellie,' he says softly, allowing the air to rush back into my lungs. To keep me alive for another moment. 'But can we please talk about this in person when I arrive? It's . . . I'm exhausted and I want to do this right.'

'Okay.' I nod, biting down on my lip. 'Sure.'

'I'll see you in a few hours.'

When he hangs up it's like there's a hole left in me – a

great, gaping space that needs to be filled. Mitch is the only man who's ever made me feel safe. I dated a woman once, briefly. It was magic but she hated my lifestyle. Hated my being away all the time. But the men, all the others I've encountered aside from Mitch, seemed out for themselves. My father, Antoine, a good chunk of the directors and producers and studio bigwigs in Hollywood.

Mr Quinn.

I close my eyes, trying to stop the image of that day from popping back into my head. The sounds. The dawning of what was happening at our school. That look on Sofia's face . . .

Haunted. It's the only way I can describe it.

Chapter Thirteen

2013

Sofia

The rubber soles of Ellie's battered runners squeak against the floor as we walk through the empty hallway. Lockers line both sides and a few have dents in the middle. Above the lockers, pieces of colourful paper with large letters in black Texta spell out the student body values: *Respect, Care, Curiosity.*

I know very few people here who actually follow those values.

'Where are we going?' Rose asks nervously.

'To the admin office.' Michelle is a few paces ahead, arms wrapped around her body. 'The system where they keep grade records also tracks login information, so we need to make sure the login credentials I'm using match up with the user's terminal. If I use the login credentials on a terminal in the computer lab, it will look suspicious.'

'But won't that person know they weren't here when the record was changed? Like, if you use the principal's login details they will know they weren't on school grounds at that time?' Rose pumps her legs a little harder to catch up to Michelle, causing her long black ponytail to flick behind her like the tail of an agitated horse. 'How do we know they won't check in the morning and figure out something weird is going on?'

'If you think the teachers have time to come in early and check every record in every system, every morning, then you don't know much about teachers.' Michelle powers on, her strides short but determined. 'This is more in case someone looks back on it later, then it shouldn't immediately raise any red flags. I can't guarantee that someone won't figure out the grade was changed, however. All I promise is that the grade will be changed and the record of the old grade will be erased. Frankly, I'm not sure why you all needed to be here in person.'

'I have to make sure it's done,' I pipe up. 'No offence, but I'm not going to hand you five hundred bucks and hope for the best. This is my future we're talking about.'

'And I'm here because it's always good to have a lookout,' Ellie adds, skipping along. Her sneakers squeak with each bouncing movement. Quiet and stealthy she is not. 'I'll run interference if something goes wrong.'

Everyone looks to Rose, as if waiting for her explanation of why *her* presence is required. But she doesn't say anything. Her being here isn't about this mission, of course. It's about her desperate need not to be left behind. I know Ellie thinks I'm too harsh on her. But she gets under my skin. She has *everything* in the world and yet she's always whinging about something. Always worried, always complaining. Always playing the victim.

Yet she has *both* her mum and dad, unlike Ellie. She has her sister, unlike me. She doesn't get teased or bullied, like Michelle. She's a talented swimmer who gets pretty good grades without having to try too hard and her parents never seem to struggle for money. They pay for all her swimming stuff and whenever she asks for anything she gets it – a new pair of jeans, a new phone when she lost her old one, money to go to the movies. She doesn't have to work at fucking Muffin Break like I do, dealing with arsehole customers all weekend long. She doesn't have to work at all.

And yet she doesn't seem to appreciate any of it.

'Rose is here because she only thinks about herself,' I mutter but apparently it's loud enough for the two ahead of us to hear. A sharp elbow lands in my side along with a frustrated, sidelong glance from Ellie. 'What?'

Rose stops in her tracks and whirls around. Her eyes are filled with tears, her lower lip trembling. 'Why do you hate me so much? What did I ever do to you?'

I look at her in disbelief. Is she really so oblivious? So off in her own little world?

I feel my own eyes starting to fill. Fuck. I never cry, not in front of other people anyway. The only time I did was when Daniella died and Ellie and her mum came round to offer their condolences. Her mum made a casserole with foil on the top and it was so thoughtful that my mum started crying and so I started crying, too. Ellie had taken me to my room and we'd sat there, her arm around my shoulders while I sobbed. I'd cried so many tears that I don't know how my body could keep producing more. I'd cried so much that by the time the funeral came there was nothing left.

I'd run out of tears.

That's when the fury started.

Yes, that's better. Be angry. Fucking burn with it.

Anger was a whole lot easier than sadness. Because sadness weighed down your bones and clogged up your brain and made everything slow. It was like a tranquilliser. But anger was fuel. It was power.

And those things were productive.

'Because you *have* your sister, Rose,' I snap.

'Shh!' Michelle hushes me. 'It's supposed to be empty here, but let's not tempt fate, okay?'

I lower my voice, needing to say my piece. 'And you don't even seem to like Lily, let alone love her. She's your family and yet you can't even stand to be around one another.' I feel a rage burning inside me. It's an inferno. It churns like devils using a fire poker to rustle the embers of my emotion, making them burn brighter. 'I don't hate you. I'm jealous! You have the best thing in the world right there and you don't even give a fuck. You have the only thing I truly want.'

'Oh, Sof.' Ellie tries to give me a hug, but I brush her away. It hurts sometimes, her sympathy.

'Daniella was my best friend.' I stare through the tears, my body rigid like stone, refusing to let them fall. I will not be weak. I will not be a victim. 'But do you know what the last thing I said to her was?'

This is when the shame comes, like it always does when I think about my last conversation with my big sister. It's molten hot, like lava being poured through me. It burns me from the inside, eroding my strength and turning me to ash.

Earlier in the evening we lost her, just hours before she snuck into my room and kissed my head, we'd had a fight.

'I said she was stupid.' I've never told anyone this. I don't know why I'm telling them now. But I'm struggling to keep it all together. Everything feels so hard lately – school, home, getting up in the morning. The anger feels like it's starting to give way, weakening like a plank of rotten wood beneath my feet, brittle and breakable. 'I said she was turning into one of those stupid girls who changes themselves for a boy. That I didn't even know who she was anymore.'

I remember it as clear as if it were yesterday and not last year.

She'd lost so much weight that her arms looked like matchsticks and her cheeks had hollows in them. The sparkle was gone from her eyes. Her hair, once a shiny chestnut brown, look dull and her skin – which used to tan to a deep golden olive in summer – was washed with grey. It was because of *him*. The guy she'd been seeing.

He'd changed her. Reduced her. Turned down her light until she was barely glowing anymore.

It's his fault she's dead.

I'd been so frightened that she was making herself sick, always heading straight to the toilet after dinner and keeping a bottle of clear liquid hidden in her underwear drawer. I'd tried to talk to her, but she shut me out. My big sister, who always had a hug in her, whose kindness was the quality she held in highest regard, shut me out. She shut everyone out.

And then she was gone.

'Sof—' Ellie reaches for me again and this time I let her touch me.

But before any of us can breathe another word, a door slams loudly somewhere in the building.

We're not alone.

'Quick, over here.' Michelle has a card in her hand and she darts over to the school administration office's locked door.

Panic bubbles up in the back of my throat. If we get caught, I'm going to have a lot more trouble on my hands than a bad grade dragging my average down.

'Do you know what you're doing?' I whisper.

'Yes,' she hisses. 'I've done it before.'

Rose and Ellie are both bouncing like anxious bunnies off to my left and I crack my knuckles, trying to release some of the pressure. Punishing myself for even needing to be here. I can't let Mum and Dad down. I can't. The little pops sound like a bowl of Rice Bubbles cereal.

Michelle leans against the locked door and slips the corner of her card – a library card – into the gap. She jimmies the handle as she works the card up and down. Another door slams and this time we hear male laughter and the sound of footsteps carrying down the hall.

'Come on, come on,' Michelle mutters. 'Don't be difficult.'

I can practically feel our collective hearts beating like a percussion band. The anxiety is palpable. Just as I hear the creak of a door down the end of the hallway and the clarity of voices as people enter through it, the lock gives way and Michelle almost tumbles into the office. But she catches herself and holds the door for us as we pour inside. When we're all inside, we close the door as quietly as we can and flick the lock.

External windows line the back of the office looking out over the staff car park and frosted, textured panes line the internal wall, dividing the office from the hallway. So while anyone looking in might not be able to see details like our faces, they will absolutely be able to see movement. I hold my finger to my lips and motion for everyone to crouch down, away from the glass. Michelle stays flat against the door, leaning against it, and I duck down behind the main admin desk with Ellie. Rose huddles between a filing cabinet and a potted plant, tucking her long, swimmer's arms into her body.

We made it.

Now all we have to do is wait for these people to pass so we can get on with changing my grade. We're collectively holding our breath as the footsteps get closer. If it's the principal or the administrator or the student services officer, we're fucked. Michelle said she checked the calendar to make sure there were no curriculum meetings scheduled for tonight and the school counsellor doesn't usually take student meetings past five p.m.

We're supposed to have the place to ourselves.

'That was a really great showing this afternoon,' a male voice says. It's Mr Quinn, the PE teacher. I can tell because we only have a handful of male teachers in the whole school and he's much younger than the others. Why would he be here when all the sports stuff finished hours ago? 'I think the team has a great chance of making state comps with you leading them.'

'You think?' There's a female voice, younger. 'We've been doing so well, but the way Mill Park whipped our arses . . .'

'It was an off day. Everyone has them. But after we took

Andrea off second base and put her at third, the team has been working together so much better. Shrivani's got a hell of an arm, too. She throws that ball like a bullet out from centre field.'

'I'm really excited,' she says.

A weird trickle of intuition slides uncomfortably down my spine. I squirm on the spot, my breathing coming faster. I try to regulate it like the grief counsellor taught me to. Now is *not* the time to flip out.

'Me too, Crys,' Mr Quinn replies.

A Crys who plays softball? Must be Crystal McKinnon. She's in my homeroom. Not too bright, but she's a great athlete. Won the school's Outstanding Achievement in Sports award the last three years, which was a school record, beating out Rose and Lily who are by far the highest level athletes at school. Rose was *livid*. But Mr Quinn coaches the softball team himself and he's the one who coordinates the awards, so I'm sure that had something to do with it.

The voices are close now, and they're as clear as if they were standing in the room with us. The soundproofing is shit in these rooms so we're going to have to stay still and quiet until they go. They're probably headed towards the front gate, where the parents enter to pick up their kids. Maybe Crystal had a meeting with Mr Quinn about the upcoming school sports day. She's probably doing some kind of ambassadorial role.

They draw closer. Not too much longer now.

But the footsteps stop before they reach the door. The sound of keys jangling makes me frown – they're not close enough to be coming into the office. In this room, the principal's office as well as a secondary office shared by the vice principal and student services officer sit to the left, bracketed by couches and a small coffee table with a vase of fake flowers. To the right is a large horseshoe of desks, where the receptionist and administrator work. That's where Ellie and I are hiding currently. This area has several filing cabinets, a coat closet and a large bookshelf. It seems Mr Quinn and Crystal are going to the room on the other side of this wall – which is the 'quiet study' room.

It's a tactic that the principal is using to lure parents of potential new students into thinking the school is better than it is. They've installed bookshelves and put bean bags and small couches in the space, and they sell the idea of a 'quiet retreat' for kids who need more mental space to work on tough assignments or study for tests during free periods. And all it cost them was some cheap IKEA furniture. The reality is that I've only ever seen kids napping in there, because if someone has a free period they're generally outside or hightailing it off school grounds as soon as the bell goes.

The sound of a lock clicking next door feels like a gunshot in the quiet building, as I go light-headed from holding my breath. I look over to Ellie and mouth 'what the fuck?' to which she shrugs in return, not daring to say a word.

For a moment, the room next door is so quiet that it's almost like Mr Quinn and Crystal McKinnon have evaporated into thin air. But then I hear the sound of rustling fabric, followed by a zip. I clamp a hand over my mouth. I know what's about to happen before the others catch on. But I see the realisation of it filter through the group – Rose's innocent shock, Ellie's confusion, and Michelle's disgust. Shit.

A long keening groan filters through the wall.

The clock is ticking. We have to get our mission done and get out of here without the people next door hearing a thing.

Chapter Fourteen

2024

Sofia

Within twenty-five minutes Nikoleta has disposed of the headless gulls and is working on cleaning up the glass, all the while muttering to herself under her breath. It's not English, but I can tell she's swearing.

Tiff looks shaken.

'You okay?' I ask as we stand over the long table inside The Glass House, my laptop set up with our run sheet for tonight and tomorrow on display. I'm taking notes in my notebook.

'Yeah, I just . . .' Tiffani glances through the window to where Nikoleta is frantically scrubbing at the glass, a bucket of soapy water at her feet. Only half the message remains.

. . . what you did.

She sucks in a shaky breath. 'It's horrific.'

For a second I don't know if she's talking about the way the bloody message was written or what it means. Ellie seems to think it's all about her – that someone is trying to make it look like she's cheating on Mitch. A deluded movie fan who thinks she belongs with them, perhaps? It's not out of the realms of possibility. Lots of famous people have to deal with such things – Taylor Swift, Jodie Foster, Sandra Bullock, Jennifer Lopez . . .

The list goes on.

But there's a seed of intuition in my gut. It's taking root, tendrils burrowing further inside me, while a worry begins to blossom.

What if this isn't about her and Mitch?

'Who would *do* something like that?' Tiffani looks green around the gills. 'Those poor, innocent birds.'

I immediately think back to last night – the shadowy figure I saw slipping into The Glass House. Was that the person who did this? The thought of a stranger sneaking around the grounds while we were all sleeping . . . it freaks me out.

'I honestly don't know who would be capable of it.' I let out a sigh. 'After she's done cleaning up, I'm going to suggest to Nikoleta that we call the local cops. Ellie mentioned Dom has a small security team scheduled for this afternoon and tomorrow, but clearly *someone* got onto the property early, without being noticed.'

'No one checked in on me when I drove in,' Tiffani confirms with a nod. 'I mean, it's pretty remote out here. I don't think anyone is stumbling across this place by accident.'

'Exactly. We're several k's off the main road without *any* signage. If someone's here then it's because they know about this place.' I chew on the inside of my cheek, unsure whether that logic makes this situation better or worse.

'And if people know this is a place where celebrities come to stay, perhaps some idiot has been lurking around, waiting for someone famous to turn up. There are a lot of crackpots out there.'

'You're totally right. Lots of famous people have to deal with stalkers and stuff, huh?'

'Unfortunately, yes.'

'The world is . . . scary sometimes.' She frowns. Tiffani is the kind of person who sees the best in everything and everyone. Our clients adore her sunny albeit naive personality.

She's twenty-two, has waist-length hair bleached to within an inch of its life and wears so much fake tan she could keep Bondi Sands in business all by herself. Yeah, she's a bit of a bogan. But Tiff is as hard-working as they come and I liked her the second I met her when she approached me for a job almost a year ago, her only qualifications an arts degree and a deeply romantic nature. I haven't for one second regretted taking a chance on her.

And after years of doing it all myself, it's a blessing to have good help.

'Maybe we should keep someone with her,' Tiffani suggests. 'Safety in numbers and all that.'

'Good idea.' It occurs to me, however, that she's on her own right now. 'You know what, I'm going to call her and make sure she's okay.'

I set my notebook down and try Ellie's number but the call goes immediately to voicemail as if she's cancelled it. A few seconds later a text pops up.

ELLIE: Sorry I didn't answer the door before, just talking to M.

I'm not sure exactly what she's talking about, since I haven't knocked on her door. But I don't want to disturb her while she's talking to Mitch. It's an important conversation.

SOFIA: Lock your door, k? At least until we figure out what's going on.

I've seen enough serial killer documentaries to know that dead animals are bad news. The image of the seagulls' white feathered bodies, broken and splattered with blood, makes my stomach lurch. For some reason, it makes me think of my sister. Of the image that's haunted me for the better part of my life.

Shattered glass – a broken windscreen – my sister's body pitched through it, face-down on the car's bonnet. There's blood splashed across the silver paint, which shimmers in the morning light, sun catching on all the flecks of mica. Her dark hair is fanned around her head, a nest of espresso curls, obscuring her face. But then she looks up, eyes vacant, the side of her face caved in so that there's bone and muscle and tooth all poking through. My beautiful sister, reduced to a horror show. A skeleton. A nightmare.

'Sofia,' she rasps, reaching for me. 'Be my revenge.'

'Sof?' Tiffani touches my arm and I yelp, thrown back into the present with force.

'Sorry.' I shake the image free, my heart pounding.

It's not real, it's not real, it's not real.

I know it's a figment of my imagination, because I never saw Daniella die. I never saw her body until after it had been patched up, the evidence of her car accident hidden away with heavy post-mortem makeup and hair styling and the modest outfit my mother picked out for her. But that vision – of her on the car bonnet – haunts me. Ellie says it's likely trauma. PTSD or something. From the age of seventeen to nineteen I lost someone every year – first my sister, then my nonno, then my father. Our family was whittled down by half, lives shaved off like curls of wood by a sharp hand plane. Why did the universe see fit to bestow so much tragedy on one family's shoulders?

At one time I'd asked God over and over. Why did you take Daniella? Nonno? Pa? But there was never any answer. Never any response. Any reason.

My phone vibrates.

ELLIE: The door is locked.

I put my phone down, shoulders sagging in relief. At least I can put that out of my head for the moment – she's safe. My mind feels like an ocean, so much depth and darkness. So many things lurking beneath the surface. I close my eyes for a moment, trying to find my centre.

Work.

It's always the thing that brings back my equilibrium. Being busy, being productive. It can help me forget anything.

I use my Swarovski pen to tap at my notebook, where I've scribbled some things I don't want to forget. The crystals glint in the sunlight, the copper barrel gleaming like a piece of rose gold. For some reason, holding this pen makes me feel like I can manage everything. A person skulking around The Glass House last night? Probably just Nikoleta doing her job. The dead seagulls? The work of a deranged movie fan. The unsettling bloody message? No better than a star sign prediction, vague enough to mean anything.

But the pen also makes me feel connected to Daniella – she loved anything glittery or shiny, and crystals were her favourite embellishment. She was a proper magpie.

Whenever things feel hard, I hold my pen and think of her. She's the reason I have to keep going.

'Until the security team arrives we stick together and keep in constant contact,' I say to Tiffani, squaring my shoulders. 'Now, run sheet. Go.'

I see Tiffani click into 'work mode' the same as I have done, her eyes sharpening and her posture straightening.

'I built in an extra ten minutes here,' she says, pointing to the run sheet. 'For the time between the solo bride photos in the cottage and her coming down the aisle. I figured you wouldn't want to be running around checking that everything is ready for the petal toss and making sure the celebrant is good to go, and risk missing Ellie making her big appearance.'

It's such a thoughtful inclusion – more for me than our client. She wants to ensure I get to experience the wedding of my best friend, instead of just feeling like I'm at work.

'Great idea, Tiff.' I nod. 'Any other changes?'

'Nothing major for tomorrow. We had a last-minute guest cancellation – from the groom's side. His aunt is unwell and can't make the flight over from the US. But since we're having a cocktail reception, it doesn't really affect anything.'

The one good thing about cocktail weddings are the lack of seating plans and, therefore, lack of drama around who is sitting where. I can't even tell you how many times I've planned weddings where the seating charts have been redone multiple times to accommodate all the selfish arseholes who can't put their differences aside for a single evening.

'She did have a request though,' Tiffani says, her button nose crinkling.

I rub at my temples, wary. Guest requests are almost aways a pain in my arse. 'What?'

'She asked if I could print a picture of her and put it in a frame and have it sitting in the spot where she was supposed to be.' I can tell by Tiffani's expression that she thinks this is as ridiculous as I do. But honestly, I've heard worse. 'I tried to explain that there isn't anywhere to put a photo since we're not having a seated meal. But she was insistent – I think she's quite old – and she said she was Mitch's favourite aunt.'

'They all think that.' I snort.

'Then she asked if we could put her photo next to the cake so everyone can see her.'

I scrub a hand over my face. 'Please tell me you didn't agree to that.'

'Well, she was very pushy and . . .' She cringes when I groan. 'But I have an idea! I've called the cake place and asked if we could push delivery forward by half an hour. They were very nice on the phone and said that would be okay. So I printed the picture and thought I would come in, put it down next to the cake, take a photo for her that I can email after the wedding is done, and then we can remove the photo before the wedding kicks off.'

I raise an eyebrow and nod. That's what I appreciate about Tiffani – she thinks on her feet.

'It's like you always say, Sof,' she says with a firm nod of her bleached blond head. 'Compromise is the art of dividing a cake so that everyone thinks they have the biggest piece.'

It's not my quote. It's from some German dude post World War II – an economist, I think. Or maybe a politician. The first time I heard it the words seemed carved into my bones. A life hack, if you will. It's simply about presenting ideas in the right way, framing things so that everyone is happy with what they get while you walk away with exactly what *you* want.

'You're a fast learner.' I twist my pen up and down, mind racing with everything that needs to be done before the guests start arriving.

But I really want to check on Ellie. I'm worried about her.

With these old paparazzi photos suddenly surfacing and the weird fake Google reviews of my business and the bloody message, it almost feels like . . .

Someone is trying to fuck with us.

Is that dramatic? Maybe. After all, if someone is targeting us for what we did all those years ago then Rose hasn't mentioned anything bad happening to her. Why target Ellie and I, and leave Rose alone? That doesn't make any sense. It must be a coincidence.

'Can I leave you to start setting up for tonight?' I ask. 'You've got everything you need, right?'

During the rehearsal dinner, Ellie and Mitch want to do a speech to thank everyone for coming, including a slide show featuring photos of them growing up and of their relationship, since many of Ellie's friends and family here in Australia have only met Mitch once or twice. That tends to happen when you get engaged overseas after only knowing a person for a few months! The slide show is corny and cute and very Ellie. But Nikoleta was adamant that they didn't do AV support when we'd asked her – *we're not a Novotel,* she'd replied snobbishly – so I've charged Tiffani with securing a portable projector and making the slide show with photos Ellie and Mitch provided. We need time to set it all up and ensure there are no technical hitches tonight.

'Yeah, uh . . . but . . .' Tiffani shifts her weight, almost squirming.

'Spit it out.'

'There's something else.' She bends over my laptop and navigates to my inbox, looking through the new emails that have come in overnight, ones I haven't yet checked on. With the fake reviews rolling in, I've been a little scared to look, to be honest.

Day to day, Tiffani monitors the inbox and takes care of basic tasks like website updates, media enquiries, invoices management and account administration, client appointments et cetera. She goes through the emails and flags the ones that need my personal attention so I don't have to wade through the muck myself. It's a great help.

Now, there's even more 'muck' than normal.

'This one.' She clicks on an email to open it and points, holding her body away like the screen is a wasp or a snake or a big, hairy spider.

I glance at her, a growing feeling of unease expanding in my gut. I register the sender's name immediately – it's from a client whose wedding is late next year. She's getting married at the Plaza Ballroom. Four hundred guests. Her husband-to-be is part of a well-known Italian family who runs a construction company, building some of the most high-end towers in the city. It's a big wedding, on all levels.

Hello Sofia,

I am writing this email with regret. I thought we really clicked during our meeting where my husband and I agreed for you to become our wedding planner. But I can't put up with this kind of behaviour. It's totally inappropriate for you to write me these kinds of emails. I shouldn't be shamed for the way I am, especially not by someone I am paying to help me navigate one of the most exciting events of my life. I am, therefore, terminating this agreement with you. I expect my deposit returned in full within 48 hours or you'll be hearing from our lawyer.

Mariella

I almost want to close my eyes as I scroll down to see the email she's responded to. I know for a fact that I haven't emailed this client recently – not after the contract was signed and the venue was booked. Her name sits on a neat little card on my project management board as a 'to-do' item for next week. Mood boards for the wedding's theme.

But there's an email from me, with my signature and a little graphic featuring my business logo at the bottom, under my name. The words, however, are not mine.

Hi Mariella,

Thanks for sending over the link to your wedding inspo Pinterest board. It's super cute! However, I would re-think the dresses you've got pinned there. Given you're quite large, those styles won't suit you. They're designed for someone with a slim figure and that's not you, unfortunately. I'd try something that covers you up a bit more. We don't want anyone running out of the church in horror now do we? I can send you some links if you like.

Ciao!

Sofia

I want to vomit. I think I'm about to. I hunch over and look around for anything to catch it. But thankfully nothing comes up. I breathe heavy, clamping my eyes shut and trying to will the nauseous wave away.

'That email was sent yesterday from your real email address,' Tiffani says in a small voice. 'Eleven thirty-four.'

'I was driving then,' I reply numbly. 'We didn't make it here until after lunch.'

'P.m.,' she corrects. 'And I know you would never have sent something horrible like that.'

Eleven thirty-four p.m. I cast my mind back to last night – we'd gone to bed early, about five minutes to eleven. I'd tossed and turned for almost two hours before getting up for a drink of water, and when I'd checked my emails nothing had seemed out of sorts. Everything looked normal.

Although admittedly I didn't check my 'sent' folder, since I had no reason to.

Tiffani eases the computer away from me and navigates to another email. I'm not sure I want to know what she's going to show me next. First the fake reviews, now this! Someone is trying to sabotage my business. I would never say something like that to a client. Okay, sure, I can be a bitch. I know that. But I would never – *never!* – criticise a client's weight. What would be the point?

'I managed to find this email in your rubbish folder. It's a notification saying someone was trying to change your password.' She points again. 'I think someone hacked in.'

Holy shit.

'You should change your password,' Tiffani suggests, picking at the split ends on her hair.

'But if the hacker changed the password, then I wouldn't be able to log in now, right? Because the password would be different. It would have bounced me out.' I rub at the back of my neck, my mind spinning. 'Maybe they tried to change it and couldn't, so they got in another way?'

But what other way would that be? Physically accessing my laptop? I'd left it in the kitchen last night, plugged in to charge unattended. I was asleep when the email was sent, so it *was* possible someone snuck into the cottage and used my computer.

The thought of it makes me feel ill.

Tiffani shrugs. 'I don't know much about hacking.'

The attempted password change notification was from a week ago.

'Let's change *both* our passwords, just to be sure.' Hopefully that will prevent any further emails impersonating me from being sent. As for this one client, I'll have to call her later and try to explain the situation. The reviews are another story. I doubt Google is going to be helpful.

'Can I leave you to keep going with the set-up?' I ask, my mind already drifting to the next problem. Making sure Ellie is safe.

'Of course. I'll bring the projector and stuff in from the car and get it all set up.'

'Take the laptop with you. I don't want it left alone, okay?' I say and Tiffani nods. 'Thanks.'

I glance over to where Nikoleta continues to scrub at the window, the message and red swirls now mostly gone, leaving behind the expansive panes of shiny glass that make me suddenly feel very exposed, like a little goldfish in a bowl.

Yesterday The Glass House had felt like a shiny, beautiful bubble reflecting the glitter of the ocean and the pearly softness of the clouds and the blinding, warming sunshine.

Today it feels like a microscope – a way for someone to look in, to examine, to assess. I don't like it.

I make my way outside to where Nikoleta is climbing down from a stepladder. She throws a bloodied sponge into the bucket of soapy water, which has turned an unappealing shade of murky light brown. Her dry, steel-wool curls have been pulled away from her face, but a halo of shorter strands have sprung free around her forehead. Without the full cloud of her hair visible, her face looks bigger – broad features enlarged without anything else to balance them. She has a strong brow, a large nose, big eyes, and wide cheekbones. Not to mention hands like dinner plates.

She could easily have beheaded a few seagulls.

I shake my head. Why would Nikoleta do something like that? She doesn't know us.

'Thanks for uh . . . cleaning that up,' I say, a little unsure how to approach her. 'It was quite a mess.'

She frowns. 'What else was I going to do? Leave it?'

'Of course not.' I shake my head. 'But we should inform the local police precinct and have them come by to check the place out. It's possible since Ellie is famous that—'

Nikoleta cuts me off with a snort. 'Please. Your friend might have been in a few movies, but we've had far more famous people than her stay here without incident. If we had dead animals smeared on our walls every time someone from the industry stayed here, then I would be cleaning this place a lot more often.'

I'm taken aback by the blunt response. Anger bubbles up inside me, hot and fast, like roiling water waiting for a handful of spaghetti. My temper isn't my best quality – I know that. But it's natural to me. Comfortable.

'She's done more than "a few" movies, actually.' I fold my arms across my chest. 'And it's *your* responsibility to ensure the safety of the guests on this property. If someone was able to come here, behead a load of birds and write a threatening message on the glass without anyone seeing a bloody thing that means your security system is deficient and that's on *you*.'

Nikoleta's face hardens. Her already cold, brown eyes turn to solid ice.

'I don't suppose you have some CCTV set up? Security cameras on the road that comes into the property?' I ask, already knowing what the answer will be.

'Our guests value privacy. They know the damage that can be wrought from photos being leaked to the press.' She raises an eyebrow, looking a little smug. She must have heard about the shots of Ellie circulating.

I want to snap that people wouldn't bother taking pictures of Ellie if she was just some woman who'd 'been in a few movies', but I hold my tongue. Stirring that pot is pointless. All I care about now is making sure that whatever sicko left this message stays the hell away from us.

'All the more reason to involve the police,' I say.

She lifts one shoulder into a shrug. 'I'll give them a call, but there's not much for them to look at now.'

Her large hand lifts as she gestures to the now spotless window, birds cleared away. All that remains is some sticky red-brown moisture on the ground outside, that could be mud or anything. It occurs to me that Nikoleta has just wiped away the evidence of what happened.

A stone settles into the pit of my stomach. Something about this situation feels off. But she's right – if we called the cops now . . . I can't even show them a picture of what was here. No one thought to take a photo of it. To get some evidence. Would the police even believe us now? Or would they see a famous woman and her gaggle of friends and their assistants and label us attention-seeking bimbos? Probably.

I can't believe I didn't think to take a picture.

'What time does the security team arrive?' I ask.

'Three p.m. I'll introduce you to Stavros when he arrives,' she says, picking up the bucket so quickly that some of the blood-stained water sloshes over the edge, right where I'm standing. I jump back out of the way, gasping. 'He'll take you through their procedures.'

Without waiting for my response, she turns and walks away.

'Nikoleta,' I call out. She stops and looks over her shoulder, her body language telling me she's giving me only minimal effort. 'Were you in The Glass House last night? Around midnight?'

'No. I have to be up before the sun, so I'm always asleep by ten o'clock.' She turns away from me and mutters, 'This place doesn't run itself.'

As she lumbers away, it occurs to me that she never actually answered my question about whether they have security cameras on the property. She simply sidestepped by saying her guests like privacy. Why would she be cagey about that? It should be a simple yes or no response.

What is she trying to hide?

Chapter Fifteen

Rose

After a while, Morgan gets a text from Ellie saying she's finished talking to Mitch, and she heads off to help her boss get ready for tonight. When I'd pointed out that it was only just past noon and the rehearsal dinner wasn't for, like, *seven* hours, Morgan had rattled off the list of things on their to-do list: spray tan application, hair mask, facial, gua sha (whatever the hell that is?), nails, toenails, hair styling, makeup, false lashes, some body-contouring thing . . .

I must have looked completely bewildered because Morgan simply laughed and said Ellie usually has a whole bloody team of professionals to get her ready for big events. But Ellie doesn't want a parade of people around her for the wedding – that would feel too much like work, apparently. Instead, she has a friend coming to do hair and makeup – someone who's previously worked with Ellie for a *Vogue Australia* shoot and who is also a guest at the wedding. The rest, Morgan said, is up to her and Ellie to figure out.

Is it really that hard? When did we get to a point that even someone who is naturally gorgeous needs seven fucking hours to prepare for a night that's supposed to be in their celebration? Does the pressure to be perfect never end?

I stand at the edge of the ocean, staring out at the waves, water dribbling up and over my toes as a mostly dissolved wave comes to greet me. The day is bright and clear, warmth beating down onto my shoulders now that I've allowed them to go bare in a singlet top, since no one is around to see me. It feels good. It feels . . . free.

For a moment I have the urge to dive into the water. To submerge myself in its cool refreshment and feel that wonderful weightlessness. To feel my arms stroke against the resistance of it, to streak powerfully through in a direction of my choosing. Away, maybe forever. The tug is so strong it brings tears to my eyes. The grief of what I have lost – not only what could have been an incredible career and public adoration, but the joy of being in the water and the purpose and pride of following one's passion to its end – is a weight on my chest.

I crouch down and wade my fingertips through the water, feeling another gentle wave roll in and then retreat. God, I even miss the gruelling pre-dawn drives to the pool, shivering in my trackies afterward with wet hair, and the deep ache in my muscles from pushing to my limits.

Most of all, I miss who I was back then. Whole. Motivated. Hungry for more.

Maybe if you were still that person, Malachi wouldn't be looking at pictures of beautiful, young blond women on his phone.

It's not just the dirty photo. There's more. Other niggling little things . . . like my gut feeling that there was *definitely* someone at the house with him yesterday.

My face flushes hot with shame and I stand, turning away from the shoreline and walking back towards the stairs. Standing here and wondering what might have been is pointless. I have to focus on the here and now. On what's going on with my husband. If he left me for someone else . . .

Fear curdles in my stomach like sour milk as I shrug my cardigan back over my shoulders, covering myself up and preparing to find the others. That's when my phone rings again.

I see the name – Jamie Hazlehurst – on my screen and I let out a frustrated cry. Does he have no mercy? No empathy? This time I'm so wound up that instead of cancelling the call, I answer it. When I bring the phone up to my ear, I'm almost seeing red.

'Stop calling me, Jamie.'

'Rose . . .' His voice is cajoling, like I remember. I fell for that last time and talked too much. 'I'm just doing my job.'

'And I'm trying to live my life.' I stare out at the ocean. Maybe I could throw my phone into the water and be at peace. No more Jamie Hazlehurst. No more calls from Lily. No more family group messages making me feel like shit. 'Can't you respect that? I've moved on.'

'With your sister in the news, people want to know. They're curious,' Jamie replies. 'I'm sure it was exciting news for the family to hear that Lily has been named torch bearer . . .'

This is a soft-ball statement, something I can't really refute even if I want to. Because I know what I'm expected to say.

Yes, I'm so proud of her.

Of course it's an exciting moment for our family.

No, I'm not jealous at all.

'Of course, we're all very proud of Lily's achievements.' My voice is robotic. Rehearsed. I've said these things a thousand times before. 'This is a huge honour for her.'

Because there's only one thing people hate more than a cheater – and that's someone who's jealous. I can't let anyone see the seething green monster inside me. The ugly part of me that would rip everything from my twin sister's hands, given half a chance. That I *am* jealous of the whole country worshipping her. That it *was* my dream. That I *hate* having to watch her live the life I wanted.

I need to be seen to be happy with my lot, repentant and calm. Reformed.

But I am not.

'You're a good sister, being so supportive even though it was your dream at one time,' Jamie says, testing the water.

'That's what sisters are for,' I say dully.

'Rose, if you'll allow me to record this call, then I can put your words into the article instead of my own. People genuinely want to know what you're up to.'

I could keep fighting it. I could tell Jamie to bugger off and leave me alone. But he's right – the article will still go ahead whether I say anything or not. That's life, as I understand it. I have minimal influence. Minimal control. The world keeps turning no matter what happens. No matter how much pain or regret or failure one person has.

'Fine,' I say, resignation washing through me like the waves lapping at my feet.

'Thank you. I'll begin recording now.'

I wait for a click or some other sound of confirmation,

but there's nothing. Maybe he was already recording before he asked for my permission.

'Is it something you ever talk about at home?' Jamie asks. His voice is so reassuring, so calm. Like we're two friends chatting. But I won't fall for it. 'The doping?'

The word makes ice crystals form in my chest, cold spreading through me and numbing me from the inside out. For a second I'm a teenager again. Shocked. Judged. Vulnerable.

'I still maintain that I never knowingly ingested or came into contact with a banned substance,' I say, my voice barely a whisper. Images flicker in my memory – my mother's eyes, disbelieving, and my father's, bewildered, my coach's, stunned. The media swarming us outside the courthouse for the Court of Arbitration for Sport, microphones jabbing at me like accusing fingers. The articles, calling me a liar and a cheat and a fraud. 'And I have the ongoing support of my family. They have always believed me.'

Have they, though? I know my father does, still to this day. He's never wavered on that. Mum refuses to talk about it, so I don't really know what she thinks. And Lily . . . well, she's made her stance clear.

'Tell me a bit about your life now.' Jamie backs off from the hard questions, playing soft ball again. 'You're a mother. What's that like after years of having a single-minded goal?'

'It's wonderful.' I think of my little boy and my heart swells. 'It's hard, of course. Physically gruelling, exhausting. But waking up every morning knowing that I have the perfect little soul to care for . . . it's given my life a whole new purpose. I want to teach him everything I can. Help him be smart and happy and successful.'

'Have you got him in the water, yet?' Jamie asks. I get the impression that question wasn't on the prep sheet for this interview, that it's more personal curiosity.

'He's only six months, so we're going to start him at lessons soon. But he loves the splash pad. I have a feeling he's going to be just like me – a water baby.'

I don't mention how Malachi and I have already discussed that he will take Isaac to swimming lessons. How when I walked into the local pool to enquire about their program that the smell of chlorine hit me like a tonne of bricks, stealing the air from my lungs and crushing me from the inside. That I'd had such a severe panic attack the manager had called an ambulance and Malachi had almost had a car accident racing to get to the hospital after they called him.

It's better if he takes our baby boy to the swimming lessons, we figured. Keep me away from the things that trigger bad memories.

'Did you ever think about returning to the sport? You were only banned for a few years and I know you had so many people wishing you'd come back to the Aussie team. I'm sure your coach would have been delighted. Was it a hard decision to stay away and have you ever regretted it?'

I'm going to keep treading carefully.

Most people have not experienced an ounce of the scrutiny in their lives that I have. The fact that anyone expected me to dust myself off and get back into the pool shows how ignorant they are. No matter what I did – if I went on to win a gold medal or become the most decorated swimmer Australia had ever seen, I would *always* have an asterisk next to my name. Any win would come with questions dangling from it.

Did she cheat?

Did she have 'help'?

Can we ever trust her?

'I haven't ever regretted it,' I say. 'That part of my life is over. I . . . that's all I'm willing to say.'

I end the call suddenly, my hands trembling. I clutch the phone to my chest and turn away from the water, eyes searing with unshed tears. Being alone with my thoughts isn't going to do me any good today. I need to find someone to distract me. I gather my things and charge up the beach towards the stairs.

But I halt when I see someone on the steps. They look as surprised to see me as I am to see them.

It's a woman. She has a short helmet of dark curly hair, light brown skin and she's dressed for the beach – a red and black rash top over skimpy bikini bottoms, a body board tucked under one arm with a thin strand connecting it to a solid black cuff at her wrist.

Isn't the beach supposed to be private? We're the only ones here – Ellie, Sofia, Tiffani, Morgan and me. Well, and Nikoleta.

The woman is frozen, almost as if she knows she's not supposed to be here. I feel my hackles rise. Has someone been sneaking onto the beach while we're here? That's not okay. For a second fear grips my chest as it dawns on me how utterly alone I am – the secluded beach surrounded by rocky cliffs. It's almost like someone has taken an ice cream scoop to the coast or maybe a shark has taken a bite out of it, creating this perfectly private pocket of sand and shore – just ripe for long languid days with nothing to do and nowhere to be. No wonder people want to use it.

Something could happen down here and nobody would see. She could brain me over the head with her body board and drag my unconscious body out to sea. I'm prepared to raise hell, should things turn ugly. Make noise and scream bloody murder.

'Oh my God, it *is* you.' The woman squints at me.

That I wasn't expecting.

I hold a hand up to shield my eyes from the sun so I can get a better look at her. At first I don't recognise her face – she looks like she could be my age, around about. Was it someone I met through swimming? All those years have been shoved to the back of my brain as hard as possible. But then something catches my attention.

There's a large mole right on the end of her chin.

'Michelle?' I gape at her, like sometime has torn a hole through time and I'm looking back into my high school years. Only, this is here and now. 'Holy shit.'

It's the first time I've talked to her since . . .

That day.

After it happened she never spoke a word to us and we never spoke a word to her. Even Ellie stopped defending her in class. It was like we wanted nothing to do with one another, because if we acknowledged each other's presence then it would be like admitting something really happened that day. That we were all involved. That we *knew*.

'When Nikoleta said there was some actress here this week I had no idea it was you lot.' She puts her board down and leans on it. 'This is a blast from the past I do *not* need.'

'What are you even doing here?' I shake my head. This feels like the mother of all coincidences.

'I live here.' There's a fire in her eyes. Like I'm invading her turf. Like *I'm* the interloper.

'You live here?' I shake my head. 'Why?'

'Accommodation comes as part of the job. Means the pay is shit, but I get a place to live that doesn't cost anything and I have the beach on my doorstep. Plus, there's lots of time when no one is here, which means my work is light and I can spend all day in the water or going for walks.' She shrugs. 'The best part of all, is that I never run into people I know . . . usually.'

'What do you do?' Don't ask me why, but I'm insatiably curious all of a sudden.

I'd assumed, after we all graduated, that Michelle had gone off to conquer the IT world.

'A bit of everything. I take care of the grounds themselves, like keeping the grass cut and looking after the plants. I clean the cottages, do some of the handiwork for anything small that needs fixing, and then I do all the tech stuff like manage the Wi-Fi, security cameras . . . fixing the printer every time Nikoleta breaks it.'

Wow, looks like none of us quite ended up where we thought we would when we graduated. I stopped swimming, Sofia quit her law degree, Michelle didn't storm the tech world. Ellie got the best of that deal – the girl who felt like she was going nowhere is now on her way to being one of the hottest actresses in the whole country.

As my mind leaves that thought behind, a little alarm bell goes off in my brain.

'Security cameras,' I say, my shoulders hiking up. Could she have been watching us? 'Where?'

'There's one in The Glass House, one out the front

of the private residence where Nikoleta and I live and where the catering staff stay when they're here for an event. I think Dom has one out the front of his cottage, too.'

It feels like there's something she's not telling me.

'How did you even end up with a job like this?' I ask, a strange creeping sensation moving up my spine. It's an awfully big coincidence that she's working here. Like, what are the odds? After not talking for over a decade, suddenly we all end up in the same, remote place.

I don't like it.

'I've always wanted to live by the beach. Then an email just popped into my inbox one day – rare job opportunity. I thought it was a scam, at first. But now here I am.'

As she says those words, something strikes me as false. Untrue. Like a key in a song that's been hit incorrectly, a subtle vibration of dissonance that tells me something is going on beyond what she's telling me.

'Wow, that's . . . lucky.'

'It's kismet, I guess.' She looks at me, eyes searching my face as if trying to hunt something out.

I don't believe a single word she's said.

'I should . . . ah, leave you to your swim,' I say, awkwardly stepping around her. I need to tell the others she's here. 'See you around, I guess.'

'See you around,' she echoes.

I head back up to The Glass House quickly and without looking back. By the time I reach the top of the stairs, I'm hot and out of breath. I really need to start exercising more regularly. I've never felt so unfit before. Isaac isn't yet at the age where I'm racing around after him too much, so while holding him every day keeps my arms strong I'm not doing enough for my cardiovascular health.

My sweet boy.

I get a pang so sudden and so strong it almost knocks me off my feet and I pull out my phone to see a picture of the three of us, faces mushed together. My loving family. Malachi's eyes are rich and his smile is so bright, mimicking the delight on Isaac's small, chubby baby face.

He'll be here this afternoon. You'll see him soon.

Sweat drips down my spine and the fabric of my singlet top and cardigan clings to my skin. The sun is beating mercilessly down, driving the temperature up. The weather can be temperamental this time of year – wildly swinging between blistering summer-like days to thunderstorms and back again. I'm grateful we'll be inside tonight, with air-conditioning to stop me from looking like a soggy mess.

At first I think The Glass House is empty as I hurriedly approach but then I spot Sofia and Tiffani in one corner. I open the door. The projector is set up and they're bent over a laptop, looking frustrated. Sofia lets out an irritated huff. All of a sudden, and before I can announce my arrival, loud music booms through some speakers I didn't even know were there and we all jump. Tiffani lets out a shocked squeak.

Then the music cuts out.

'How's it going?' I ask.

Sofia looks up. This might be the first time I've ever seen her looking dishevelled. Her dark hair started the day being pulled back into a plait, but now there are fine and frizzy strands popping out all around her face. At some point she's changed out of her bathers into a pale green shirt and white denim skirt, but her shirt looks creased and a little damp under the arms. It's unnerving, the usually always-in-control Sofia looks like . . . she's lost her grip on something.

'We're trying to get this bloody laptop to sync up with the sound system for tonight. I asked Nikoleta for help but she said they're quote "not a Novotel".' Sofia mimics Nikoleta's deep, gruff voice. 'Bitch.'

Tiffani looks warily at her boss, as if she's a ticking bomb about to go off, and says nothing.

'This is why I prefer doing weddings at trusted venues where they have staff to do this shit,' she continues, her cheeks red. 'Honest to God, they operate this place like it's not even a business. They won't even confirm if they have security cameras! She just dodged my questions.'

I open my mouth to say that they do, based on my conversation with Michelle just now, but she barrels on before I can get a word out.

'Celebrities' privacy? Bullshit. They're probably running a paedophile ring or orgies or something.' She grunts. 'And why would Dom put someone in charge who talks to their clients like that? It's ridiculous. She stomps around like a bloody ogre, acting like we're an inconvenience when we only came here because her boss bloody invited us. And all these rules, like asking for one little thing is the biggest fucking ask in the world. Not a Novotel, my arse.'

It's been a long time since I've seen her this angry – not since I followed her and Ellie to the school grounds that day.

She suddenly looks up, giving herself a little shake. 'Anyway, what do you need, Rose?'

It's ironic that she's complaining about Nikoleta treating

us like an imposition, since that's something she makes me feel on the regular. But I need to talk to her. It's more important to keep the harmony right now – not just for Ellie's wedding but because Michelle's presence makes me think there's something weird going on.

'We need to talk. Now.' I use my firmest voice, the one usually reserved for dealing with Lily, and she raises an eyebrow in surprise.

'Looks like we got it paired, Tiff. But can you figure out how to adjust the volume? I don't want to deafen anyone tonight.'

Tiff nods. 'Sure thing.'

Sofia follows me outside and I lead her around the back of The Glass House. I'm feeling anxious about anyone overhearing us. We've never talked about what happened that day. But I feel like now, something needs to be said.

South of The Glass House, the view is incredible. We're up high, standing above the curved section of private beach and the sparkling blue expanse stretches on for what feels like forever. My loose hair whips around my face for a second, the smell of brine and salt and grass filling my nostrils, before it dies down. The wind feels like it has a force to it. It wants to dance around you, tease you, push you closer to the crumbling edge.

I turn to Sofia.

'We have a problem,' I say before she can open her mouth. 'A *big* problem.'

'You have no fucking idea,' she mutters, shaking her head. Something is up with her, but I don't even bother asking – she wouldn't confide in me anyway. Besides, we have bigger fish to fry right now. 'What's going on?'

'Michelle is here.'

At first, there's confusion in her features. Knitted brows, pursed lips, eyes darting to and fro like she's flipping through photographs in her mind. 'Michelle who?'

Is that day really *so* far back in her mind? Has she forgotten it? Repressed it? Buried it away with her sister and grandfather and father? I think about it more often than I want to admit. I dream about it – about the stillness, then the chaos.

'Michelle *Smith*,' I say and when that doesn't seem to register either, I sigh. 'Smelly Shelly Smith.'

Sofia's dark eyes go wide. 'You're shitting me.'

'Nope.' I shake my head. 'She *works* here. *Lives* here.'

Sofia suddenly looks behind her, turning all the way around, as if expecting Michelle to jump out from behind a bush like the bogeyman. When she turns back to me, her face is as pale as the one lone cloud overhead.

'How did you find out?' she asks.

'I bumped into her on the beach. She said we're a blast from the past that she doesn't need.'

'No shit.' I notice the muscles working in Sofia's neck, like she's trying – struggling – to swallow. 'Was she here last night?'

'I don't know.' I shrug. 'If she lives here, then I guess so. Probably.'

'We should tell Ellie but . . .' She looks around again, sighing. 'I don't want to ruin her big day. She's already dealing with so much.'

'Yeah, I know.'

For a moment it feels like Sofia and I are finally on the same page. We both care about Ellie a bloody lot. It might be the only thing we have in common at this point, and it feels nice to be in sync for once. To be united instead of on opposite sides of some divide that I wish wasn't there.

I remember Sofia from when we were young – before her sister died, before *that* day, before I became a punchline. We were *truly* friends back then. She used to come to my house and we would play with my Barbie dolls and eat the wontons in broth that Mum made from scratch. Sometimes Lily would join in, too. We'd all laugh, making the dolls do silly things like try to ride the stuffed porpoise Dad bought me from the Melbourne Aquarium. When we got a bit older we'd flip through *Girlfriend* magazine and swoon over the pictures of our crushes.

I'd liked her a lot. And she liked me.

But after Daniella died . . . she changed. Something inside her broke and I don't think it's ever been fixed. She resented me so much for having my sister while she didn't have hers and it morphed into something physical between us. A wall. A divide.

I want to say something real. To let her know I forgive her for being mad and mean and angry, even though there's nothing anyone could have done to stop Daniella from dying that night. Nobody could have prevented her from having a car accident. It was just one of those horrible things in life – a tragedy with no point.

I open my mouth, but nothing comes out. I never know the right thing to say or how to say it and I always end up saying the dumb thing. Putting my foot in my mouth. Making myself look like an idiot.

'I don't like that she's here,' Sofia says quietly, almost to herself. She smooths a hand over her hair and looks out to the water, like she might find answers there. Then she takes a step back from the edge, which falls away into nothingness – no barriers, no protection, no support. Just a sheer drop. 'It feels like something is coming to a head.'

'I agree.' I nod. 'Do you think . . .'

'What?'

'Do you think she ever told anyone?' I ask, looking closely at Sofia. But her expression gives me nothing.

'No way.' She shakes her head, resolute. 'If anyone knew what really happened that day we would have heard about it by now. She needs to keep it secret as much as we do. None of us can afford to tell.'

I want to say more – to ask more – but it feels dangerous, like the words might escape our mouths and drift into the ears of someone who could punish us.

Someone who could make us pay for what we did.

Chapter Sixteen

Ellie

I stand in the bathroom, arms out like a scarecrow, legs spread, wearing only a skimpy pair of bikini bottoms. At this stage, most of the world has seen my boobs, so there's no point trying to hide them from Morgan. She's crouched at my feet, carefully painting me with an aerosol can of tanning product, which fills the room with sickly-sweet artificial coconut scent and fine brown mist as she turns me into a bronzed goddess, step number five of the 'Make Ellie Beautiful Enough to be a Wife' plan.

I must pretty, pretty, pretty to lock down a husband.

It's exhausting always having people looking at you. Every time I leave my house I'm conscious that someone will try to take my picture, whether I want it or not. Whether I consent or not. Imagine having your worst body image day ever – on your period, bloated and pimple-faced, feeling like absolute rubbish – and you need to run an errand. But the second you leave your house someone snaps a picture and sells it to every media outlet for a killing.

Ellie McLeod, unrecognisable without makeup!

Caught! Blond bombshell Ellie McLeod looking less than glam. Already too old for leading lady roles?

Working out or heading to rehab? Stars looking tired and dishevelled without hair and makeup team to cover their flaws.

It's relentless.

And then there are the opposing, but equally frustrating articles: *Stars set unrealistic beauty standards for the average woman* and *Are celebrities responsible for rising mental illness and body image issues?*

I literally can't win.

Now there's someone trying to tell the word I'm a liar and an adulterer . . . and another (or maybe the same person) leaving gruesome, threatening messages. My world is a tornado and Mitch still hasn't arrived from the airport.

Part of me wonders if he's gotten cold feet and hasn't figured out how to tell me yet.

'Ellie? You still breathing up there?' Morgan asks.

'Huh?' I look down at her.

Morgan's furrowed brows and perceptive blue eyes stare up at me. 'I asked you to turn around and you totally blanked on me.'

'Sorry.' I shake my head and turn. I jump a little when the cool spray hits the backs of my thighs.

'Did you talk to Mitch?' she asks. The gentle *woosh woosh woosh* of the tanning spray fills the air.

'It was just a quick conversation because he was getting into the car. Sounds like the airport was rammed.'

'He'll believe you,' she says softly.

Tears fill my eyes and I blink rapidly to make them go away, because we've already done my face and I can't have tear tracks staining my cheeks.

'I don't know what to make of all this,' I say, my shoulders feeling heavy. 'I really don't.'

'Talk it through. Sometimes that helps to clarify things,' she says. 'At least, that's what I do.'

She's right. I've always been that person who needed to externally process things, because words in the air make more sense than they do inside my head.

'If someone sent the photos directly to Fanny then they *wanted* to make sure I was off *Heartland*, right? Because if it was just about money, why bother with her?'

Paparazzi don't give a shit about ruining an actor's career, they simply want a payday. Whoever sent the photos to Fanny wanted to *hurt* me. Punish me. Maybe that was the main goal and forwarding the photos to the media for cash was just a bonus?

'That's a good question,' Morgan replies. 'Oh, by the way, I had to dispute a submission to your Wikipedia page this morning that put the affair in your "personal life" section,' she says with a huff. 'Arseholes.'

'Seriously?' I groan.

'Like, at least wait for someone to make a statement before you get all *Current Affairs* on them.'

I roll my eyes. 'They don't waste any time.'

'Personally, I think you should set everything to private for a while. Take some time away from the public. The comments that got through on Insta before I managed to change the settings were uh . . . well, let's just say the vibe check was not it.'

'Maybe I just won't go back.' I sigh. 'To any of it.'

'Margot doesn't do socials,' Morgan says, standing up behind me and beginning work on my back. 'None of them really mean much outside TikTok these days, anyway. Facebook is Boomer central and Insta is mostly bots and people photoshopping their arse. You could happily be in your luddite era.'

'Luddite era. I like that.'

'And then you wait a little while, publish the beautiful wedding photos where you look insanely gorgeous, and Mitch looks happy and totally in love with you . . . and anyone who has an issue with it can go jump.'

'If *only* it was that easy.' Ironically, while Hollywood demands women stay young forever, being there has aged me. It's made me cynical. I understand Sofia's ruthless outlook on life more these days than ever before. 'I have to convince Mitch to believe me, first.'

'He will. He's a total simp.'

'He's *not* a simp.' I turn around to look at her and she's grinning like the Cheshire cat. I figure she's only saying that to get a rise out of me in the hopes I'll laugh and lighten up a bit. 'Mitch and I love each other equally. He does not trail around after me like a puppy dog.'

'Whatever you say, boss.'

'Just because you think any guy who wants more than a situationship is a simp, doesn't mean they are. Real men embrace commitment.'

Jesus that makes me sound old.

Morgan doesn't reply. I know about her feelings about commitment – it's not for her. Like me, she grew up without her dad. He died young, from what she told me and her mum was never the same afterward. But loss impacts everyone differently. For Morgan it means being in her 'ho era' as she flippantly puts it, jumping from one noncommittal bloke to the next. For Sofia, losing her sister and father meant creating a life for herself that filled the holes in her heart – a business she was passionate about, a husband to love.

Everyone handles grief differently.

'Yeah, yeah,' I say, teasingly. 'To you I'm just an old lady. I get it.'

'I wanted to be married when I was a little girl,' she says from behind me, her voice catching. 'I used to dress up in Disney princess costumes and rip handfuls of flowers out of the garden to make a bouquet and set up my toys in two neat rows in the backyard so they could watch.'

I can imagine her, a little blond girl with pigtails, dressed as Belle or Snow White or Cinderella, holding a bouquet of flowers with the roots still dangling off the bottom.

I laugh. 'That's adorable.'

'Yeah, except I wanted to marry my dad.' The pain in her voice makes me glance over my shoulder to see if she's crying. She's not. When I catch her eye, she looks away. 'Sorry, I shouldn't talk about the dad stuff knowing your situation.'

My situation is more complicated than hers – after all, my father is still alive. And after years of acting like I didn't exist he wants back into my life. Wants my money, more like it. But we've invited him to the wedding, much to my mother's disgust. It was Mitch's idea.

You don't get a second chance to have your father at your wedding, Ellie, he'd said. *You don't have to let him walk you down the aisle. But if you lock him out, you can't ever take that back.*

It's a very Mitch way of looking at the situation – he's

from a big, close family where they do super American family things like big Thanksgiving lunches and reunions with more than a hundred people and throw family watch parties for the Super Bowl. He could never imagine not having one of his parents at his own wedding.

Oh God, his parents.

Do they know about the pictures of me and Antoine? I've only met them a handful of times and they seemed nice, but who the hell would approve of their son marrying a woman who appeared to be cheating on him?

What if they protest the wedding?

Should anyone present know of any reason that this couple should not be joined in holy matrimony, speak now or forever hold your peace.

The panic begins to set in again. I need to see Mitch. I need to set things straight.

I drag in a deep, wobbly breath and let it out slowly.

'Shit, I shouldn't have said anything. Sorry, El,' Morgan says, thinking I'm upset about my dad. Honestly, I couldn't give a shit about my dad and his money-hungry ways right now. 'Forget I opened my big mouth.'

'It's okay.' I try for another breath. 'Everything will be okay.'

But even as I will my happily-ever-after into existence, something foul curdles in my stomach. A feeling – intuition – that this is only the calm before the storm.

*

'Glow-up complete! Well, aside from hair and makeup . . . and wardrobe.' Morgan looks at the mess we've made in the bathroom. All manner of beauty products are scattered across the countertop – spray bottles of tan, a pot of facial mask, oils and serums and other skin potions, a loofah mitt, nail polishes, cuticle oil, razors, tweezers, and *two* LED light therapy masks – one for my face and one for my neck and décolletage. 'I did the best I could with your nails, but . . . we should have sent you to get some tips put on like I suggested. Then you wouldn't have been able to bite them.'

I'd rejected that idea because I *hate* the feeling of fake nails. I can't scratch properly, can't pick up small things, can't put my own jewellery on. But now that I look down at the bitten-down edges and slivers of exposed nail bed, the polish looks a little bit like lipstick on a pig.

I frown. 'Too late now.'

'You should listen to me, I know what you're like,' Morgan grumbles. 'But anyway, nails aside Mitch is going to fall over when he sees you.'

I glance at myself in the mirror. It's always strange to see the transformation – the pale, dull-skinned, hollow-eyed regular version of me turned into Ellie McLeod, award-winning actress. It's like putting on a mask. A very time-consuming, coconut-scented mask.

'What else needs to be done?' Morgan is already tidying up in that busy bee, super-productive way of hers. 'It'll just take me a minute to clean up in here.'

'I could do with some time by myself, to be honest,' I say, feeling a twinge of guilt about kicking her out after all she's done to help me. I know I pay her for it – *well*, I might add – but Morgan has been a permanent fixture in my life the last couple of years, so she's a friend as well as an employee. 'I need to think about how I'm going to broach the conversation with Mitch.'

I have to get it right. Otherwise I might not walk down the aisle tomorrow.

For a long time I believed I would never get married. After all, all men are bastards, right? That's what Mum told me. They lied, they manipulated, they hurt. They took advantage of you.

But then I met Mitch.

It was a chance meeting – a party. The host was a big-name director. Someone I should have been trying to impress, but instead I ended up talking to this sweet, funny man who rescued me from a dire conversation with some Wall Street bro about cryptocurrency. Mitch was the opposite – clearly doing well for himself, if the glittering Rolex was anything to go on.

But he was as down to earth as could be. I was smitten.

'Are you sure you should be here by yourself?' Morgan asks, a little groove forming between her brows. She huffs a rogue strand of blond hair out of her eyes as she continues packing up the beauty supplies. I spy a streak of fake tan on her T-shirt and another on her arm.

'I'm not going to fall to pieces,' I say, which *might* be the truth. Who knows? Between the pictures and the rumours and the bloodied message, I'm so stressed that I haven't eaten a thing all day.

I'm tired. I'm shaky. I'm hollow.

'As much as I, like, care about your mental wellbeing, Ellie, I'm a little *more* worried that there's some dude out there *bloody murdering pigeons* and writing creepy messages on the walls.'

'They were seagulls,' I correct.

'Whatever. That's not the point. But the message . . . I

know what you did? That's high-key creepy AF. What if some crazy fan is running loose out there? Remember that singer who was shot by their stalker? She had a fan obsessed with her and he shot her right in front of a whole group of people. If being in public isn't safe, then being on your own sure as shit isn't.'

I go to rub at my brow and then stop, not wanting to disturb Morgan's handiwork. Plus, if I get my skin all angry and irritated when my friend Marni arrives to do my hair and makeup, I'll cop an earful.

'Who?' I ask, confused. I don't remember a singer being shot.

'Christina Grimes. No, Grimmie . . . I think. I saw it on a documentary a while back.' Morgan is shorter than me by almost a head and so she tilts her face to look up at me, worry brimming behind her chunky black glasses. She looks like a concerned owl. 'Celebrity murder victims.'

'You have to stop watching those shows.' I shake my head. 'Besides, everyone is going to start arriving soon and—'

We're cut off by a loud *bang*. I jump and Morgan shrieks at the top of her lungs, skittering closer to me and grabbing my arm. We stand there, pressed together, breathing heavily.

'What the fuck was that?' Morgan whispers, her eyes darting to and fro. She jabs at her glasses, pushing them back up the bridge of her nose. She always does that when she's nervous.

'I don't know,' I whisper back. I have no idea why we're whispering because she screamed loud enough to let people in Europe know we're in this cottage.

I'm barefoot, wearing only a loose, silky robe to prevent

transfer from my fake tan, and when I creep out of the bathroom towards the front door of the cottage, my soles make soft suctioning noises against the polished boards. Morgan is behind me, close as a shadow. So close I can feel the heat and anxious energy radiating off her.

The front door itself doesn't have a view to the outside – no windows, no peephole. There's a thin sliver of window on either side of the door, but the glass is textured to allow the light in without anyone being able to peer inside. It's designed for privacy. There's a larger window further down with thin, gauzy drapes pulled across. They billow gently from the air-conditioning unit, which hums quietly on one wall. The back windows – floor-to-ceiling glass with a single sliding door facing the ocean – however, are uncovered.

I press my ear to the door, but hear nothing outside.

'Check the back?' Morgan suggests and together we pad quietly towards the back of the cottage. My heart hammers in my chest, like a fist punching the back of my ribs.

What if there *is* someone here, looking for me? Wanting to punish me? A crazed fan? Who else could it be?

My heart is in my throat as I move as silently as possible towards the big glass windows. I'd kept the blinds on this side open, wanting to delight in the view as much as possible – the bright, white lighthouse to my right, the vast, empty blue beyond – but maybe I should keep them closed from now on.

I taste something warm and metallic on my tongue. Blood. I've broken the surface of my lower lip from biting down to keep from making a noise. I swipe at it with my thumb, watching the vibrant red smear across my skin. I can't see anyone outside. It's silent, save for Morgan's breath puffing against my arm as she huddles close to me.

'Should we go outside?' I whisper.

Her eyes widen. 'I . . . I don't know.'

'Stick with me.' I hook my finger around the handle of the sliding door and ease it open a fraction at a time, cringing at the soft scraping noise it makes.

'Why wasn't that locked?' she hisses at me. 'Jesus, Ellie. You're not security-conscious *at all*.'

I'd locked the front door when Sofia texted, but I'd totally forgotten about the back. Typical scatterbrained Ellie, I can practically hear her say. I shoot Morgan a look and she holds up both hands, shaking her head at me. But she's right. These days privacy, anonymity and feeling safe is a luxury I have forgone in favour of my career. But here on home turf, around Sofia and Rose, I sometimes forget I'm 'the' Ellie McLeod and I just revert to being normal, old me.

I step outside and look around, my palms growing sweaty and my throat feeling tight and dry. My heartbeat is a steady *thump, thump, thump* growing quicker with each breath. If someone were to come charging with a knife around the corner of the cottage . . .

I'd be dead.

I take another step, hands tucked up close to my body, clutching at the edges of my silky dressing gown. Please let it be nothing. Let this all be a bad dream.

Please, please, please.

As I take another step, something moves suddenly at my feet and I squeal, jumping back and bumping into Morgan, almost toppling her over. She grabs the back of my robe, hiding behind me. But it's only a bird on the ground, looking dazed. A blackbird with silky feathers and a little yellow beak.

As I exhale in relief, my knees almost buckle.

Sing a song of sixpence, a pocket full of rye. Four and twenty blackbirds baked in a pie.

I almost laugh out loud at how absurd I'm being – since when do I freak out over some poor bird hitting a window?

'It's just a bird,' I say and I feel Morgan relax behind me. 'It must have flown into the window.'

The poor little mite struggles to its feet and tries to fly, stumbling and anxious. I crouch down and slowly reach out a hand but it skitters – stumbles – away from me, probably terrified. Confused. But it's moving. That's a good sign. It's when they make no attempt to move that they've really hurt themselves.

'We should watch him a minute,' I say, glancing at Morgan. 'To make sure he flies off okay. Otherwise we might need to find a box to put him in until he recovers.'

'How do you know it's a *he*?' Morgan asks, peering down.

'The black feathers and yellow beak. Female blackbirds are brown all over.'

'Girl birds always get the boring colours,' she muses. Then she gives herself a shake. 'Can I just stay with you, Ellie? Please? At least until Mitch arrives. I don't like the idea of you being here by yourself.'

Maybe *she* doesn't want to be on her own, all things considered. And by 'all things considered' I mean the very likelihood someone is here watching us. I stand to my full height and sweep my gaze around. In the distance, I spot

Rose going for a walk towards the lighthouse. But when I follow the path she's walking with my eye, I think I see someone else already standing there. Is that Sof? I squint. It's hard to tell.

But when the person spots Rose, they duck around the side of the tall white structure, out of view. I feel that strange prickling sensation again.

'You know what,' I say, turning to Morgan. 'Maybe it is a good idea if none of us are alone right now.'

Chapter Seventeen

Sofia

Talking to the 'security team' yielded nothing. First of all, the term should be used in only the loosest possible sense, since these were not trained professionals and my frail, eighty-two-year-old nonna would have a better chance of scaring potential predators away. One of the guys had a barely post-pubescent face covered in patchy bum fluff, making his jaw look like a sad neglected garden. The other guy looked like he'd be stumped by a rhetorical question.

Nikoleta had given us the B team, that was for bloody sure. Either that or there was some nepotism at work, because I couldn't imagine two people less suited to the job.

They'd tried unsuccessfully to placate me.

Yes, we check every car that arrives against the guest list.

Yes, we'll be posted outside while the rehearsal dinner is going on.

No, there's no need to worry. Everything is under control.

Apparently Nikoleta warned them I would be coming to have a word, undermining me before I'd even had the chance to speak with them. I bet she painted me as some uptight prissy princess, high on her friend's success and making a mountain out of a molehill. When I'd told them about the seagulls, I was sure the younger guy was trying to hold back a smirk.

Did they think a pile of dead birds and a message written in blood was funny? Or did they simply not believe me?

Whatever the reason, I can't afford to waste any more time on it now. Tiffani and I finally got everything set up for tonight – after more than forty minutes trying to figure out the sound system for the video – as well as setting up the party favours that Ellie plans to give out. For some reason, she and Mitch wanted to do favours for both the rehearsal dinner *and* the wedding, so Tiffani spent a few hours assembling them and doing the handwritten calligraphy tags. Tonight, small bags made of a sheer, gauze silk will contain a set of two Gucci dessert forks topped with tiger heads, which cost somewhere in the vicinity of $700 to 800 a pop. Tomorrow night guests will receive the matching cake server, which cost close to a thousand dollars each. The server has been engraved with her and Mitch's initials, along with the date of the wedding.

I've planned plenty of luxury weddings in my time but this is probably the most extravagant bonbonnière I've ever seen.

Ellie is determined to treat her guests to something memorable. Better that she spends her money, I reckon, before her mother and father get their hands on it. I try calling her to check in again, but there's no answer. She texts a moment later to say everything is fine.

When I make it to my cottage I'm surprised to find

the front door ajar. Did Rose leave it open? That's not like her. My heart rate kicks up a notch. I press my fingertip to the door, easing it open and listening for any indication that there's someone inside. Music. Talking. The sound of cupboards opening and closing. Maybe one of the husbands has arrived? I glance around, but I don't see either Rob's car or Malachi's.

I know what you did.

A prickling feeling extends up the back of my neck, like a bug is crawling over my skin. I squirm, batting at the sensation even though I know there's nothing there. It's the feeling of being watched. Observed. Plotted against.

'Rose?' I call into the house, hoping she's inside and that I've just contracted her paranoia. But there's no response. 'Anyone in there?'

I glance back over my shoulder, but there's nobody about. I haven't seen Nikoleta since our discussion – if you can call it that – earlier, and the security guards must be elsewhere. Not that I feel super confident they would do much for me, anyway. There's no sign of Ellie or Rose . . . or Michelle.

Talk about an unexpected turn of events.

I look for anything around me that I could use as a weapon and come up empty. There's a small terracotta pot containing bright pink and yellow flowers, but I doubt it would work for anything other than a distraction if thrown. It's not heavy enough to do any damage. I decide to nestle the cottage's key through my middle and pointer finger the way I used to when I would walk from the train station to my car late at night when I still lived at home in Lalor. It's better than nothing.

I slip into the cottage and leave the door open behind me. The main room is clear, left exactly as it was this morning, the spare charging cable for my laptop sitting limply on the breakfast bar. Rose's slippers are by the front door so she can change out of her shoes immediately upon entering, a leftover habit from living with her parents. There's a mug on the coffee table, along with a half-consumed glass of water, and in the kitchen the knife block is full, no sharp implements missing.

The open curtains show off the glorious view outside. I stand still and listen, but only the distant sound of the ocean and a lone bird crying fills my ears. Nothing seems out of the ordinary.

I walk hesitantly into the living room and creep towards Rose's bedroom, the door half open. I peer inside. In one corner sits a small white cot and for a minute I cringe, having forgotten until now that she was bringing her son. Hopefully the soundproofing is good enough that I don't get woken up if he's crying in the middle of the night. Tomorrow is going to be a long day and I need to be on my A game. Ellie and I talked about making the wedding eighteen plus, but she said Rose was the only one with a young child and she didn't want her to feel targeted.

And Rose *would* feel targeted, too. If something could even remotely be taken as a personal affront, then that's exactly how she would take it. Plus she's sensitive about being the only mother in the group. She constantly sends baby photos to our group chat – Isaac with his favourite toy, Isaac eating spaghetti, Isaac in his pram. And that was just last week! I always respond with the requisite heart emoji now, because Rose gets testy if I don't, even though she knows that neither Ellie nor I have any interest in motherhood.

I head back out of her room and towards the shared bathroom. A quick peek tells me it, too, is empty. The only remaining room in the cottage is my bedroom. The door is pulled firmly shut and I don't remember if I closed it or not when I left after getting changed a few hours earlier.

I press down on the handle and ease the door open as quietly as possible. My suitcase sits against one wall, empty after I'd unpacked it yesterday. On the floor are all the shoes I've brought with me – too many – rubber thongs and leather sandals, a pair of wedge espadrilles, gold strappy heels for the wedding, and some jewelled flat slides in case my feet get sore from dancing.

I almost don't see the small envelope sitting on the bed, the pale colour of the paper blending in with the rumpled linen doona. Cautiously, I reach for it. Inside is a card with a single flower on the front – hand-painted, it looks like. A sprig of lavender. Maybe Ellie wanted to give us our thank-you cards early?

But when I open it, I frown. There's not much inside. Certainly nothing to indicate who sent it.

To Sofia, I've got a surprise planned for you tonight. I hope you enjoy it.

Someone has been here, in my room. Touching my bed. Writing this note that's meant to frighten me. The bloodied message . . . it's not for Ellie. At least, it's not *only* for her.

What do they have planned next?

Chapter Eighteen

2013

Ellie

We're all frozen to the spot as the two people next door make the kind of noise that can only mean one thing. There's a long keening moan – masculine, guttural. Animalistic. Sofia goes green, like she wants to spew, her lips curling back into a disgusted sneer. Across the room, Rose slowly pops up from her crouched position, looking equally repulsed.

I'd heard rumours about Mr Quinn but hadn't wanted to believe them. He's always been nice to me and I figured since he was the only good-looking male teacher in the whole school, maybe it was just meaningless gossip.

But it looks like those whispered words were true.

He's having it on with a student. Crystal McKinnon, no less. She's one of the most popular girls at school. I had a crush on her briefly in year ten, before she turned into one of the mean girls. I crushed on her brother, too. Good genes in that family.

My eyes flick to the wall that separates us from the grunting. I listen to hear if Crystal is . . .

God. I don't even know what I'm trying to listen for. If she's being forced? If she's hurting? Scared? If she . . . wants it. He's our teacher. Even if she *does* want it, what he's doing is wrong. I know it. Sofia and Rose and Michelle know it. *All* students and teachers know it, even if some of the girls in my year level hike up their dresses when he's around. They say lewd things and wink at him and he takes it in his stride . . . or so I thought. The principal would have a bloody conniption if she knew about this – because the high school in the next suburb over had a huge scandal last year, when one of their teachers got caught sending 'sexually explicit' messages to a student.

This is *so* much more than messages.

'Oh yes, Steven.' Her voice, thick and sultry like spiced honey, makes me want to stick my fingers in my ears. 'Yes, like that.'

I can't believe what I'm hearing.

I mean, I *can* believe it but I also can't, you know? Something rattles against the wall and next to me Sofia shudders. Her cheeks have gone pink and her hands are balled into fists. She looks like she wants to punch someone. I want to tell her that it's going to be okay. That we'll still get her grade changed and everything will be fine. We'll achieve our goal in coming here.

Across the room, I see Michelle quietly stand and test the lock on the door, making sure it's closed. She barely makes a sound as she creeps over to where Sofia and I have been squatting down, behind the main administration desk. There's loads of junk food back here – bags of lollies and chips, soft drink cans, some Gatorade bottles, a box of the Freddo Frogs they sell for a gold coin for fundraising. The little bin on the ground overflows with empty containers and bottles and torn, foil wrappers. KitKats, Crunchies, Mars Bars.

And they have the nerve to tell us not to eat so much sugar!

'I'm going to get started,' Michelle whispers, her voice so quiet I have to strain to listen. 'Keep watch on the door.'

I frown. 'Shouldn't we wait until they're . . .'

'They're plenty distracted,' she replies, gesturing to the wall, where the bookcase rattles again. 'Just keep quiet and make sure the door doesn't open.'

Like the leader of a police Special Operations Group, Sofia uses her hands to direct me to stand by the door and Rose to keep watch out the window that faces the car park. She puts two fingers together and swings them from her eyes outward, telling everyone to stay alert.

Michelle goes to a computer that sits on the back part of the horseshoe desk and brings up a login screen. Without missing a beat, she types in a username and password and is immediately granted access. As she does this, I make my way over to the door and take up the position Michelle had a moment ago. In the room next door, the moans and groans continue. There's a loud smack and it makes me jump, but there is no sign of distress.

I nervously chew on my nails while we wait, energy building up inside me like a bubble swelling. Keeping quiet and still is not my forte. A little strip of skin near my cuticle peels away and I stifle a hiss of pain as a drop of bright red blood blooms there. I stick my thumb in my mouth and suck on it, cursing myself for not being able to leave it alone. I always do that. I bounce on my heels and it makes the door rattle a little, and Sofia pops up with her finger planted in front of her lips.

'Sorry,' I mouth, holding up both hands.

There is a very faint *click, click, click* as Michelle's fingers tap softly over the keyboard, but I doubt you would be able to hear it outside the room. At least . . . I hope so.

I look around trying to distract myself, but there's nothing of interest to settle my eyes on. I watch as Rose peers out of the window, the side of her lip sucked inward and her jaw working as though she's trying to chew her way out of this situation. The minutes tick by at half-speed as Michelle types slowly, probably trying to minimise the sound. I shake my hands out, trying to dispel the jittering energy that's cranking up and up. I want this to be done so we can get out of here.

For some reason, I've got an icky feeling in my gut. There's badness in the air. It's thick, suffocating. I can almost taste it.

The sound of a long groan next door signals that . . . uh, things might be done there. I watch Sofia as her head swings to the wall, a look of pure venom on her face. I frown. I mean, I think it's pretty gross that a teacher and student are having sex, too. But it didn't sound like she was being coerced. Does that make it better? I'm honestly not sure. All I know is that it's wrong . . . but what we're doing here now is wrong, too. A different kind of wrong, sure, but Sofia and Rose both have something to lose if we get caught.

So, all I care about now is making sure we get out of

here without getting caught. Oh, and that Sofia has her grade changed so she still has a chance for being named dux. That's what matters. I just want her to be happy again.

There's rustling next door, a zipper being pulled and a soft girlish giggle. All of a sudden, Michelle looks up and gives us two thumbs up. It's done.

Time to get out of here.

I make a motion to the girls that I'm going to listen through the wall of next door. Michelle is shutting down the computer and Sofia sits there with a palm pressed to her head. Maybe she's sick. She doesn't look so hot. A fine sheen of sweat glistens across her forehead and her eyes look unfocused, glassy. Her usually warm and tanned olive skin has a pale, waxy quality to it.

Something is wrong.

I head to the wall, tiptoeing so as not to make any noise and find a space between a bookshelf and a filing cabinet. The soundproofing in this room isn't great, but I can hear more detail with my ear pressed to the wall.

The rustling I've heard might be someone shifting on a bean bag. There's a distinct sound to all those little polystyrene balls, almost like plastic rice grains squeaking against one another. There are footsteps now, and another soft laugh along with an oof. Maybe one person was helping the other up off the bean bag? The rustling stops.

'We should do this again.' It's Mr Quinn, his voice low. 'But I have to know I can trust you not to say anything.'

'I won't tell anyone. But I'll be eighteen in six months. Then I can do what I want.'

'The school doesn't see it like that. Not while you're still a student here. For both our sakes I need to make sure this stays our little secret, okay?' There's a smacking sound, like they're kissing. 'Promise?'

'I promise.'

'You go out the front and I'll wait a few minutes to leave, just in case.'

Light-footed steps are followed by a slight creak as the door opens in the quiet study room. I creep back to the girls to tell them what I heard.

'She's gone but he's waiting,' I whisper. 'We should give it another minute or two.'

Michelle nods, raking a hand through her close-cropped curly hair. 'We'll wait until he goes, and then head out through the side entrance near the labs.'

That door was locked before – hence why we didn't use it on the way in. But going out, we can unlock it, then snib the lock and pull it closed behind us, leaving no trace we were here. I go back to the wall and press my ear to it again. Now that Mr Quinn is on his own, there's no noise. He's probably on his phone or staring out a window, maybe. Not moving. The only footsteps I can hear are the now mostly faded sound of Crystal leaving.

I glance back to look at Sofia, who is sweating visibly. Her breathing looks like it's coming a little fast and shallow, and she's knotted her hands together so hard her knuckles are white. I remember her looking like that one time when she got food poisoning and had to run to the girls' bathroom at school. I make a little motion with my hand to catch her attention.

'Are you okay?' I mouth. She nods in response, but I'm not convinced.

Something weird is going on with her.

All of a sudden I hear movement in the next room, footsteps striding with purpose and the squeak of a door opening. I motion to the girls and point enthusiastically. We all slink over to the office door, holding our breaths. But then there's a soft *thunk* and everyone freezes. Rose throws both hands up, mouthing 'sorry' as a potted plant wobbles. She steadies it with her hand. Probably caught it with the toe of her sneaker or something.

Not one of us moves and we strain to listen. But there's nothing outside – no sound, no voices. Just eerie silence. I can't hear Mr Quinn at all. He must be gone.

Letting out a slow breath, I place a hand to my chest. My heart is beating wildly, like fists sending rolling punches to an overhead boxing bag.

We wait a few seconds more and then Sofia flicks the lock on the door with a soft *click*. Still, we wait. But there's nothing. I'd expected Mr Quinn to walk past the office, because that's the quickest way to the staff car park. But perhaps he put his car somewhere else. Or maybe he was going to get something from the gym before he leaves.

'I'll go first,' Sofia whispers. 'You guys wait until I give the all clear.'

She eases the door open and slips out, leaving the door partially closed. At the sound of her gasp, I know something has gone horribly wrong.

THE NIGHT BEFORE THE WEDDING

Chapter Nineteen

2024

Ellie

I wonder what they're all thinking. What they all believe. Most of all, I wonder what Mitch believes.

We stand together – Mitch and I – talking to my mother and Auntie Pat. The Glass House has filled with our guests, the vast majority of whom are staying on the lighthouse grounds or in the nearest town. There are a handful of people arriving early tomorrow morning, as well.

I spot Sofia, elegant in a straight-cut bronze silk midi dress, standing with Rob, who has his hand at her back. It keeps drifting down to her arse and I watch as she shoots him a sultry look, admonishing him in a way that says if they were alone she would totally give in.

Then there's Rose and Malachi and little Isaac, who's cute as a button in his tiny suit pants and blue collared shirt. He's grizzly though, probably tired from the long drive and Rose keeps taking him outside to placate him. He'll likely have to go to bed soon. Rose's sister Lily is standing with them, their faces mirror images. Morgan and Tiffani are chatting – getting along like a house on fire, which makes me happy.

Everyone seems to be having a good time. Waitstaff in black and white circle about with trays of food – it might be a cocktail event, but the food is abundant. I wouldn't expect any less from Dom, being Greek. To him, food is love. It's life. His movie had the best craft service I've ever seen.

Outside the sun is starting to set and people have gathered by The Glass House's windows to watch the sky's shifting watercolour hues. A reddish orange bleeds into blue, creating a purple haze in the distance. Pink-tinted clouds streak across the sky, like tufts of fairy floss torn from a fairground dessert. Everyone has champagne flutes and the liquid seems to glitter, matching the jewels hanging from my friends' ears and the sparkling shoes and dresses and tiny, impractical handbags.

It's all so beautiful. So perfect.

But I can't seem to escape the churning worry in my gut that no matter how beautiful it looks, it's all an illusion. That tomorrow, the spell will be broken.

My soon-to-be-husband looks effortlessly handsome tonight, even though he's running on little sleep and high emotion. Like me. Since this is the rehearsal, we're not dressed to the nines like we will be tomorrow. I'm wearing a short white dress with dramatic laser-cut fabric and a pair of flat gold sandals. Mitch is dressed in tan slacks and a white shirt with the sleeves rolled up. His hair is mussed and there's stubble on his jaw, but I like him that way. A little rough and tumble. Natural.

But our conversation hasn't given me the security or closure I was looking for. Mitch took way longer to arrive than the drive should have taken and when he finally showed up at our cottage, he went straight off to the shower and stayed in there for almost forty minutes. Then he needed to take a call. By the time he was done, we barely had time to talk before I needed to get my dress and shoes on.

He's angry – I can feel it in the air around him – but I don't know if it's with me or the situation.

I glance over at him, trying to scan his face for extra information. He laughs at something Auntie Pat says but the smile doesn't quite make it up to his eyes. That's not like him. I reach for his hand and he gives me a quick squeeze before releasing me almost immediately, his eyes staying straight ahead.

I can't stand this.

I catch Mum watching me out of the corner of her eye. She's been weird all night, too. I was anticipating as much, since I know she doesn't want me to get married. She's protective like that. Wants to keep me away from the pain she experienced while being with my father. Speaking of which . . .

I catch Dad walking towards our group, a slight sway in his step. He's been drinking. He's *always* been drinking.

'Ah, there's my darlin' girl.' He beams. These days his hair is long, swept back into a greasy ponytail at the nape of his neck. The edge of a tattoo peeks out from the collar of his unironed shirt. I guess wife number two doesn't fuss about his appearance. Thankfully, he's listened to my request not to bring her to the wedding. 'Aren't you a right vision, my love. All grown up.'

I feel the tension rise in the group as though it's a physical thing – an electrical current charging the air, ready to make lightning. It sizzles and pops and makes my already queasy stomach churn even harder. I feel a little faint.

'Hi, Dad. Uh . . . you remember Mitch,' I say awkwardly. Dad's only met Mitch once and only because Mitch insisted on meeting him before the wedding.

'Good to see you, sir.' Mitch extends a hand.

'See, now those are some real manners. Most of youse lot can't get a proper sentence out these days.' Dad shakes his hand enthusiastically and Mum rolls her eyes. The irony of him complaining about the poor grammar of kids today while using 'youse' in a sentence is not lost on any of us. 'Too bloody right. You did good picking this bloke, Ellie girl.'

'Thanks, Dad.' I force a smile.

His eyes slide to my mother and harden. 'Rhonda.'

'Dale,' she replies, gritting his name out through teeth so clenched it's a wonder anything makes it out at all.

'Still seeing that floozy, Diane?' Auntie Pat asks, her voice a thousand needles behind a brittle, insincere smile.

She knows full well that Dad and Diane have been married for years at this point.

'Oh fuck off, Pat.' Dad makes a shooing gesture.

I shoot my mother a look. She guides her sister away, who throws a nasty glare over one shoulder towards my dad. Mitch's parents watch us warily. They've been a little cool all night, so I guess they *did* see the pictures.

Shit, shit, *shit*.

'Dad, can you just . . . not.' I press my fingers to my temple.

He looks indignant, like he hasn't done anything wrong. I regret inviting him. Mum barely spoke to me for a week after I told her. I can't blame her. He's done fuck all for us since he left and meanwhile she's done everything, yet he still scores an invite. She has a right to be mad.

'Mind if I talk to my daughter for a minute?' Dad asks Mitch gruffly.

I glance at Mitch imploringly, begging him to read my mind and make up some story about how we need to speak to someone together right now. Begging him to know me and what I need. But he nods and is already walking away when he says, 'Sure thing.'

He doesn't even lean down to kiss me on my cheek before going. Nothing.

I catch Sofia's eye across the hall and notice her start coming towards me, a frown etching lines between her brows. At least *she* knows what I need without me having to say a thing.

'Darl, I hate to bring this up on the eve of your weddin' but . . . I'm in a spot of bother.' Dad rubs at the back of his neck, seeming almost sheepish. That's a new look for him. The man wouldn't know remorse if it slapped him in the face with a raw salmon filet. 'I need to borrow some cash.'

'You're doing this *now*?' I look at him incredulously. My nerves are far too frayed for me to brush it off like I've been trying to do. 'How can you walk out of my life without looking back and then waltz back in asking for money like it's nothing? The night before my wedding, no less.'

God, why don't I have a champagne in my hand right now? Actually, stuff that. Give me a vodka martini, extra dirty. Make it three.

'I know the divorce was hard on you, Ellie. But it *really* was for the best.' He rubs a hand over the top of his head, shifting his hair in a way that reveals a patch of scalp. The once-blond strands are now coarse, sparse and mostly silver. He was handsome once – I've seen photos. But now he carries some paunch and his face is dry and sagging from years of sun and boozing. 'Your mother and I . . . we never meant to have you.'

I let out a bitter laugh. 'Wow. You're doing this now, too.'

'We might not have meant for your mother to get pregnant, but I loved you with everything I bloody had. Leaving you was the hardest, most painful thing I've ever done.'

Dad has never said anything like this to me. In fact, for the longest time, he never said anything to me at all – not even a call for my milestone birthdays, no cards at Christmas. Nothing. Now, though, he looks truly regretful. Or maybe it's just a very well-prepared act to add extra zeros to the 'loan' he's going to ask for.

'It's what put me on the drink,' he adds.

'You could have come to visit me . . . had shared custody, even.' My resentment simmers like water coming to the boil. I feel the pressure building. 'You could have come to see my plays at school or sent me a birthday or Christmas card. Anything other than disappear for almost *fifteen* years with barely any contact.'

'I shoulda started coming around sooner.' He nods. 'I shoulda stopped listening to your mother's threats.'

The waiter attempts to come back to us now that Dad isn't telling people to 'fuck off' anymore, but I wave him away. My appetite has been absent all day.

'What threats?' I scoff. 'I've never heard about any threats.'

'She said she was gunna turn you against me, Ellie. When she found out about me and Diane, she told me to get out and if I ever contacted you she was gunna tell you that I was abusive and a drug addict. I might like my drinks and my ciggies, but I never did no drugs. And I certainly never hit a woman.'

The words are like a slap in the face.

Because Mum *had* said those things. And I'd believed them without hesitation.

'I'd rather you think I was a shit dad than an abusive one,' he adds, his voice sad.

I have no idea if I can trust *anything* he says or if this is simply a technique to win my sympathy. I mean, this is the guy who carried on an affair with another woman for years before Mum finally got proof to confront him. Prior to that he lied about everything.

That's what she *told you.*

Maybe she *did* want to turn me against him. That's not uncommon in divorced households.

'*If* that's true,' I say. 'And that's a big bloody if, then why did you think it best to disappear instead of fighting for me? I'm your daughter.'

'You don't know what she's capable of, Ellie. And what the fuck was I going to do? If I argued with her, she'd call the cops on me. Make up some story. She *did* one time, almost got me arrested. She's *manipulative*.' He looks at me imploringly. 'She knows how to get what she wants.'

I'm finding it hard to believe him because he could have told me this years ago if it were true, not just *after* I came into money. The timing makes me suspicious.

'So do you, Dad.' I shake my head. 'After all, you're trying to ask me for money right now.'

At that moment Sofia appears, slightly pink in the cheeks and looking frazzled.

'Hello, Mr McLeod,' she says cheerily. She has her beautiful crystal-encrusted pen in one hand and she taps it against her palm like a ruler or a pointer. It makes her seem very official. 'I am *so* very sorry to steal Ellie away, but she and Mitch have planned something special for everyone and it's my job to keep things on track. It's so good of you to make the drive out for tonight. Such a long way. You're looking very well, too! I'm so glad to see it. Thanks again.'

She whisks me away in a cloud of words and a sweet voice I've never heard come out of her mouth before and Dad stands there, looking rather bewildered but also puffing his chest out in pride like she'd bestowed some amazing compliment on him.

'That is quite a talent,' I say as she hooks her arm into mine.

'I just say a lot of things and most guys can't keep up.' She grins. 'How are you doing?'

'Well, Dad just told Auntie Pat to fuck off and he and Mum are about to throw down and Mitch's parents are avoiding me like the plague and Mitch himself can barely look me in the eye . . . so, you tell me.' I sigh. 'At least there are no more messages written in seagull blood.'

It was supposed to come out as a joke, but neither Sofia nor I are laughing.

'I checked with the security team about thirty minutes ago,' she says, her lip curling as if she's tasted something sour. 'They said all vehicles on the grounds are accounted for and have been checked against the list we provided. They've done a walk around the property and haven't seen anyone here who shouldn't be.'

I frown. 'So whoever did it came on foot?'

There's doubt in her expression.

Because if that's *not* what she believes, then it means that she thinks the person who did it is *here* right now, hiding in plain sight. I glance around the room, narrowing my eyes. There are thirty guests here and ten kitchen and waitstaff, from what Nikoleta has told us.

'Well, the security guards weren't here until this afternoon. It's possible the person parked outside the gate and snuck onto the property on foot.' She shrugs as though trying to appear relaxed. But the way she white-knuckles her pen belies that. 'I mean, it isn't *that* high. It would absolutely be possible to climb over.'

'Unless they had the code, then they could have driven in.'

'Yeah, but we would have noticed,' she replies. 'There was no one else around so it would have been obvious if some random car was driving in.'

'What do you think happened?' I prod.

Usually Sofia is in control – she either has a plan or is in the process of making one. If she has any negative emotion it's usually anger, not worry. So seeing her like this, the frown, the way she's sucking on the inside of her cheek, the way she's twirling her pen between her fingers, making the crystal cap catch the light, is concerning. Highly concerning.

'I don't know what to think.' She shakes her head. 'Something bad is going on. Earlier . . . '

She looks like words are dancing up a storm on the tip of her tongue. Her dark brown eyes flick back and forth, like a laser scanning my face.

I touch her arm. 'What?'

'Nothing.' She shakes her head. 'I'm just worried about making sure everyone is safe, that's all. Promise me you won't go anywhere on your own. Take Mitch or someone else with you. None of us should be alone.'

None of us . . .

She doesn't think the message is about me and the paparazzi pictures. At least, not *only* about that.

'What are you not saying?' I ask, narrowing my eyes at her. She practically squirms. It's a very *un*-Sofia-like thing to do.

'It's just a hunch, Ellie. I don't know anything . . . that's the problem.' She looks around, glancing back over her shoulder. 'Michelle is here.'

'Michelle who?' I frown. But when she looks at me meaningfully, understanding filters through my body like a slow-moving toxin. I feel it run along my limbs, slowing me down. Turning the world to molasses. '*That* Michelle?'

'She works here, apparently. Rose bumped into her. Strange, right?'

'I haven't seen her.'

'Me either.' Sofia pulls me closer. 'But what if she's behind all this? She knows what happened. She was there. Maybe now she thinks it's time to cash in – you're a famous actress with everything to lose and I'm running a successful well-known business. Maybe she needs the money.'

I glance to the windows that face the ocean. It's dark out now. The sun has disappeared below the horizon, turning the sky an inky velvet black. The windows have turned to mirrors, reflecting the gently glowing lights that hang overhead and showing the faces of people who stand close. It feels like everyone is watching me. Something slithers down my spine. Foreboding.

'If she's part of the staff then security would have no reason to flag her vehicle, right?' I say. 'But wouldn't outing us hurt her too?'

'Not if she's the first one to talk,' Sofia says. 'And not if she thinks we'll pay up instead of risking our livelihoods.'

'You don't know it was her who killed those birds,' I say. I can't imagine it. Michelle might have been an outcast, but she never showed *any* signs of violence. In fact, prickly as she had been from years of bullying, she'd always struck me as thoughtful and kind. She used to feed the sparrows that flittered around the school grounds, breaking off tiny pieces of her sandwiches or muesli bars and tossing them towards the scavenging little creatures. She seemed . . . kind. 'We have no evidence.'

'If she's smart, we won't,' Sofia says. 'All the more reason to be careful and stick together.'

'Good idea.'

'Now, go and grab Mitch. We need to do your speech and slide presentation before we fall behind on the schedule.'

Michelle being here seems like way too big of a coincidence, all these years later. And coincidences, I have learned, are almost never about fate and almost always about motivations.

Chapter Twenty

Rose

Isaac is grizzling again. I jostle him in my arms, cooing softly and rubbing my cheek against his head. His wiry little curls scratch against my skin in a way that's soul-soothingly familiar and comforting. I haven't been away long, but being separated from him makes me feel like part of myself is adrift.

'Mummy missed you so much, little man.' I kiss his chubby cheek. His broad nose screws up and it looks like he's about to let out a shriek so I bounce him a bit more energetically. 'Okay, okay. I know you're tired, sweetie. It won't be long, now.'

I should have taken him back to the cottage half an hour ago, but Ellie and Mitch still haven't done their speech and I don't want to miss it. I've been watching them all evening, trying to work out if everything is okay between them. I'm still not sure.

Compared to Ellie's bright and shining aura, Mitch strikes me as . . . a little dull. Nothing stands out about him. Medium brown hair, medium brown eyes, white skin that's got a weak, pinkish tan and a smattering of freckles. He's not skinny but not bulky, moderate height. I'm not sure a composite sketch artist would be able to do anything with a description of him.

I'm being harsh. Mitch is extremely successful in his own field. He's a professional golfer and he's been ranked top ten in the world more than once. It's nothing to sniff at. But outside his career, he hasn't got much else going on.

When they started dating I asked Ellie what attracted her to him. He was steady, she said. Grounded. Didn't buy into the hype and flash of her rising stardom since he had his own thing going on, so if the bubble of her Hollywood dreams popped and it all went away, Mitch wouldn't be fazed. Not once did there seem an ounce of passion in her voice. An ounce of excitement or thrill or . . . even love.

I'd never say it out loud, but I think she wants someone who is the complete opposite of her father – someone who is successful, steady, reliable – and passion didn't even factor into the decision. It feels like she's settling, frankly. And love might be the only area in my life where I've made good choices, so I feel entitled to that opinion even if I won't ever share it with anyone.

Isaac grizzles again and I bounce him, soothing him with a soft *shh*.

Next to me, Malachi stands close, always protective even when there isn't a specific reason to be. I catch a waft of his aftershave and it warms my belly, making some darkly delicious feeling stir low there. I missed him, too. Terribly.

'You look bloody fit in that dress, Rose. Legs for days.' Malachi grins. The way he looks me up and down, rich brown eyes filled with hunger, makes my cheeks turn instantly red. He's dressed in all black tonight, like the dark prince in some gothic fairy tale, and a simple gold chain gleams around the base of his throat, glowing against his deep brown skin. God, he's so handsome. 'Too bad we have to share the cottage with Sofia and Rob.'

He leans down and snakes an arm around my waist, making out like he's coming in to give Isaac a peck on the head while trying to cop a feel of my bum. I nudge him with my elbow. 'Behave yourself, man. We're in public.'

But there's no reprimand in my voice. Fact is, tonight might be the first time I've felt anything close to beautiful since I got pregnant. I'm wearing a simple red dress that hits mid-thigh and has loose fabric gathered around my waist with a tie. I've always thought I looked my best in red, although maybe that's because I associate it with luck and good fortune. I went shopping for the dress alone, not wanting Mum's well-meaning but harsh critiques of my body nor wanting Sofia suggesting things that were totally out of my budget. Lily is *never* any help with that stuff, either – something that hasn't changed tonight judging by her plain black pants and simple green shirt. Being a decorated Olympian and having sponsorship deals has never improved her sense of style and she dresses for function over form.

That's one area where we don't have to try to look different. We just do.

She's currently chatting with one of Mitch's mates – another golfer. Trust Lily to sniff out the other athletes in the room.

'We could skive off for a bit,' he suggests, breath whispering over my skin. 'I've got the car. We could take it close to the edge, look out over the ocean, 'ave a little romance.'

He always amps up his British accent when he wants to get me going. It works a treat and I feel the thrum of desire ripple through me.

'But what about Isaac?' I ask, my insides warring. What I want to do and what I have to do – the eternal push-pull of being a mother. 'I want to go with you . . . but we can't. We have responsibilities.'

There's a flash of disappointment in his eyes, the dimming flame of his hunger. But he covers it with an easy smile and pops a kiss on my cheek, letting me know that all is well with us. He never makes me feel bad for saying no, whatever the reason. Still, that doesn't stop guilt welling in my gut . . . and something else. Worry. Fear. The perpetual drumming *what-ifs* that have plagued me all my life.

What he gets tired of me and leaves us?

What if he's thinking about fucking other women?

What if he wasn't *alone last night?*

I hate rejecting him. But if we got caught – having sex in a car like two teenagers . . . I'd never live down the shame. It would be tacky. Disrespectful. And we really *do* have to consider Isaac, of course. I can't just leave him in the cottage alone or with Sofia. She'd probably let him cry forever.

Funny how you never even considered leaving him with your sister.

As if sensing my unease, Isaac grows even more grizzly. He squirms in my arms, cute little nose scrunching up and his eyes screwing shut. Then he lets out a loud, bellowing cry that has everyone in the room snapping their heads to look at us. My face heats. Isaac is the only baby here. The *only* person who's not even of drinking age. There are no children, no tweens or teens. I'd debated whether we should bring him, to be honest, and I'd contemplated asking Mum and Dad to take him for two nights so Malachi and I could be here as adults.

But Ellie hadn't put 'no kids' on the invite, so I'd expected there to be some young guests. Enough to make me feel like I wasn't a pariah for bringing my baby along. But apparently not.

Someone in a glamorous silver dress scrunches her nose slightly at us, before turning back to the person she's talking to. Ellie's mum, who I'd expected might be excited to see a baby here, looks at me without any empathy as if my little boy is a stray dog who's wandered in. Even Lily looks annoyed by the sound.

It's so bloody hard being the only mother surrounded by women who believe they've chosen something 'more' by not having kids. They don't understand how hard it is to feel like people look down their noses at you for doing the 'expected' thing. I want to scream sometimes, *I'm not boring and I could have done something else but I* chose *to be a mother.*

Is it true, though? In my darkest moments, sometimes I wonder if I had Isaac because I *couldn't* do anything else with my life. Was he the child I wanted or simply a way to prove to the world that I hadn't failed at life? That I might not be famous and successful like my twin and my friends, but I am someone's mother? That counts for something, right?

I shake the thoughts off. Of course I had my son because I wanted him. To think otherwise is silly and I'm just letting the judgement get to me.

Isaac cries again and I bounce him up and down, willing him to be quiet and not to draw any more unwanted attention towards us. But the tears are coming and I know my little boy has lasted as long as he can. He needs to be put down for bed, despite the fact that the speech and presentation hasn't yet started. I glance anxiously towards where Sofia is talking with Ellie, their heads bowed.

'Why don't I take him back to the cottage?' Malachi says, holding his hands out.

'You can't leave him there alone,' I say, clutching Issac close to me.

After being away, I have this instinctual need to cradle him, to let him know that I didn't enjoy leaving him behind. That I don't want to do it again any time soon. But he kicks and wriggles, his temper building. If we don't get him out of here now, it's going to be a full-blown meltdown and then people will really stare.

'I know that, Rose.' Malachi's voice is slightly clipped, like I've insulted him. But before I have a chance to apologise, he comes closer and lifts Isaac from my arms. 'Alright, off to bed with you, mate. Say goodbye to Mummy and Auntie Lily.'

Lily waggles her fingers for a second before turning back to her conversation. Isaac's eyes are filled with tears and his pouty lower lip trembles. He really is at the end of his rope, poor mite.

'Goodnight, baby boy.' I bend down and blow a raspberry against his round, pudgy cheek. Then I fish the cottage key out of my bag and hand it to Malachi so he can let himself inside. 'Mummy will check in on you soon. Be a good boy and go down easy for Daddy, okay?'

Malachi turns and heads towards the exit without looking back. My stomach turns to stone. A lot of people say having a baby can be hard on your marriage – what with the sleepless nights and the endless demands and the kaleidoscope of hormones making me feel every emotion to maximum strength – but I naively thought Malachi and I wouldn't suffer from that. We're a good team. We love each other.

I stand around awkwardly trying to insert myself into the conversation with Lily and Mitch's friend – Aaron, Adam, Adrian? – for a few moments before I pull my phone out of the little glitzy shoulder bag I picked up at an op shop and fire off a text to my husband.

ROSE: Let me know when you get him in bed. I'll come over as soon as the speeches are done.

A waiter comes by and it occurs to me that I'm famished. My tummy rumbles at the sight of a tray of fancy little pastries topped with prawns and curls of citrus. I eagerly catch the young woman's attention and grab two, popping one into my mouth whole and keeping the second one in my hand. Holding Isaac all night has made it impossible to eat.

Ellie and Sofia are still talking. For some reason, my mind irrationally jumps to them bitching about me bringing Isaac tonight. Ellie wouldn't do that, would she? But as I think this, they both glance back and look at me, brows furrowed.

I hustle over to them while eating my second prawn pastry, hating to be left out, and desperate to confirm my suspicions. If the conversation stops suddenly, then I'll know they were talking about me. But before I can make it over, Sofia leaves Ellie and heads to the front of the room, decisive strides saying she has a plan and is on a timeline. Ellie is looking around the room, pressing her hands nervously to her stomach.

'Hey, Ellie,' I say as I approach, dusting the crumbs from my fingertips. 'I uh . . . were you guys talking about Isaac?'

I blurt the question out before I can even think of how it makes me sound like a paranoid idiot. I hate that my insecurities are insatiable like that. Once a thought burrows its way into my brain, nothing can pluck it out.

'What?' Ellie blinks, confused. 'Uh . . .'

Her hesitation is like fire in my blood. It makes me feel small and insignificant, feeding my doubts and letting them grow. Shame and anger wells inside me. How *dare* they try to judge me for—

'Sofia told me you saw Michelle.'

'Oh.' The fire in my belly extinguishes in an instant. 'Yeah, I did see her.'

'Do you think she . . .' Ellie glances around, eyes looking a little wild. She seems strung out. Has she eaten anything today? She goes off her food when she's stressed. 'Do you think she killed the birds and wrote that message?'

'I honestly don't know.' I suddenly think of Malachi and Isaac, walking back to the cottage in near darkness. They should have arrived by now – it's not that far. I pull my phone out. The screen is blank. No return message. 'Do you think she's capable of something horrible like that?'

'Do you think *we* were capable of something horrible like that?' she asks.

It's a good question – because theoretically I would have said no. But the truth is yes, we were capable of something horrible like that. We were capable of lying about what we heard. What we saw. What we did. We were capable of helping to bury a disgusting, painful truth.

I stare at my phone.

What if it *was* Michelle and she's out there now? What if she's following my husband and my child? The tornado of paranoia always begins small, like a breeze kicking up dried leaves and skittering them along the ground. It builds – that breeze turning to a wind, a gust, a squall. It grows and grows and grows, whipping and churning.

I shoot Malachi another text.

ROSE: Can you let me know you're okay?

'This is your rehearsal dinner, Ellie.' I place my hand on her arm. She looks a vision – a white dress with these cool cutouts to make a starburst pattern, gold sandals and matching gold and diamond earrings, hair like champagne silk and the most exquisite diamond on her finger. But her face is a mess of worry and frustration. 'You should be enjoying yourself.'

It's a weak thing to say, but honestly I don't know if *anything* can bring the tension down right now.

'I just wish I knew why this was happening,' she says tearfully. 'Mitch can barely look at me and his parents probably think I'm a cheating whore, just like everyone else does.'

'Not everybody thinks that, Ellie. There's no actual evidence you were cheating.'

'The photos are "evidence",' she says.

'There's nothing to show when the photos were taken, so you could share your flight itineraries with Mitch. If you haven't gone to Paris while you were dating him then . . . that's all the proof you need.'

'The photos could have been taken anywhere, though. *I* know they were taken in Paris, but there are no street signs in view. It could have been an apartment in the French Quarter of New Orleans for all people know. Or anywhere else with a similar architecture.' She sighs. 'The conversation with Mitch is one thing. What I want to know is why someone took those photos and held on to them for so long. And why is Sofia getting flooded with fake reviews for her business? I would think someone was targeting us, if not for the fact that your life seems perfect.'

I almost laugh. How can someone target me? What I wanted most in life was already taken away. The only way someone could hurt me now is if . . .

I swallow and look down at my phone. Malachi still hasn't responded.

'Anyway,' she says, shaking her head. 'For all we know the seagull thing was some nutter who gets their rocks off torturing famous people and Sofia's fake reviews are the work of a salty competitor. It could be nothing. And we've got security on the grounds, just in case.'

My phone screen remains black and silent.

'Are you guys about to do the speeches? I really need to go check on Malachi and Isaac,' I say.

'You've probably got ten minutes. I need to grab Mitch and have a quick talk to him before we get started. Sofia is trying to rush us along to keep on schedule, but if he wants to call the wedding off . . .' She sucks in a shaky breath. 'I'd rather we send everyone back to their accommodation now.'

Her words are wavy and distorted, like my head is underwater. I hear her, but it doesn't penetrate. It doesn't have meaning. I find myself drifting towards the door without saying goodbye – without giving her any words of encouragement. I feel like a terrible friend, but something in my gut is telling me I need to see my son and my husband healthy and unharmed. The worry is growing roots inside me, strengthening. Fortifying.

I almost stumble out of The Glass House into the night. One of the security guards stands a few metres away from the door, quiet and serious in his dark uniform. I'd almost have missed him if I didn't know he was supposed to be there.

'Careful on the grass,' he says. His voice is slightly high-pitched. Jesus, how young are the guys they hire to look after this place? He's so skinny even Ellie couldn't fit into his uniform. 'It's been spitting and it's slippery.'

'Thanks,' I mutter, as I hurry off towards the cottage.

The grounds are sparsely lit in areas and our cottage is a short walk, but the waxing and waning glow of the lighthouse gives enough light to make do. I step carefully. The grass is speckled with light rain and every so often I feel the slick underside of my sandal slip across the surface, but the cottage is soon in reach. Without my key, I can't go through the front so I head around the back and find the lights on. Someone has tried to pull the blinds shut, but there's a gap between them.

Malachi is here, which means everything is fine. I feel my shoulders drop in relief.

He's pacing back and forth in the living room. He does that sometimes when Isaac is crying and Malachi is trying to see if he'll settle himself – something I refuse to do. If my little boy cries I go to him, no questions asked. But I don't hear any wailing. The wind is starting to pick up, however, and my hair whips across my face. I shiver suddenly. The temperature has dropped and the air feels like it's filled with bustling electricity, a sign that we might get some lightning.

I'm about to wave to get Malachi's attention when someone else appears, coming up beside Malachi and slipping an arm around his waist. He turns to face her and she rises up onto her tiptoes and presses into him, their lips meeting.

I stumble back, hand pressed to my chest. Here I was worried out of my mind that something bad might have happened because he didn't respond to my message, when instead he was here meeting someone. *Kissing* someone.

My eyes brim with tears and I blink, trying to clear them. It's like looking at a scene underwater – only the big details make it through at first. Colours. Shapes. His all-black outfit and her vibrant, unmistakably red dress. It's almost exactly the same shade as mine. Long, golden hair tumbles down her back.

I wipe the back of my hand across my eyes, trying to clear the tears. It's . . . oh my God, it's Morgan. Ellie's assistant.

A memory rockets through me like a bolt from Zeus himself – the picture on Malachi's phone. The woman with the sun-bleached blond hair and naturally perky tits and smooth, flat stomach. She'd been wearing a skimpy bikini with straps so thin they looked as though they wouldn't withstand the barest tug of someone's teeth.

It's nothing, Rose. Just a dirty picture on the internet. Why are you making a mountain out of a molehill, love? You know you're my number one.

But it wasn't just a dirty picture on the internet. It was Morgan! It was *her* picture.

I didn't recognise her earlier today. With her hair pulled back, wearing big chunky glasses and her figure hidden in a baggy T-shirt, loose jeans and Birkenstocks . . . my eye kind of glossed over her. But I can't mistake it now – it was definitely her in that photo on his phone.

Was she at the house last night? At *my* house? I'm standing there, barely aware that the rain is coming down harder. Barely aware that my red dress is steadily getting soaked through while I watch this woman cajole my husband. He's resisting – but he does that. Likes to be chased as much as he likes to be the hunter, sometimes.

I don't know what to do. I'm frozen. Petrified. My whole world is crumbling right in front of me.

Distantly, there's a warning rumble, like fists beating a drum. But then it's closer. Right overhead. I almost hear the sizzle of electricity as the lightning starts, streaking through the sky like pure, blue fire, and striking the ground somewhere close. Can I smell the burning, or is that my imagination?

The lightning streaks again, this time brighter. Whiter. It illuminates the area with flooding light intensely for a brief moment, just long enough for Morgan to see me standing outside the window. Her shocked expression alerts Malachi, who turns, swearing and shoving Morgan away. He looks furious. Morgan tries to grab him but he shakes her off, making her stumble. Maybe he's told her to go, so he can pretend I'm imagining things.

But I know what I saw.

With a shake of her head, she spins and storms towards

the front door of the cottage and disappears out of sight, while Malachi comes towards the sliding glass door, his eyes on me, hand outstretched.

But I don't give him the chance.

I take off running.

Ahead of me, inside The Glass House, I see the party going on, everyone facing the front of the room while Sofia, Ellie and Mitch stand there. Sofia looks like she's pleading with Ellie. No one is smiling. In fact, it looks like something has gone very *very* wrong.

Chapter Twenty-One

Sofia

Tonight is . . . well, it's supposed to be fun. A delightful amuse-bouche of happiness and celebration before the main event. Instead, Ellie looks like she wants to be anywhere else and Rose has suddenly disappeared and twice I've caught Ellie's dad hitting on women half his age while her mother looks on in disgust.

And I can't stop thinking about the note left on my bed.

To Sofia, I've got a surprise planned for you tonight. I hope you enjoy it.

I have no idea what this psychopath has planned. More fake reviews? More dead birds? Something worse than either of those two things? My stomach churns as I glance out of the windows, my eyes looking for a shadowy figure, a threat. But there's nothing, only blackness beyond The Glass House and the reflection of lights and glitter and celebration.

Ellie and Mitch don't seem to be making a move to come up to the front where Tiffani is sitting at my laptop and the projector is ready to go. She glances at me, waiting for a signal, but I hold up a finger, asking her to wait a moment longer. Tonight she's wearing a light blue maxi dress that enhances her deep fake tan and makes her eyes look nice and bright. She taps her wrist as if tapping a watch and I nod. Too much longer and we're going to be completely out of sync with the itinerary and next food course.

I approach them cautiously, catching the strained expression on Ellie's face. Is Mitch going to pull the plug right here in front of everyone? God, I hope not. Thank goodness we have a tightly controlled guest list and *zero* media, something Ellie and I had agreed on from the start. And that was before the Antoine fiasco. Lucky foresight, I guess. I've been thinking about broaching the topic of selling her wedding pics to some select media outlets in case it might help put the affair rumours to bed. But right now I'm not sure we're even going to *have* wedding photos.

'El?' I give a little wave as I approach. Neither Ellie nor Mitch smiles. Uh-oh. 'Are we still going to do the speech and slide show?'

When Ellie glances at me, I see her mascara is slightly smudged like she's rubbed at her eye. Mitch looks solemn. The air around them is thick enough that my deadly Shun Hikari chef's knife wouldn't even cut through it.

'Uh yeah.' She gives herself a shake and attempts a smile, though I think it's mostly for my benefit. I want desperately to give her a hug, but I don't want to draw attention to the fact that anything bad might be going on. 'But I have a favour to ask.'

'Whatever you need,' I say without hesitation.

'Can *you* give the speech? Well, *a* speech. I guess you

can't read mine because that wouldn't make sense.' She looks at me pleadingly. 'I'm just not sure I can hold it together.'

She wants *me* to give the speech? I don't have anything prepared. I barely know Mitch, certainly not well enough to talk about him in any detail. I look to him, hoping he might step up and be the bigger person, but he avoids my gaze, looking stonily outside.

Fantastic.

I frown. 'Maybe it would be better if we just skipped—'

'Oh, but it's such a sweet slide show,' Ellie says, looking at Mitch. I can feel the pleading in her expression calling out to him, begging him to love her. To listen to her. To believe her. But he gives her nothing. 'Mitch and his mum found such amazing photos. Besides, we've already told the families about it . . .'

I scrub a hand over my face. 'Okay.'

'You'll do it?' Ellie's relief is palpable and I nod. I know I'm going to regret this. 'You're the best. Thank you.'

'You have to at least stand at the front with me. Both of you.'

I head over to Tiffani and give her a nod so she can turn the microphone on, but when she goes to hand it to Ellie I take it from her instead. She looks confused and I place my free hand over the mic, muffling it.

'Change of plans, I'm talking.'

'What's going on?' Her eyes – heavily rimmed with black eyeliner and layered with lash extensions – slide to Ellie. 'Everything okay?'

'Ellie's had enough of reading off a script.' I nod to the laptop. 'Ready to go?'

'Say when.' She settles on a stool by the table where the laptop and projector sit.

I glance at Ellie and she nods. Then I give Tiffani the signal to pause the ambient music and tap the microphone to get everyone's attention. 'Good evening everyone, the bride and groom would like to request your attention.'

A ripple of anticipation goes through the room as people turn to the front. I always find saying the bride and groom request their attention gets a better response than simply asking them to pay attention to me – a stranger to the guests, usually. Although tonight I know more people than usual.

'Ellie and Mitch are thrilled to have you all here to help them celebrate this momentous occasion,' I say. The words roll easily off my tongue. I've spent the last few years listening to speeches about love and commitment and partnership every single weekend, so there's plenty to draw on. Even totally off the cuff. 'Tomorrow might be the main event, but we have many guests who've travelled a long way to be here, so Ellie and Mitch wanted to make sure tonight was special, too. On behalf of the bride and groom, let me present some important images from the two lives that will be forever entwined by this time tomorrow.'

I nod to Tiffani and she first hits the music selected specially for the presentation, which plays softly in the background, easy enough that I will be able to speak over it. Then she starts the slide show. The first picture fills the screen – it's baby Ellie with a tuft of white-blond hair and her mum, beaming down at her.

'Here we see the makings of the beautiful woman we all know and love today. For Ellie's mum, Rhonda, I'm pretty sure it was love at first sight.' I search for Rhonda in the crowd – easy to find in a skintight Barbie-pink dress. She raises her champagne glass up and makes a little whoop. 'She knew Ellie was someone special from the day she was born.'

The picture changes and there's six-year-old Ellie, blond pigtails, big ears and a gap-toothed smile, wearing her blue and white checked school dress with frilly ankle socks. On either side of her are Rose and I, in identical school uniform dresses. Rose's long black hair hangs in a plait over one shoulder and she's smiling so hard her eyes are squinted shut. I've got my arm around Ellie, my hair a mess of wild brown curls and a yellow Band-Aid stuck on one knee.

'I'm here in a double capacity tonight,' I say. 'Both as Ellie and Mitch's wedding planner, and as one of Ellie's oldest friends. She's like a sister to me and it has been a privilege to grow up alongside someone with such a big, kind heart as Ellie has.'

There are a few more photos from our school years – Ellie dressed as the Good Witch Glinda from the *Wizard of Oz* for a dress-up party, wearing striped bathers from a holiday in Queenscliff, and standing with Rose and I again in skater skirts and off-brand Ugg boots, looking every bit the tween fashion victims we were.

I talk through the pictures as best I can, pausing for *awws* and *ahhs* and doing my best to say the right things about Mitch. I must have done okay, because I see his mum well up at some of the baby photos. Maybe everything will be okay. Maybe tomorrow will go ahead perfectly and we'll later find out that the bloody message was a big misunderstanding and someone will be able to timestamp the Antoine photos and my fake bad reviews will get flagged as spam and be removed.

Maybe it will all work out okay in the end.

'Ellie and Mitch are about to embark on one of the most rewarding partnerships a person can take in life – marriage. And as any married person will tell you, it's hard work.' I catch Rob's eye and wink and he laughs, raising his champagne flute. 'But the work is where the gold lives. The work you do together – to trust one another, to lean on one another, to learn from one another, to fully believe in the capabilities and motivations and the *heart* of the other person – is where you find the true joy in married life. I know this is the path that Ellie and Mitch will take tomorrow. The path to a beautiful lifelong union filled with more happy memories than either of them could ever know in this moment.'

In the audience, I spot several misty eyes. Okay, job well done. I glance at Ellie and Mitch and they're looking at one another now, for the first time all evening, and there's a soft smile on his lips. Relief lowers her shoulders and she tilts her face up to him, inviting him closer. He leans down for a kiss and the room erupts in cheers.

Thank fuck for that.

'Now we're going to play a short video of Mitch and Ellie, before we let you get back to your evening,' I say. Ellie supplied me the file last week – it's a short clip filmed by a director friend of theirs, all hazy afternoon light and a glowing sunset, palm trees and blurry shots of holding hands. Californian romance at its finest. I embedded the file in the PowerPoint with all the photos so Tiffani could click it and have it play, without needing to hunt for the file in front of everyone.

We often do this for clients who want photos playing on a screen during their reception. Not many opt for it – but some do. We collect the photos and video files and compile them into a presentation for the venue. I'm not normally running it, mind you. But here, with Nikoleta and her 'we're not a Novotel' attitude, it's up to Tiffani and me.

Tiffani drags her finger across the trackpad on my MacBook, clicking the video. The file opens up and fills the screen. But instead of the sound and image I'm expecting, the unmistakable groan of someone in the throes of pleasure fills the room.

Two people are writhing, grunting, and groaning on a bed. I recognise the designer lamps on each nightstand, bracketing the king-size bed, topped with shades in Italian linen that cost a small fortune. I can practically feel the subtle embroidery on the doona and feel the plush, high-quality mattress. A photo of my wedding stares back at me from my side of the bed and my long, dark hair trails down my back as I ride the taut body of the man beneath me, his hands firmly gripping my arse. My back arches in ecstasy and the sound of my voice carries clearly to the speakers of whatever device was recording me.

A device I had no idea was there.

Someone planted a camera in my home. My stomach lurches. Because it's not only my naked form on screen that's making me feel ill. It's not only the violation of being filmed without my consent, in my own home, my own bed.

It's the fact that the man with me is not Rob.

It's Mitch.

The second it takes me to react, disbelief rooting me to the spot, feels like an age. Time slows the way it does in movies, becoming syrupy and stretched. But then it's like I've been jolted by an electric shock and everything speeds back up.

'Tiff!' I scream, darting forward to try to make it stop. But she reacts at the same time as I do, our hands knocking against one another as we try to stop the video from playing. Shocked gasps ripple through the audience. The microphone clatters to the floor, letting out an ear-piercing squeal. 'Get out of the way.'

I almost shove my assistant off her stool in my mad scramble to make the video stop playing. Ellie has whirled around to face the wall where the image is projected onto. 'What the fuck? Sof . . . ?'

My hand slides around the trackpad, slipping as I try to click the little red x in the corner of the video. Tiff sits next to me, looking on in horror, blue eyes wide as dinner plates and both hands clamped over her mouth. I finally get it, on my third attempt stabbing at the button to close the video. It cuts off the sound of one of my moans halfway through and the bone-chilling silence left behind filters like ice through my veins.

I couldn't have foreseen that this was the surprise . . . because I have *never* slept with Mitch.

In fact, I've only met him a handful of times in person, always with Ellie there. The video is a deepfake. I don't know enough about technology to say for certain whether there would be the right amount of content available on Mitch to make a deepfake . . . but given this is only supposed to imitate an amateur home sex tape, they probably didn't need much. What I do know is that *someone* created this video to make it look like I was sleeping with my best friend's fiancé.

For a moment, I don't dare look up.

Where would I even look first? Rob? Ellie? Mitch?

I stand there, hands braced against the table where my laptop sits, my body and face so hot it feels I could melt anything I come into contact with. My heart pounds and I sway, overcome by shame and horror. My throat is on fire. When I slowly raise my head, the entire room is looking at me. Their faces are a mix of emotion – shock, confusion, disgust, bewilderment. Rob has a hand at the back of his neck – a telltale sign he's trying to work through something in his head.

I suddenly feel fingernails digging into my arm. It's Ellie.

'What the fuck did I just see?' Her voice wobbles. I can't look at her. 'What. The. Fuck. Did. I. Just. See?'

Out of the corner of my eye, I see Tiffani going for the microphone. It squeals with feedback again when she gets too close to one of the speakers. 'Uh, sorry folks. Looks like we've had a bit of a stuff-up here . . . uhh, technical difficulties. Please go back to your evening.'

She pulls the plug on the projector, yanking the cord out. Then she reaches for my laptop and starts the music up again, so that it drowns out the beginnings of the whispers rushing through the audience like a wave. Outside, thunder rumbles and there's a flash of lightning over the water. It feels like an omen. Rain has begun to patter against the glass and I still haven't looked at Ellie.

'Sofia,' she says, her hands tightening around my arm. I'll have little half-moon-shaped indents in my skin if she squeezes any tighter. 'Tell me.'

My lip is trembling and it takes me a moment to work up the courage to look at her. When I do, I don't see anger. I only see the unbridled confusion and betrayal that's somehow worse than if she's slapped me clean across the face. Beside her, Mitch is scratching his head, looking anywhere but at me. I got the video down quickly – only a few seconds – maybe I can pass it off that it was a shoddy home video of Rob and me. Maybe people were so surprised by what they were seeing, that they didn't spot that it was Mitch's face on the man's body and not my husband's. Maybe they didn't even know it was me at all.

Maybe I can claim I'm a porno addict and it was something downloaded off an amateur sex video website. Jesus, when did I ever think claiming something like *that* would be a good option?

'Tell me *now*.'

I open my mouth, but no words are coming out. I gape at her like a goldfish.

She leans closer, looking me in the eye as if searching for something on my face. 'Because that video was shot in your bedroom. I know it's your bedroom because I was with you when you bought those lamps. And I swear, the man in that video looked a hell of a lot like . . .'

'It's not what you think, Ellie. Someone is messing with us,' I hiss, shaking my head over and over like denial might make it all go away. 'The video is fake. A deepfake. You have to believe me.'

She releases me, a look of horror washing over her face. Then she takes a step back and it feels like the foundations are crumbling beneath me where I stand.

'Ellie, please. You know that things aren't what they seem right now! Someone is doing their best to drive us mad. To punish us.'

Out of the corner of my eye, I see Rob storming out of The Glass House and rounding the corner of the building as if heading towards the ocean. He's raking a hand through his hair, his strides long and purposeful. My heart jolts as I think of him getting close to the edge. Who am I kidding? They saw everything.

'I need to think.' Ellie turns on her heel and heads straight for the door, Mitch trailing behind her.

People are watching us. Ellie's mum is burning holes into Mitch with her laser-focused gaze, her hands knotted tightly in front of her. Mitch's parents are arguing, hands flying in the air, though I can't hear what they're saying. Ellie's dad looks confused and he scratches his head, like an oaf.

'Keep things going here,' I say to Tiffani as I grab my phone from where it's been sitting on the table next to my laptop. My glittering Swarovski pen sits on top of my notebook, which has all my notes to myself for tomorrow written inside. It's probably going to be all useless now. 'Text me updates if anything goes off the rails . . . more than it already has. I need to speak to Rob.'

I rush out of The Glass House before she can respond, my heels clicking on the floor and my dress swishing against my knees. It's dark outside and lightning streaks across the sky. The rain immediately splatters against my skin, making dark droplets on the bronze silk of my dress and the wind thrusts my hair back. I shiver. Mitch and Ellie are heading towards their cottage, arguing, their voices carrying on the wind. Rob is nowhere to be seen. I follow the path he took around the side of The Glass House, my feet slipping and sliding on the slick grass.

Nikoleta's warning drills into me.

Stay away from the edge.

The sharp sound of a text message cuts through the air and I pull out my phone, expecting it to be him. But it's not. The number isn't saved in my contacts and it doesn't ring any bells. But the words strike fear right into my heart and I stumble on the slick grass, dropping the phone.

'Shit.' I crouch down, hands sliding through wet blades until I catch the edge of the hard plastic and glass. I tap at the screen to light it up. The text sits there, still.

You like vows, Sofia? Here's one for you: I vow to make you pay for what you did.

Before I even have the chance to contemplate whether I should write back to try to get more information, I hear footsteps behind me, and then someone grabs me.

I scream.

Chapter Twenty-Two

2013

Sofia

'What are you doing here?' Mr Quinn says, eyes wide.

'What am *I* doing here?' My chest heaves. Pain explodes inside my heart. It's like fireworks, *boom, boom, boom, boom.* The flashes of it almost leave me blinded. Like someone is reaching into my chest and tearing me apart from the inside. 'What are *you* doing here?'

It had taken everything in me not to scream while I listened to him having sex with another student. I didn't even want to know *who* it was. To picture it. His hands on her. His mouth on her.

The rage inside me is like a beast. I can barely contain it.

'You were having sex with someone else.' Tears fill my eyes and my whole body trembles. 'Another student.'

If I wasn't about to have a panic attack, I'd find the look on his face priceless. Mr Quinn thinks he's *so* good-looking. Blond shaggy hair, brilliant blue eyes, tanned skin, square jaw and biceps that make most girls go weak at the knees.

He does triathlons in his spare time and he wears these tight T-shirts to show off how fit he is.

'I wasn't—'

'Don't lie to me,' I scream. 'You were preying on more students, you fucking paedo! Wasn't it enough that you had to break my sister's heart?'

Behind me I hear gasps as the other girls spill into the hallway.

'You *ruined* her!' I feel the tears I've been holding back for half an hour finally break free. They stream down my cheeks as I charge forward. I want to hurt him. Make him hurt like I've been hurting ever since Daniella took her own life. 'You took her from being a beautiful, bright soul and you made her think she was worthless. You let her believe you loved her and then you discarded her like she was a used tissue.'

He gapes at me, soundless. The idiot had no idea anyone knew about him and Daniella. About what he does with the girls here.

'What's wrong, huh?' I'm baring my teeth like an animal. 'She got too old for you? Too hard to control? You like 'em young, don't you?'

He's thirty-two years old and he has *no* business sleeping with students. Oh, and did I mention that he's married with a kid? Apparently they're in year seven. *Here*. At our school. He's screwing one student while his own child goes to the same school. It's fucking disgusting. And yeah, if you do the calculations right that means he got a girl pregnant when he was nineteen. What a fucking role model.

Why the hell does a man his age even want to be with a girl who hasn't finished school yet? Because he can control them. Manipulate them.

Just like he manipulated Daniella.

Mr Quinn catches me by the wrist as I come at him, ready to swing. His eyes are wide with fear. He knows he's in deep, deep shit. Because if it was just me, then he'd probably overpower me. Bully me into silence. Or worse. *Make* me be silent.

But we're four to one.

It's far too easy for one of us to make a break for it and call for help. He's fucked.

And not like in the way he enjoys with his female students.

'I have no bloody idea what you're talking about,' he says through gritted teeth. But I detect the panic behind the growl. The wolf has been backed into a corner. 'You're not making any sense.'

Ah, denial. The tool of the idiot. The person with no plan. I bet he thought he could get away with this forever.

'You're a paedophile,' I sneer. 'You have sex with underage girls. Your *students*. I bet you thought no one knew about you and Daniella, huh? But I saw you once. Here, at school. She was sad all the time and I was worried and wanted to know what was going on. So I followed her here after hours and overheard you arguing – about how you seduced her after softball practice when she was sixteen. You made her fall in love with you and you said you were going to leave your wife. But you had no intention of ever doing that, did you? And when she finally realised what a piece of shit you are, it was too late. Her heart was broken. She drove herself into a tree and you replaced her like she was nothing!'

My voice is raw from screaming. I'm like a wounded animal. Broken. Irreparable. Inconsolable. He took the most important person in the world away from me, and now he's moved along to someone else like Daniella never even existed. My throat is scratched up, clawed to pulp with my emotion. I'm crying, snotty and furious, and he holds my wrist in a vice-like grip, but his face has grown steadily whiter and whiter, that tan fading out like someone mixed his skin tone with grey paint.

'How many have there been?' I yell. Tears stream out of my eyes, the dam broken. There are creeks on my face. Rivers. The tears I'd thought were all dried up because I'd been so irrevocably broken . . . they're back. I'm awash with the pain I've repressed since my sister died. 'How many since her? Since Daniella?'

He says nothing, his eyes darting back and forth between us, weighing his options. The way I see it, he doesn't have any good ones. If he runs, we tell the principal what we heard. If he fights, the odds are in our favour.

'No one will believe you,' he snarls, jerking me towards him. But I stand tall, eyes wide and unblinking. He's already done the worst thing he can to me. 'I'll make sure of that.'

'You think I didn't keep her diary?' I'm bluffing, Daniella never wrote his name down. Otherwise I would have gone to the police by now. But he doesn't know that.

'That can be faked.'

Behind me, I hear soft tentative footsteps. The girls are coming closer.

'Yeah, but this can't,' Michelle says.

The sound of carnality fills the school hallway, gasps and groans and furniture rattling. There's a loud smack. A sultry *Oh, Steven.*

If I thought he was pale before, now he's ashen. He looks

like death. Like decay. All I can think of is my poor sister rotting in the ground in Fawkner Cemetery. For what? For a monster who moved on to his next victim without a care in the world?

'That could be anyone.' His voice is fading, like the colour in his skin. His grip tightens on my arm, but I won't flinch. I won't cry out. 'You can't prove it was me.'

'We can certainly try.' Ellie comes up beside me, hands by her sides. She would never take the first swing, not like me. But I know if things turn bad she'll have my back. Rose moves silently to my other side, showing her support.

'The recording plus the diary makes for a strong case,' Michelle says. 'Plus, I'm sure once we pass Crystal's name on to Principal Wright she'll be able to get *something* out of her. That girl isn't exactly a steel trap. Not if her position on the softball team is threatened.'

'What are you all doing here anyway?' He gives me a shake, bringing his face close enough that if he hisses I'm sure I'd feel the fine mist of his spit on my skin. 'There's no good reason for you to be here after hours by yourselves.'

'Wouldn't you like to know,' I say, trying to pull my arm free of his grip, but he holds on tight. It's starting to hurt where he's cut the circulation off from my hand.

'Whatever you're up to, I'll find out. And I'll make sure you're expelled.'

'Not if you're in jail,' I sneer. My hand is tingling now, crying out for blood. 'And sleeping with an underage girl *is* rape, even if she says yes. The law says so.'

We'd learned about it in Legal Studies last year – statutory rape. That lesson was burned into my brain. Likely would be forever.

'Under Section 49C of the Crimes Act, it's an offence for a person to engage in sexual penetration with a child aged sixteen or seventeen who is under their care, supervision or authority,' I parrot. 'The penalty for which is up to ten years in jail. More, if we find out you've been sleeping with girls under sixteen.'

Suddenly and without warning, he releases me. He's going to run. I can feel it in my bones, probably the same way a wolf smells fear in the air around a rabbit. Disappointment floods through me like a tidal wave. I want him to stay. To fight. I want an excuse to lash out and cause him pain. Physical pain.

'You're going to regret this,' he says, his brilliant blue eyes flicking between each of us. 'All of you. I'll make bloody well sure of that.'

He turns on his heel and walks – *walks!* – away, like he's got nowhere to be and nothing to do and no cares in the world. The furnace inside me ignites. How dare he simply walk away like this is nothing! Like he'll be fine. Like he'll be able to worm his way out of this. All this time I kept Daniella's secret, because I didn't want to break my mother's heart.

She thinks Daniella's death was an accident. That she was driving too late at night and fell asleep at the wheel.

But I know the truth. When the police showed up early that morning . . . I knew.

She'd been too sad for too long. And she might not have mentioned Mr Quinn by name in her diary, but she mentioned other things. How a man broke her heart. How she couldn't feel joy anymore. How she could never trust another person.

How she didn't know if she could keep going.

No amount of trying to talk to her helped. She shut me out. And I was too inexperienced to know what to do. I didn't want to betray her trust by spilling the beans to Mum and Dad because they would have *flipped* if they knew she'd slept with a teacher. I was worried that Daniella would never speak to me again if I dobbed on her.

It's the thing I regret most in the world. Because how can I tell my parents *now* that she left us on purpose? That she chose to go? That I could have said something and I didn't?

She'd left behind no proof.

So I kept my mouth shut, inadvertently protecting Mr Quinn. But I know it was the wrong thing to do. I saved him. I let him hurt someone else – Crystal, even if she doesn't know yet that she's being hurt. She will one day.

He's past the quiet study room now, not looking back. Still walking. Still on his way to get away with it all over again.

I can't let it happen this time.

Chapter Twenty-Three

2024

Sofia

My scream is cut off by a hand clamping down over my mouth. Strong arms hold me tight and, try as I might, I can't wriggle free from their grasp. I attempt to suck in air, but the hand is suffocating me. Panic rushes like a drug through my veins, lighting me up from the inside.

'Shhh!' The harsh snakelike sound turns my veins to ice. The arms feel smooth against me – strong but wiry. Woman's arms. 'It's me, Michelle. I'll let you go but *don't* scream.'

Michelle? The person who's possibly following us around and leaving messages in blood?

She waits a minute before releasing me and I whirl around to look at her, holding my hands up to defend myself. In the dim light – visibility provided by a mixture of moonlight, the glow from The Glass House, and the sweeping lens of the lighthouse – I see the familiar elements of her that I remember from high school. Lanky frame, hair that's dark and curly and cropped close to her head.

A slightly hooked nose. The unfortunate mole placement. The main things are the same, yet she's more attractive now – not pretty, but definitely striking. Almost as if she's grown into the features that overshadowed her as a teenager.

She certainly doesn't look like a psychopath.

'We need to talk,' she says, motioning. 'Come with me to the staff accommodation.'

She makes a move to go, but I don't budge.

'I'm not going anywhere with you,' I say, folding my arms across my chest. 'Do you really think I believe it's a coincidence that you're here just as our lives start turning to shit?'

'Of *course* it's not a bloody coincidence. The second I confirmed you three were here, I knew for sure it wasn't. Someone orchestrated this.' Her eyes look a little wild. Is it fear or something else? 'I'm wrapped up in this as much as you all are and my life has turned to shit recently as well.'

I should be wary of her. She knows too much.

'What happened to you?' I ask, still keeping my arms protectively wrapped around my body. The wind whips off the ocean, cracking coldly against my skin. I feel myself sway from the force of it.

'I was doing so well . . .' She looks down at the ground.

Before she can continue a voice emerges as someone appears to be coming around the corner to where we're standing.

'Hello? Lily speaking. Oh, hi Jamie . . . yes, it is late but I can talk. Is this about the article?'

'Come on.' Michelle motions for me to follow her, a look of desperation in her eyes. 'I have to show you something. Please.'

I look back towards Lily, torn between wanting to know what Michelle is alluding to but also being aware it could simply be a trick to lure me away from everyone.

'How do I know you aren't the one screwing around with us?' I hiss. 'How can I trust you?'

'I kept our secret all this time, didn't I?' She glances around, eyes quick and sharp. There's a nervous energy to her. A jittering, wound-up, cranked kind of energy. 'What good would it do to tell the truth now?'

Lily is getting closer and Michelle is backing away, motioning again.

'Five minutes,' she says. 'That's all I ask.'

I know I should go and find Rob – my marriage hangs in the balance. But there's something in my gut telling me that if I don't figure out who's targeting us right now, then worse things than a deepfake video will be in my future.

If I have a future at all.

I follow Michelle along the back of The Glass House, towards the direction of the building where Nikoleta told us not to go. The one marked 'private' on the map. The staff accommodation is housed in a plain, squat building painted white, with a cheerful blue roof and lots of windows. It's a bit of a walk along a roughly paved path, but I imagine the views – like from all the other buildings here – are exquisite during the day.

Overhead, a warning grumble of thunder makes me jump and we scurry along the path as rain mists over us. When we get to the front door, Michelle pulls out a set of keys and lets us inside. The building is still and quiet. I assume all the staff are currently working – either in the event kitchen connected to The Glass House or ferrying food back and forth between it and the party.

I have no idea what's happening there now, with Ellie and Mitch storming outside, abandoning their guests. My stomach vaults as the memory of the video flashes before my eyes and I almost bump into Michelle as she pauses inside the door, listening. The building creaks from the force of a gust of wind coming off the ocean, the sound whistling through the building like a ghost calling for an old enemy. But there's no sign of life inside.

The foyer is simply decorated, a worn rattan rug on the floor and a tall ceramic pot holding long blades of dried grass. The walls are painted a light, earthy shade and there's a bench by the door, pale wood and low, above which hangs an old black and white photo of the lighthouse.

'Quickly,' Michelle says, her voice hushed. 'We're not supposed to bring guests in here.'

I follow her past a staircase into a hallway lined with doors on one side. Down the end, I can see a small kitchen. Not the commercial kind used for events, but a personal one. Likely the staff kitchen. I imagine the sleeping quarters are upstairs, because the doors along the bottom are marked with simple signs – *cleaning*, *laundry*, *storage* and, finally, *office*. Michelle still has her keys in hand and she unlocks this door, too.

She pushes the door open and reaches inside, flicking a light on. As I step in behind her and the door swings shut after me, a frisson of worry shoots along my spine. The building is empty – far away from the rest of the party – and *anything* could happen. This room is fully enclosed. No windows, no other exits than the one behind me.

There's a long desk against the far wall, bracketed by filing cabinets, with a single desk chair, a computer and little set of drawers, the top one secured with a lock. Aside from the computer, there's another screen off to the side, which shows nine neat square images.

Security cameras.

I gasp. 'I knew it was suspicious that Nikoleta dodged my question about cameras.'

'The guests aren't supposed to know about them,' Michelle says, running a hand over her short curly hair.

'Why?' It seems highly unethical to me.

'How do you think Dom got to where he is making the weird, artsy shit he does? He had one huge movie and then a series of flops that almost ran him out of Hollywood. The mortgage on this place was going to kill him. So he invited a few people here, let them stay for free, kept the cameras rolling . . . and all of a sudden, he's working again. One of the girls here told me a famous studio exec got taped doing some weird sex shit and . . . boom. Instant career revival for Dom.'

'There are cameras *inside* the cottages?' I shudder.

'With my login credentials all I can see are the ones positioned outside the cottages and by the front gate, plus the one that covers the entrance of this building. But I'm positive there are more that he and maybe Nikoleta have access to.'

Tonight I'm going to get changed with the lights off.

'Oh!' I suddenly realise the importance of this information. 'Any chance there's one looking at The Glass House?'

Michelle shakes her head. 'There's one inside The Glass House, but not one that covers the area outside it.'

'Shit.'

'I did see something weird from the gate footage from late last night, however.' With a few clicks she brings up a grainy image – it fills the screen, black and white. It shows a large car rolling up to the gate at the entrance of the property. The vehicle is a four-wheel drive of some kind, old. The time on the screen reads eleven-twenty-eight, dated yesterday.

'Do you know who it is?' I ask, peering closer.

'Not a clue. The car doesn't belong to any of our employees – at least, not according to our records. I checked this morning.'

'Why were you checking?' I ask, leaning against the table.

'Because you three being here is a big fucking red flag.' Michelle looks up at me from the office chair, her eyes brimming with worry. '*Someone* brought us together.'

I agree it's a red flag, but I'm not sure how much to reveal to her. So instead I ask, 'How do you figure?'

'Because of how I got this job.' Michelle glances back at the door, as if nervous someone is about to ambush us. 'Six months ago, everything was going great. I was working for a boutique tech firm making a killing as a machine learning engineer—'

'What's that?'

'It's creating the environment to enable AI to imitate the way people learn so it can become smarter over time,' she says. I don't know exactly what that means, but I wonder if there's a link with that and deepfakes.

An uncomfortable feeling unfurls in my gut.

'And I was living with a woman who—' She breaks off,

shaking her head bitterly. 'She was out of my league and yet, for the first time in my life, she looked at me like I was someone worth knowing. I wasn't Smelly Shelly Smith anymore. I was successful. I was in love.'

'Then what happened?'

'One day I got called into my boss's office and he *fired* me. Totally out of the blue. Said there was evidence that I had leaked proprietary information to one of our competitors – had photos of me at a café with the guy and everything. Only they were fake. I'd never met him.'

'They fired you over photos?' I ask.

'It wasn't just that – they had emails sent from my work email address. Like I would be stupid enough to send them from a work email address if I was selling trade secrets,' she scoffs. It makes me think of the emails sent to my clients from my address that I definitely did *not* write. 'So I lost my job. Then, a week later, my girlfriend's cat turns up dead. Someone cut it open. The cat and I never really got along – it scratched me up a few times – but I tolerated the bloody thing because I loved her. But when she found the cat, there was something on the ground near it. One of my earrings.'

'And she blamed you?' I already know the answer.

'She sure did. Called me a psycho and ended things right on the spot.' She lets out a frustrated huff. 'She owned the unit, of course. Told me to get out. I had to sleep on my sister's couch while I looked for a new job. Not easy, when I couldn't get a reference from my last employer.'

I can see how all the puzzle pieces are starting to fit together. I know what happens next even though I shouldn't.

'Let me guess,' I say. 'Someone contacted you about

this amazing employment opportunity with onsite accommodation.'

'Got it in one.' She nods. 'At first I thought it was a scam, like one of those fake will beneficiary emails. I didn't respond. Then I got a call from a recruiter. She said they'd been given my name by someone I used to work with and they were looking for a technology and operations manager for a boutique coastal accommodation business. It was a short contract – only six months. The person who worked here previously had been struck down with an unexpected illness.'

'I wonder what kind . . .' I muse, almost to myself.

'Turns out she'd been taking tainted supplements – almost poisoned herself to death . . . by accident.'

'By accident, *sure*.' I shiver as another gust of wind makes the building groan. The rain has picked up outside, I can hear it drumming on the roof.

'I thought it was serendipity – it gave me a job, somewhere to live, but I didn't have to commit to it forever. I could move by the beach for six months and lick my wounds, even if the job was well beneath my skill level. They were offering a generous signing bonus if I could come and start right away.'

'Too good to be true,' I whisper.

'That was almost a month ago. I've been looking into things, trying to figure out who got me fired and killed my girlfriend's cat. Then you three show up and I start to wonder . . . huh, isn't that weird? We're all in one place again. Then someone beheads a bunch of seagulls and when I look up your business online, you've got all these recent weird one-star reviews. And photos of Ellie looking like she's having an affair are in the paper.'

I'm not sure if it's comforting to know my paranoia has basis, or if it's terrifying to have my suspicions supported.

'But *who* would do this?' I shake my head. 'What happened back then . . . *nobody* knows. I never told a soul.'

'Me either.'

'And Ellie and Rose didn't talk, either.'

'You never told your parents.' She looks at me sceptically. 'Even after—'

'No.' I shake my head vehemently. 'I could *never* tell them the truth. Dad's gone now, but Mum wouldn't get over it if she found out about my sister and everything else. It would kill her.'

It would be the last straw, the snapping of the final thread between her and the will to live.

The lights flicker overhead and for a second I'm sure we're about to be plunged into darkness. But they remain on and a sigh of relief rushes out of me. Michelle is right – we need to stick together. My gut tells me that she's a victim in all this, same as I am. Same as Ellie.

For a moment my mind ventures to a dark corner. Nothing bad has happened to Rose, that I'm aware of. But I shake the thought off as quickly as it comes. Rose isn't capable of masterminding a revenge plot. She's subtle as a hammer, that one.

'Did anything else weird come up on the cameras?' I ask.

'No.' She shakes her head. 'The person who came last night drove onto the property and left about an hour later. Nothing else they did was captured on the cameras. But all the lights were off in all the buildings, so . . . who knows. I might have missed something.'

She shows me the footage of the person getting out of

their car to plug the security code into the electronic lock at the gate. They're dressed in dark clothes, with a hoodie pulled up over their head, obscuring their face. It's impossible to tell if it's a man or a woman, and the camera doesn't give much indication of depth or height. I catch a glint of something as they get into their car – something twinkling in the light. But it's gone before I can figure out what it is.

And *all* of the wedding guests have the gate code – it's part of the welcome pack Tiffani and I put together, detailing the accommodation, directions and a map, the weather forecast and information about surrounding sights and activities in case people wanted to make a longer trip of it.

It could be any of them on the video. Or it could be a staff member.

'You've worked with AI, what do you know about deepfakes?' I ask her. 'How hard are they to make?'

'Not as hard as one would hope. There's a program called Deep Face Lab that VFX artists use, so you could probably find someone on Upwork to make one.'

That doesn't help me narrow down a suspect.

'But why bring us all here?' I ask. 'If the point is simply to torture us for what happened, then why do we *need* to be in the same place?'

'That's what I'm concerned about.' Worry passes over Michelle's face like a drifting cloud, blotting out the light in her eyes for a moment. 'That dead cats and seagulls and bloody messages are just the beginning.'

Her fear is palpable. I can taste mine like a piece of metal on my tongue. Something worse than bad is yet to come.

Then the lights go out.

Chapter Twenty-Four

2013

Rose

'Sofia, stop!' Michelle calls out but Sofia is too fast.

Her legs and arms pump and she reaches Mr Quinn before anyone can stop her. He was walking away, leaving. But he freezes in his tracks at the sound of Michelle's warning, whirling around and eyes widening as Sofia crashes into him. If he was prepared, there was no way she could have taken him down. He's tall, strong. Towers over us. Even Ellie. But because he's partially in motion, not expecting the full force of an almost-adult woman to come at him with the ferocity that only grief can fuel, he goes down.

'What the fuck—?'

The cracking sound his head makes when it connects with the floor is unlike anything I've ever heard. I clamp a hand over my mouth as Sofia stumbles and overbalances, pitching forward, a surprised squeak ripping out of her as she lands hard on her hands and knees next to him. There's a tiny flicker of light and the sound of tinkling metal as if something has dropped onto the floor. But I don't see what it is.

Michelle, Ellie and I all skid to a stop at Mr Quinn's feet.

He doesn't move.

Confusion, fear and disbelief create a swirling dust storm inside me, one emotion melting into the other. Morphing and shifting like a kaleidoscope. We all stare. Ellie gingerly takes a step forward and crouches down next to Sofia, who pushes back so she's sitting up on her knees. No sound comes from him; there's no flutter behind his eyelids, no attempt to move a hand or an arm. He's deathly still. I think his chest might be rising and falling, but it's hard to tell. I don't want to touch him.

'Shit.' Ellie shakes her head, reaching a hand out but then yanking it back before she touches anything. 'Is he . . . unconscious?'

'I don't know.' Sofia's voice is dull.

Michelle comes around the other side and leans down, waving a hand over his face to see if he reacts, but there's nothing. 'I think so.'

'We have to go.' I keep my distance, worried he's going to wake up and grab me. It always happens in the movies - the villain executes one last sneak attack. 'This is our chance to get out. If he wakes up, anything could happen. He could try to kidnap one of us; he could call the police; he could pull out a gun!'

'A gun? Really?' Michelle shoots me a look. 'You've been watching too much American TV.'

'You think people like him play by the rules? No way. He could do anything to us.' I fold my arms stubbornly over my chest. It's bravado, in the hopes I don't look like I'm going to burst into tears. I should never have come here. Ellie was right – it's too risky.

Now it's too late. You're involved. You're part of this.

I don't want to be. I can't let this ruin everything. When Mr Quinn wakes up, he could tell the police we attacked him. Then they might find out about Michelle changing Sofia's grade. We're screwed. I could get in trouble with the swim team. Get kicked off. Get expelled from school.

This is a disaster!

'If you guys don't come with me, fine. But I'm leaving,' I say, my voice wobbly. Inside I'm hoping – *praying* – that they'll come with me. I don't want to go home on my own. 'I don't want to be part of this anymore.'

'We told you not to come,' Sofia snaps. Her cheeks are a bright, almost unnatural red. She looks funny and not in a ha-ha kind of way. Shakily, she gets to her feet and Ellie follows suit.

'What are we going to do with him?' Ellie asks, her hands fluttering at her sides. She hops from foot to foot, unable to keep her weight in one place.

'Nothing. We have to go – right, Michelle?' Panic is starting to set in. 'We have to go *now*.'

'Agreed,' Michelle says. 'But first I have to lock up the office and make sure we haven't left anything behind.'

I'm still staring at Mr Quinn, weirdly feeling like I'm floating outside my body and looking down at what's happening from above. I have a sudden vision of Sofia climbing on top of him and wrapping her hands around his neck.

'Shouldn't we call triple 0?' Ellie asks softly, her eyes still on the prone, unmoving body of our teacher.

'No,' Sofia, Michelle and I say in unison, strongly enough that Ellie steps back with her hands in the air. Conceding.

'Ellie, we can't.' I shake my head vehemently. 'If we call triple 0 then someone will know we were here. We'll get in trouble. We could get *expelled*.'

'Or worse,' Michelle mutters.

'What if he's hurt?' Ellie asks.

'What if *he's* hurt?' Sofia asks incredulously. 'How could you even ask that? Who cares if he's hurt? He's the one *doing* the hurting. This is karma.'

Mr Quinn *still* hasn't moved.

Being knocked out doesn't usually mean death – unless there's bleeding or swelling in the brain. Most people wake up in under a minute. I learned that when I got my first-aid certificate through the swimming centre. How long has it been? Thirty seconds? Forty? More?

What if he's not just unconscious?

'He's a grown man. When he wakes up he can call for help himself,' Michelle says. 'We need to go. Now.'

'We could call anonymously,' Ellie protests quietly. Her blond brows are knitted together and she's picking at a hangnail. There's a smear of blood on her thumb and a strip of rawness where she's pulled the skin away. 'And leave before . . .'

As we stand there, frozen by panic and the possibility of all the terrible outcomes of this moment, Mr Quinn's finger twitches.

There's a low, guttural groan from the crumpled body at our feet as he appears to be coming to consciousness. His hand moves slightly to the side. Michelle skitters back, letting out a shocked gasp, knocking into me and I almost topple over from the surprise.

'Oh my God, he's coming to.' I jump back, hands up in front of me in a defensive stance although I don't know what I'm exactly preparing to do.

Mr Quinn's eyes blink groggily. 'You fucking—'

Before he can finish his sentence Sofia lunges at him, teeth bared, her hands going straight for his head.

'No!' Ellie makes a grab for her, but she swipes at air. Sofia is too fast. Again.

She's on her knees in an instant, grabbing a long tuft of Mr Quinn's blond hair and rearing his head forward, slamming it back against the floor with such force I'm shocked she doesn't split it open like a cantaloupe. It's like she's become superhuman. Stronger than a titan. Rage burns across her face, hatred and grief twisting her features into a grotesque mask. One hard slam is all it takes. He goes limp on the floor, eyes rolling back in his head. There's a speck of blood at the corner of his mouth, a tiny splash of crimson against skin that suddenly looks too pale.

'No!' Ellie reaches out, shock forming her eyes into saucers and making her lower lip quiver, pulling Sofia off him. 'Sof, please stop.'

Sofia is trembling, tears now streaming out of her eyes although she doesn't seem to be actively crying. Her face is frighteningly devoid of expression. She's trance-like. Vacant. Awash in nothingness. I stand there, horrified, as Mr Quinn's body is eerily still once more. His hand rests limply by one side.

'We're going.' Michelle's voice jolts us into action. 'Right now.'

She jogs back to the office, disappearing inside. Ellie is cradling Sofia, turning her away from Mr Quinn. But I can't stop staring at him. He looks like a life-like mannequin that's been toppled over on the sales floor at Myers. As Ellie drags Sofia away, she accidentally kicks his foot.

He doesn't respond.

I back up, unable to tear my gaze from him. Is he alive? Dead? What's going to happen to us if he wakes up? Will he tell the school principal that we attacked him? That we broke into the office? Will he lie, make up something worse to have us kicked out? To make sure no one believes us when we say he's having sex with students?

The questions come faster and faster, like rain pelting against my brain. Each droplet is another worry, another fear, another possible terrible thing. It's coming thick and fast and it threatens to drown me. I feel my breathing grow shallow as the mental rain gets heavier. The world tilts, wobbles. My vision narrows to a pinprick on the floor in front of me. Everything is dark at the edges. I plant my hands against my knees, bent over, heaving.

'No, no, no.' It's Ellie. There's a hand on my shoulder. 'Rose, please don't do this now. I can't drag two of you out of here.'

But the panic is pressing me down, squeezing me. It's like that time I got demolished at a swim meet when I was twelve and Mum ripped me to shreds in the car. She was so angry. So disappointed. Said I was lazy. Stupid. Didn't try hard enough. A failure.

Can't. Breathe.

'Fuck.'

I vaguely feel Ellie beside me, trying to get me to move.

But I can't. There's too much pressure in my chest, too much rain in my head. I'm drowning in it.

'Rose, come *on*. Not now. Oh my God, please.' Her voice sounds like it's coming through water. It's muffled, distant.

I clamp my eyes closed and try to suck in another breath, but everything is tight. Painful. Why am I like this? Why am I always the weak link? If only I'd listened to them. If only I'd stayed home.

There's a crack across my jaw so sharp and so unexpected that my head rears back and I suck in a lungful of air. Breathing deep, after those shallow breaths, is like fire. But I've been yanked out of my spiral. My eyes fill with tears – I don't know if it's from the pain or the shock.

'Sorry.' Ellie is in my face, brows wrinkled in concern. She has Sofia under one arm and wraps her free one around me. 'You can be mad at me for slapping you later. I'll take it. But we have to go now.'

I stumble forward, dizzy and unsure on my feet. Ahead of us, Michelle comes out of the administrator's office and closes the door behind her. She rattles the handle, testing to make sure it's locked. It is. Her expression is grim. She motions for us to follow her and we do.

I look back at Mr Quinn and he's still on the ground. Still unmoving. Still . . . still.

We cut through the creek and the fresh air helps to bring me out of my head. Out of the mental rain. We pick our way through brush and bush, stepping over rocks and twigs and sending cockatoos scattering into the air. The whole time we follow the creek I keep turning around, sure that Mr Quinn is behind us.

It's like there are eyes on my back. Someone watching. Following.

But he's not there.

About five minutes after we leave the school grounds, Sofia suddenly skids to a stop. 'My keyring, it's gone!'

'What?' Ellie stops so suddenly I almost plough into the back of her. 'Did you drop it?'

'I don't know,' Sofia groans.

I glance around the ground. Trying to find a tiny crystal-studded bar here is going to be like looking for a needle in a haystack. Unless the light manages to catch it just right . . . that thing is *gone*.

'You didn't drop it at school, did you?' Michelle asks, eyes widening. 'Does it have your name on it? Or anything that says it belongs to you?'

'Not my full name, but it has my initials.' She scrubs a hand over her face.

'Maybe you dropped it at my place?' I offer. 'When you were getting changed.'

'Or it might be caught up in your clothes,' Ellie adds.

'We can't go back now,' Michelle chimes in. 'It's too risky.'

Sofia looks overwhelmed. I've never seen her like this – dark eyes wide and unfocused, her skin pale but flushed. 'You're right. We need to get back to Rose's place before her parents get home.'

Not one of us speaks the whole way back after that moment, not until we reach my house and hurry down the hallway – past Lily's closed door, music pulsating behind it – and into my room. Then it's just us. Ellie, who looks like she wants to cry although I know she won't. Michelle, who seems to be shrinking into herself by the second. Sofia, whose eyes are vacant like black holes as though she's staring backwards in time.

And me.

'We can't ever speak about this,' Sofia says suddenly, her voice soft. Usually she speaks with authority and arrogance, but now it sounds like she's a little girl, the one I first made friends with years ago. 'No matter what happens.'

In the silence, we all contemplate what that might be. It encompasses so many things – Daniella, Crystal McKinnon, what Michelle was doing on the administrator's computer, what Sofia did to Mr Quinn. All of it.

'Do we make a promise?' I ask. 'A pact.'

'No.' Sofia looks up, her eyes suddenly clear and determined once more. There's a hard set to her jaw and her hands are balled into fists. 'We need something stronger than that.'

'A vow,' Ellie suggests.

'Yes, a vow.' Sofia looks at each of us in turn. 'Because we *all* have something to lose.'

For Sofia, it would be losing the dux position and having her sister's secret get out. For Michelle, it would be losing the money she makes from students paying her. Money, I'm sure – if the state of her uniform is anything to go on – she very much needs. For Ellie, it would be losing her friends who are the sisters she never had.

And for me, it would mean losing my parents' approval. Potentially losing the chance to compete in the sport I love – because the water is the only place in the world where I feel confident. Where I feel . . . me.

'Do you all vow to pretend like today never, ever happened? To keep your mouths shut if a teacher or parent asks what you know? To protect this group at all costs?' Sofia asks, looking to Ellie, her eyes pleading. It stings that she always chooses Ellie first and when they entwine their hands together I feel the knife twist in my gut. I'm second best again.

'I do,' Ellie says, without hesitation.

'Michelle?' Sofia turns to the only person who's an outsider here.

Michelle rakes a hand through her hair, something ticking over in her mind. I can practically hear her brain working overtime. The pause worries me.

'I do.' Michelle bobs her head. 'I won't say anything.'

Now all eyes turn to me and for the first time, it feels like I have everyone's attention. I want to wait a little, to bask in the feeling of having my words mean something. But I also don't want to risk pushing Sofia over the edge today.

I never knew about Daniella sleeping with Mr Quinn. Or that her car accident wasn't really an accident.

'I do,' I say eventually, nodding.

'And I do, too,' Sofia adds, capping the vow with her agreement.

She then proceeds to empty her backpack all over the floor to look for her missing keyring. Ellie and Michelle help by getting down on their hands and knees to scour the floor. I'm about to pitch in when I hear a sound, like a door opening and closing. Have Mum and Dad come home early? I rush to my door and pull it open, peering around the corner to look down the hallway to the front of the house. But the front door is closed. Nobody is there.

You can't be paranoid now. You can't crack. Can't break.

'It's not here,' Sofia says, her voice shaking. 'Mum and Dad are going to flip.'

We all swap glances, hoping that she dropped the keyring somewhere other than the principal's office. Somewhere other than near Mr Quinn's body. Somewhere other than the scene of a maybe-crime.

Maybe? You heard the way his skull cracked. You saw the blood at his mouth.

We can't afford to have anything tie us to this.

This kind of secret is one that could destroy us all.

Chapter Twenty-Five

2013

Beloved high school physical education teacher found dead on school grounds

High school physical education teacher and softball coach, Steven Paul Quinn, was found dead with a serious head injury on school grounds earlier today in Melbourne's north-west. Details about the man's death have not yet been released, but Superintendent John McDonald told reporters that investigating officers were currently parsing through evidence. No suspects have been named.

School principal, Melinda Wright, has announced that the school will be closed for the rest of the week, with a memorial service for the beloved teacher to be scheduled at a later date.

'To ensure Victoria Police can conduct their investigation, all students are directed to remain home for the rest of the week,' she said. 'Information about critical VCE classes will be provided.'

Police state they believe that there is no ongoing threat to the community, but wouldn't comment when asked if they believed any students or school staff were involved.

'At this stage it's too early to tell,' said Superintendent McDonald. 'But investigating officers will review all evidence.'

A school representative has advised that counsellors will be available to students and parents for professional support. Anyone with information that could help the investigation is urged to call police or Crime Stoppers on 1800 333 000.

Steven Quinn is survived by his wife, Felicity, and daughter, Sarah.

Chapter Twenty-Six

2024

Ellie

My fiancé and my best friend . . .

I can't get the images out of my head. The *sounds*. Those keening moans, the flash of Sofia's long dark hair and Mitch's face. I don't know where to go to get away from it, but my legs power on, propelling me forward. I need to be alone. To think. It's spitting and thunder grumbles in the distance like a warning.

You don't deserve happiness. You let someone take a life and you stayed quiet. This is payback.

'Ellie, wait!' Mitch is behind me, reaching for my wrist, but my skin is slick from the rain and I easily pull out of his grip. 'Please. We have to talk.'

'*Now* you want to talk?' I throw my hands up in the air as I continue walking past our cottage. I can't go back there tonight – not after this. I'll bunk in with Mum and Auntie Pat, instead. 'When I was the pariah you were quite happy to give me the bloody silent treatment and make me sweat, but now you expect me to roll over. Doesn't work like that, mate. Fair's fair.'

'Let me explain.' He scoots around in front of me, walking backwards as I charge forwards. Gosh, he looks so good tonight – even with the bags under his eyes. After Sofia's speech, when she'd said that thing about learning to trust the heart of a person, the way he'd looked at me . . .

I'd felt it. The warm, comforting blanket of forgiveness.

Only there had been *nothing* to forgive. He'd found me guilty based on a few photos and nothing more, but now the tables have turned and I have evidence. An amateur sex tape! I can't believe it. How could they betray me like this?

'What can you possibly say, Mitch?'

His eyes are panicked. They dart back and forth, searching my face. He holds up a hand to stop me but I knock it out of the way as I storm forward. I think Mum's cottage is the left-most one – she always forgets to lock her doors. Like mother, like daughter. I bet she's left the sliding glass one open. I'll slip inside and wait for her there.

'I have *never* slept with Sofia, Ellie. Never. That video . . . it's got to be fake.'

Isn't that what Sofia said? Someone is messing with us. The video is a deepfake.

It's a pretty convenient out.

'Why should I believe that?' I ask. '*How* can I believe it?'

I don't want to believe it, trust me. But it's hard to refute something in black and white right in front of you.

'Because . . . she's not my type?' Mitch offers weakly and I shoot him a look that's pure fire. 'Okay, I know that's a poor excuse. But it's true. I would *never* cheat on you – it's why I took those photos of you and that French guy so hard. My parents have been married for thirty years and that's the kind of marriage I want. Adultery is a sin.'

'So is lying.'

'I'm not lying.'

But I don't know if I can believe him.

My chest feels like it's been filled with a thousand stabbing needles and every breath hurts. Because I might not only lose my fiancé tonight. I might lose my best friend, as well. Sofia has been like my sister ever since we were little girls . . . in some ways, the potential of *that* loss is even scarier than not getting married tomorrow.

'*You* weren't willing to believe me earlier, Mitch. Do you know how much that hurt?' The cottage is almost in reach now, the dark building sitting quiet and still. All the lights are off. Instead of going to the front door, I head around the side to the back, hoping the layout is the same as mine. 'You wouldn't even let me talk to you about it. You avoided me like I was . . .'

I don't even know what to say. His sudden change in behaviour is making me feel sick. Because if he wouldn't believe me when I protested my innocence, then that ultimately means he doesn't trust me.

And without trust, love cannot exist. Not *real* love, anyway. Not the kind of love I want.

Because what if this happens again? What if rumours start about me and a co-star, like those disgusting tabloids often do to sell magazines? To get ad clicks? Will he believe me then? Will I have to spend my whole life walking on eggshells?

But he expects me to forgive him in an instant for something I saw with my own two eyes? And I *know* this isn't like my photos – the video *had* to have taken place after Mitch and I were together because he'd never been to Australia before that. And I went shopping with Sofia for those lamps on the trip when I brought Mitch home the first time.

'I need time to think,' I say, shaking my head. It's all too much.

'Ellie, please. I love you. Listening to the speech . . . It made me realise what a fool I was not trusting you. Those pictures could have been taken at any time.'

Funny how it didn't mean anything when *I* made that point.

I reach the glass door and test the handle. Sure enough, the door has some give. Mum forgot to lock it. If nothing else, she's predictable.

'Look, Mitch, I need to process what I saw. We'll talk in the morning, okay?'

I'm suddenly bone-tired. The stress of the last twenty-four hours and my lack of eating has been more than enough to wear me down. I'm feeling shaky. Weak. I need to sit and think until I know what to do next.

'Right now I'm hurt and I'm confused and I want to be alone,' I finish.

The grooves in his forehead look even deeper than usual from the shadows playing overhead. Thick, dark clouds drift across the near-full moon. It blots out the light for a second, but then the clouds continue to float on by and the lighthouse turns in long, slow blinks. Everything keeps moving even if I want to freeze it all so I can have a moment to think.

'I'm not going to sleep tonight,' he says, looking at me with a pathetic expression.

'Me, either,' I say. For a moment we stare at each other, so much and yet so little to say. It feels as though irreparable damage has been done tonight.

I pull the sliding door open and slip inside, yanking it shut behind me and flicking the lock. When I look up, I meet Mitch's eyes and his mouth pulls into a flat, disappointed line. But I need to be alone right now. I need to get my head straight.

Sofia – how could she do this to me?

It's dark in the cottage and I fumble for a light, stepping forward carefully, hands outstretched. I blink as my eyes slowly begin to adjust. Shapes take form, morphing from blobs to corners and edges and lines. My hand grazes something on the wall and it moves. I scream and jerk my hand back, almost overbalancing. A dark shape scuttles up the white paint, retreating to the safety of the upper corner.

Fucking spiders. I hate the bloody things.

Pressing my hand to my heart – which thunders like the hooves of a thoroughbred at the Melbourne Cup – I take a deep breath. Now I see something else on the wall – something unmoving. I reach out and flick on the light. Sure enough, a black spider with long legs is tucked up into the corner where the wall meets the ceiling. I eye it warily and then turn back to the glass.

Mitch is gone. I'm alone.

Worry flickers like a candle inside me. Sofia's earlier warning that until we know who's behind the bloody message that none of us should be alone echoes in my head. I let out a sigh and rub a hand over my face, not worrying now about the state of my makeup or my tan. Who cares how I look now? I'm a woman who just saw an amateur porn video featuring her best friend and her fiancé – I bloody well *should* look haggard. When I jumped into Sofia's car to come here, I felt like I had the whole world at my feet.

But now . . .

My body feels as though it's been weighed down with rocks.

I'm definitely in the right cottage, because I spot Mum's telltale pinkness everywhere, like a unicorn exploded. Pink fluffy slippers strewn on the floor, pink water bottle sitting on a table, a pink tube of lipstick discarded next to an iPad in an equally pink cover. They mustn't have had much time to unpack before the rehearsal dinner, because I can see Mum's suitcase still sitting on the bench at the end of the bed, through an open doorway.

I pad over to the bedroom she's claimed. The other – Auntie Pat's room – is shut, and I expect it will be neat as a pin inside. Mum's room, however, is a disaster. Why she needed a full suitcase for two nights I'll never know. There's a sparkly pink dress hanging from the back of the ensuite door and several items of clothing spilling over the edge of the open suitcase onto the floor: lacy underwear, the top half of a bikini, a gauzy beach cover-up. A sparkly belt drapes over the edge like a sequin-adorned tongue.

I'm shivering in the air-conditioned room. I've gotten more soaked than I realised on the walk over here. Rain taps gently on the roof for a moment, then it stops. Then it starts up again. It doesn't know what it wants to do. But the AC is blasting in here because it was hot today and now goosebumps ripple across my damp arms and legs.

I eye Mum's overflowing suitcase. I bet she won't mind if I borrow something to change into. No way am I going back to my cottage now and facing Mitch in order to get changed. I can't do that. I can't see him right now.

Gently, I dig past the beach things – bathers and gauzy cover-ups and a floppy hat – to see if there are any trackies or a pair of PJ bottoms underneath. Something dry and comfortable.

But as I'm digging, something else in the suitcase catches my eye.

There's an envelope hidden underneath all the clothes, tucked way down on the bottom of the suitcase. Maybe it's my wedding present. Although it does seem a rather large and utilitarian envelope for a wedding card. Aren't they usually pearly or decorated? This is a standard manila-style envelope.

Then I notice something odd. It's got my name and address written on it.

But it's not in Mum's handwriting.

I would know her messy, looping cursive anywhere and this writing is blocky and impersonal, almost like someone was trying to obscure any identifying details. And besides, why would Mum post something to me when she pops by the house all the time and could give it to me in person?

Without thinking, I turn it over and see it's already been opened, the lip jagged and torn. A strange feeling settles in my gut, telling me not to look.

But I have to look.

I open the envelope and a sob catches in the back of my throat as I see the photos inside – a half dozen, at least. They're printed on high-quality paper in a larger-than-usual size. Each and every one features Antoine and me. But they're not exactly the same as the ones released to the media. I could sketch those photos from memory because I've studied them so intently, looking at every little detail.

These photos were taken slightly before – showing us walking down a quiet Parisian street. We're holding hands and there's a street sign in the background – *rue* something – that clearly shows we're in France. I file the first photo to the back and look at the next one. It shows us walking past a boulangerie with a Parisian name. Another shows us walking past a newspaper kiosk, the sides featuring posters of the magazines they're selling.

My brain catches on one important detail – there's a poster showing *Le Point* magazine, a conservative French political magazine that Antoine always turned his nose up at. But the politics are not why I'm staring. Oh no, it's the cover image. The photo featured is a brilliant orange and red-tinted photo of a blazing Notre Dame, with fierce jet streams of water being aimed at it.

This proves the photos were taken in April 2019, because that's when fire broke out in the attic of the famous cathedral, setting the old building ablaze and capturing the attention of every media outlet worldwide. This *exonerates* me. I hadn't even *met* Mitch in 2019.

I flick through the rest of the photos and find the three that have been circulating in the media these past twenty-four hours. But why does my mother have these photos?

I'm about to slide them back into the envelope when I see there's a piece of paper in there, much thinner and more flexible than the paper stock used for the photos. It's a note.

I slide it out. It's addressed to me.

Ellie, you've been a bad girl sleeping around with a married man. Did you know he's married to the best friend of your dream director? I bet she wouldn't look so fondly on you if she knew you were an amoral bitch. But I already know this. I knew it a long time ago.

The note sends a shiver down my spine – it's so cold, so threatening.

But it doesn't make *any* mention of sending the photos to the media. The tone of the note seems highly personal.

I knew it a long time ago.

This isn't about money.

But *someone* sent the photos to the media. They *sold* them, undoubtedly. I bet for a pretty penny.

An image catches in my brain, flickering, a little blurred around the edges. Mum standing by the stools that line the island in my kitchen – yesterday – putting something into her handbag. I thought it was a bill or paperwork or something. But it was a large envelope.

'Your mail is here . . . it looks like you haven't checked the mailbox since you've been back. I tossed the advertising rubbish. You need to get Morgan to spray the letterbox, too. The bugs have taken over.'

No.

I shake my head even though I haven't said anything out loud. But the shaking continues. There's no way Mum would have sold the photos. She wouldn't do that to me!

But I saw her standing there, putting an envelope into her bag. She'd picked up my mail like she always does . . .

My own mother?

Mum doesn't want me to marry Mitch – I know that. She's told me so many times that marriage is a bad idea – a fool's errand, a path to pain. She's terrified that my getting married will mean I'll forget all about her.

But would she go this far to stop me?

You don't know what she's capable of, Ellie . . . She's manipulative. She knows how to get what she wants.

My father's words are like an echo in a canyon. They roll on and on and on.

At that moment I hear the door go and I'm so tired and so shocked that I don't make any move to put the envelope down or get out of Mum's room. I hear her tinkling, giddy wine-infused laugh and Auntie Pat telling her to be careful. As soon as Mum comes into view, her eyes go straight to what I'm holding and she gasps in a way that leaves no room for uncertainty.

My own mother sold me out.

Chapter Twenty-Seven

Sofia

'Tell me it was the storm that cut the power,' I whisper into the darkness.

I hear the squeak of the office chair as Michelle stands and feel her brush against me. I'm suddenly unsteady, woozy, without my sight. The room is pitch-black. Silent. There's no hum of air-conditioning or the whir of computer fans, no blinking lights or even a sliver of moonlight highlighting the crack under the door. There's nothing but the angry sounds of the rain and thunder outside and total, utter darkness.

'The power has gone out here once before.' Michelle sounds uncertain. 'But that storm was *a lot* stronger than this one.'

Shit. Because if the power hasn't gone out on its own, then it means someone turned it off. That means someone wants us in darkness.

'Could be a fuse, though. It's an old building and the wiring could be dodgy,' she adds. I'm not sure if that's meant to comfort me or her. I'm not sure she buys it, either. 'But I think we should get out of here.'

'And go where?' I blink, trying to force my eyes to adjust.

Before I can even think of using my phone's torch functionality, the screen lights up. I feel the vibration of a text message against my palm.

I hope you're not afraid of the dark.

'They're here.' I show Michelle the text and in the vaguely blue glow of the screen, her eyes widen. Now I know for sure it's not her – she couldn't have sent a text in the dark without her screen giving her away. 'What do they want?'

'I don't know.'

I can't imagine it's anything good. How many steps are there between massacring a pile of birds and murdering a human on the scale of psycho behaviour? One? Two?

Not enough, whatever it is.

'We have to go,' I whisper. 'We're sitting ducks in here.'

Using my phone's light, I illuminate a path to the office door. When we get there, Michelle presses her ear to it, listening. I hold my breath, not wanting to make a sound. Not wanting to accidentally mask any indication our stalker – because that's what they are – is close by.

Michelle looks at me, wincing as I cast the light over her face, and nods her head. 'You're right.'

She eases the handle of the door down slow and steady, and gently pushes it open. I'm reminded so much of that day, of sneaking out of the school admin office and coming face to face with Mr Quinn.

Is there someone waiting on the other side? In some weird way, a small part of me hopes there is. Because I want to know who's doing this to us. What their plans are. I want the chance to fight back instead of being taken unawares.

Michelle steps out into the hallway. There's more light here, from the moon outside, but we still can't see much. I turn my phone's screen off, just in case. But shadows creep across the floor, like long stretched limbs, and there are pockets of darkness between the windows. So many doors that someone could be hiding behind. When we pass one of the north-facing windows, I catch the very edge of one of the cottages.

The lights are on.

'Look,' I whisper, pointing. 'The power hasn't gone out everywhere.'

'That means the storm didn't knock it out.'

So it's either a fuse or something sinister.

My eyes dart around, looking for clues that we're about to be ambushed. But the building is silent, waiting. 'Do we go out the front?'

'They're probably expecting that.' Michelle huddles close to me and keeps her voice so low I have to strain to hear her. 'There's another exit, through the back of the kitchen. Keep your phone off. We don't want to alert them.'

We creep past another door – one marked 'administration'. I wonder if that's Nikoleta's office or something else. The staff kitchen is through a doorway. Light spills into this room because it's on the corner, partial windows to the left of us and a full wall of windows to the front. We're facing the coast as it curves around back towards Melbourne and the moon hovers fat and high in the sky. Thick, dark clouds drift, dipping us in and out of light. From this angle, we don't see any of the other buildings on the property. Nor the lighthouse. We're at the furthermost point of the land that Dom owns.

Outside there's a sound and Michelle and I freeze. My ears strain to listen, to put the sound in context. When it happens again I notice it's just a tree branch scratching against the windows. Some of the tension I've been holding leaks out of my body, but not enough to fully relax me. I won't be relaxed until I'm away from this place, safe at home.

Even then, will you be safe? You still don't know who's behind all this.

Somewhere deeper in the building, there's a bump.

I grab Michelle's arm, my heart thumping so fast I'm worried how close I am to having a heart attack. Quietly, we skirt around a table with six chairs, careful not to knock into anything. There are countertops along the opposite corner to the windows, with a fridge to one side. No lights blink from the oven or microwave. Nothing hums.

The door to the outside is wooden and it sits right next to the window. That gives me some comfort, because it means I can see there's no one outside waiting to jump us. But when we reach the door, Michelle swears under her breath and scrubs a hand over her face.

'What's wrong?' I ask.

'I need the fucking key.' We're whispering, barely loud enough to hear one another.

'Why? We're inside going out.'

'It's a double deadbolt – locked from both sides.' She points and sure enough, there's a space for a key on the inside. 'Bloody Nikoleta and her security paranoia.'

'Is that even legal?' What if a fire broke out in the middle of the night? Don't ask me why my mind is going there now. I'm so panicked it's like my brain is glitching. I shake myself and ask something more important: 'Do you *have* the key?'

'I do, on my key chain,' she whispers. 'But I left it in the office. Fucking stupid move.'

Panic pounds behind my ribcage. My hands feel damp. We both glance back to the kitchen door and my heart crawls up into my throat. The thought of having to make our way back through the darkened building to get the key, while there's someone running around hell-bent on hurting us, fills me with dread.

'Stay here,' Michelle whispers. 'I'll go get it.'

'We should stick together, right? Two against one and all that . . .'

Isn't that always the thing that gets people in horror movies – doing dumb shit like splitting up the party and going up the stairs instead of out the front door?

'Two people moving around is *double* the risk of noise. Look what happened last time. If Rose hadn't kicked that pot Mr Quinn might not have paused in the hallway and seen you coming out of the office.'

She's got a point. We need less risk now, not more.

'Stay put,' she finishes. 'I'll get the key and come right back.'

I make the decision to huddle down, next to the stove, in the far corner of the room, furthest away from the interior door. I don't hear anything once Michelle leaves the kitchen – no footsteps, no creaking floorboards. As I wait, my breath comes in shallow bursts and my mind races.

My phone suddenly starts to ring – but unlike in all

those horror movies, I have it on silent. It's Rob. I press the phone screen against my chest to blot out the light. I want to answer it. I want to tell him I'm in danger and to come and save me. But if I do . . . it will give my position away.

I turn the phone over and cancel the call. I can't talk but I *can* text! I try to angle myself in a way that the glow of the phone screen won't shine into the doorway.

SOFIA: I'm in the staff building. Power out. Someone is after me. Call for help!

Underneath the blue bubble of my text a little note saying 'read' appears. Three dots blink. Yes, Rob! Please!

ROB: Is this a joke?

I deflate. The dots continue.

ROB: I don't know what's going on with you right now. First the video of you with Mitch and now this? I'm hurt, Sof. I don't have the headspace for games right now. We need to talk about this. I came back to the cottage to clear my head. I assumed you would come to find me. But I guess not.

More dots.

ROB: How long has this been going on? How did you even see one another when he lives in the US? I have so many questions. I thought our marriage was solid. I'm heartbroken right now.

The three dots keep blinking.

ROB: Do you even love me anymore?

I know seeing that video would have shattered him. I get that. But I need him to trust me. I need him to believe me.

SOFIA: Yes, I love you. We will talk about it. But I need HELP NOW. Staff building. Call the police.

There's a thump deeper in the house, like the one I heard

before. It makes my head snap up. In the texting back and forth with Rob I'd gotten distracted and stopped listening to what was going on outside the kitchen. Someone is moving around – I can hear footsteps. The creak of a door. It must be Michelle coming back. I tuck my phone away to keep my hands free, praying that Rob will put aside his pain for one moment and believe me.

I slowly rise from my crouching position, still pressing back into the shadows. I'm holding my breath, not daring to make a sound. But eventually I have to breathe. I draw a shaky, slow and silent breath.

No one comes to the door.

I open my mouth to whisper Michelle's name, but then snap it shut. I'm too scared to speak. What's taking so long?

I check my phone. Rob hasn't responded. He's probably sulking, thinking I'm trying something wild to distract him from the 'affair'. What I'm telling him sounds preposterous – I *know* that! – but sometimes the truth makes for the most ridiculous story.

I strain to listen, but there's nothing. I even let my eyes flutter closed for a second in the hopes it might enhance my hearing. I read about that once, that when one sense goes away, the others are heightened – but there's still nothing. Only rain, steady. Drumming. One loud whipcrack of thunder, then back to the soft pitter patter.

I can't stay here much longer, waiting. The tension is killing me.

Moving as slowly and quietly as I can, I creep back towards the interior door that leads to the hallway. Michelle left it open on her way out, which was a good move. One less chance to make a noise. I lean the barest part of myself past the doorframe to look into the hallway with one eye.

It's empty. There's no sign of Michelle.

She must be in the office. Unless she left me here . . . but she wouldn't do that, would she?

I glance at my phone again. She's been gone more than eight minutes – that should be *well* long enough to creep to the office, grab the keys and come back. I hover by the door, waiting. The house creaks and groans as another gust of wind blows past.

The hallway remains empty.

When I hear footsteps again, this time it's from above. The stalker must have thought we went up there, this is our time to get out! I creep into the hallway and quickly hurry along, looking for the office. Ah, there it is! As my hand settles on the doorknob an ominous feeling drifts through me, like the shadow from a cloud passing overhead. It's quiet. *Too* quiet. There should be something – footsteps, rustling. A sign of life. I press my ear to the door, straining to listen. But there's nothing.

I think for a second about making a break for the front door. Surely that's not locked from the inside, too? But what if it is? What if I get there and I can't get out and our stalker comes down the stairs? There will be nowhere to hide.

I *need* those keys.

Shit. I bounce impatiently on the spot, nerves gathering like a tight fist in my stomach. This can't be happening.

I gently ease down the handle on the office door, trying to be as quiet as possible. It's dark inside. Pitch-black, still. The clouds have shifted over the moon and the little light I had is blotted out for the moment when I step inside and let the door close behind me. It's still silent. I feel like I'm stepping into someone's deepest, darkest secret.

There's so much to keep hidden.

'Hello?' I whisper.

The only answer is a deep, aching silence.

Chapter Twenty-Eight

Rose

I'm wiping tears from my cheeks as I rush away from the cottage, the image of my husband kissing Morgan burned into my mind. I stumble, almost knocked over by a wave of nausea. All that time I thought he never looked at other women . . . I'm an idiot. What do I do now? I can't face him. And I can't ask to bunk in with Ellie and Mitch the night before their wedding – that's ridiculous. Sofia is staying in the same cottage I'm supposed to be in with Malachi and Isaac, so that's no help.

Lily is my only other option.

Going to my sister for help is the *last* thing I want to do – God, I know she'll lord it over me forever – but I can't stay in the same bed as Malachi tonight. The thought of him touching me after he kissed Morgan . . . No, I can't do it.

I contemplate for a moment whether I would be better off asking a stranger to let me stay with them instead of asking Lily. But I know I won't do that. I have no other option but to go to her for help.

'Rose!' Malachi's voice rings out behind me. But not too close – it must have taken him a moment to figure out how to unlock the sliding door. The latch is tricky. 'Rose, stop!'

Tears are streaming down my cheeks as I hurry, slip-sliding over the wet grass in my sandals, ducking around the side of one of the other cottages. It's dark – I think this might be the one Mitch's family is staying in. Pressing my back to the wall, I look up to the sky, my chest heaving. I'm sheltered by the slight overhang of the roof and I see Malachi go past, head swinging to and fro. He looks panicked.

How could I have trusted him? All these years married, having a child together, building a life . . . How long has it been going on for?

'Rose!' he bellows. The sound is pained and it strikes me right in my heart, jump-starting the instinct to go and comfort him. But I hold myself back.

I love my husband, but he has betrayed my trust. My thoughts spiral out to what life will be like now – there are no good options. If I leave, I'll become a single mother, have to fight through a divorce, custody battles because I know Malachi won't be an absent father. He adores Isaac. He had a wonderful father of his own who was always there for him and wants to give our boy the same.

Our boy.

My lip trembles. But staying means . . . what? Lying in bed side by side, pretending to sleep so he won't come near me? Sleeping in separate rooms? Trying to act happy around Isaac while secretly growing to hate one another?

I watch as Malachi reaches The Glass House, looking for me. People have started to disperse now. It's early, though.

Too early. Why is everyone coming outside? I see people smoking, the white coiling tendrils disappearing up into the sky as they walk towards where the cars are parked. Shit. If I want to stay with Lily tonight, then I'll need to catch her before she leaves to drive back to her accommodation. I think about going back to grab Isaac, but there's no chance I'll get him packed up and out without Malachi catching me. For one, if Isaac gets woken up when he's just gone down he screams bloody murder. Two, there's not going to be anywhere for him to sleep at Lily's motel room.

I know Malachi will take care of Isaac tonight. I trust him with that much, at least.

I spot my husband heading back out of The Glass House, brow furrowed and strides long, and I shrink further into the shadows. He's heading in the direction of our cottage, likely guilty about leaving Isaac alone. My phone buzzes with a text message.

MALACHI: Where are you? We need to talk.

Not yet. Not until I've had time to pull myself together.

I skirt the dark, empty cottage and look around the corner, watching Malachi's retreating form. I wait a moment longer, to make sure he won't see me if he looks back over his shoulder. The seconds feel like hours as I count them down. One, two, three . . .

When he finally makes it inside the cottage, I rush over to The Glass House, looking for Lily. Inside, only a few people remain. I spot Sofia's assistant, Tiffani, standing nervously at the front of the room, hands knotted. Several waiters mill about, with full trays of food, looking confused. There's an anxious hum to the air.

My phone rings but I cancel the call. A second later a text appears.

MALACHI: Please Rose. It's not what you think. Let me explain.

I scan the room and my sister is nowhere to be found. Ellie's father stands, beer in hand, words slurring as he talks to himself and Mitch's family are gathered, looking on in disgust. Mitch's mates are clustered in one corner, chatting and drinking, and the waiters huddle together, gossiping. Everyone else is gone. What happened in here? My stomach churns, thinking I might have missed Lily already – missed my ride out of here – when I see her through the glass. She's outside, facing the ocean. I rush over to the glass and knock, waving to get her attention, and when she turns, I hold up a finger, asking her to wait. She barely acknowledges me, her mouth moving and her phone pressed against her ear. Who is she speaking to this late at night?

Another text comes through.

MALACHI: You're scaring me. Where are you?

I hold my finger up again to Lily and then turn on my heels, heading back towards the door and out into the night air, relief filtering through me. I haven't missed her. I can hop in her car and let her take me away for the night, to give me time to think about what to do with Malachi. When I'm safe and off the lighthouse grounds, I'll message him back and let him know I'm okay. I'm angry, yes. But I need him to take care of Isaac tonight and I can't have him leaving my boy to come looking for me again.

I skirt around the corner of The Glass House, stepping

carefully on the slippery grass, and catch part of Lily's phone conversation.

'Why did you need a statement from *her*? This is supposed to be about me.'

I halt in my tracks. Is she talking about me? Is that Jamie Hazlehurst on the other end of the phone line and did he tell Lily I gave him a statement already? Or am I doing what I've been accused of before – making it all about me?

'No matter what I do, no matter how *far* I go and what I achieve . . .' Lily breaks off and swears, shaking her head. 'Why does her story have to follow mine?'

I hang back, face heating. She's *definitely* talking about me.

'Jamie . . . no, I don't want to hear this right now. I want you to take her quotes *out* of the article.' She pauses. I can't hear the murmur of the voice on the other end of the line, because the *whoosh* of the waves has grown strong. The ocean is churning. 'Fine. But don't expect any exclusives from me now or in the future.'

She ends the call and her hand drops down by her side. For a moment she stands there, near the edge of the cliff we were told not to go near, looking furiously out into the inky night, her own storm clouds gathering. A little droplet splatters against my arm. The rain is going to come with force any moment now. We need to leave.

'Lily?' I say, tentatively.

'You again.' She turns to me, eyes stone cold. 'Everywhere I go it's Rose, Rose, Rose.'

Is she kidding me right now?

'How do you think *I* feel?' I'm too frayed from the night's events to hold my tongue any further. I'm filled with despair, with anguish. Filled with the hurt of betrayal and fear about what the future holds. I need to lash out. Need to make someone else hurt. 'My whole bloody life it's been Lily *this* and Lily *that*. Look at Lily winning her medals. Oh look, Lily is on TV again. Lily, Lily, Lily!'

I'm practically screeching, my heart aching so much it feels like it might explode.

'Oh come *on*, Rose. You were always Mum's favourite when we were kids.' She throws me a derisive glance. 'Always beating me at swim meets and in every sport we played.'

That time in my life – being Mum's favourite – was short lived.

'But you were Dad's favourite.' I'd always hated that, because I felt closer to him than my mum. He was more like me – the softer personality. The gentle one. But he loved her more . . . until the doping scandal. Then they both did.

I often wonder what life might have been like if only one of us made it out of the womb. Or if we were just sisters, like Sofia and Daniella, instead of twins. Because twins are born for comparison. We *are* apples to apples. A perfect match. The perfect environment to test which is truly better. And our whole life our parents compared us. They dangled one carrot in front of us to see who could get it first. Regular sisters aren't like that. There are more differences. Apples to oranges. It makes for love instead of competition. The way Sofia crumbled after her sister was gone, the way she raged over Daniella's death, the way she lived every day to honour her sister's memory . . . *that's* love. A love I have never known.

That I likely never will.

'I *wanted* to be Mum's favourite,' she says, throwing her hands in the air. A gust of wind comes off the water and it makes Lily's black hair fly away from her face, making it seem like her resentment is commanding the weather. 'Because then I would have had more say in the house. I would have gotten *my* first choice of things – the best bedroom, what we had for dinner. She always let you pick! It's because you took to sports quicker than me, always two steps ahead. Our whole childhood I was silver and you were gold.'

Until I wasn't.

'And you were the A while I was the B,' I fire back. 'She *always* sang your praises when it came to school. I could never be as smart as you.'

'Is that why you helped Sofia become dux by getting her grade changed after she flunked that assignment?' she asks. 'So I wouldn't be number one there anymore.'

It's like the wind is knocked out of me – I stagger back.

'Oh, you think all these years I didn't know about your little trip to the school to get that weirdo Michelle to change Sofia's grade on the school system?' She sneers. 'You *took* something that was supposed to be mine and gave it to your friend. A friend who treated – who still treats – you like shit, I might add.'

'How did you know about that?' I shake my head.

'That day . . . I followed you.'

My mouth hangs open. I blink, trying to remember all the way back. I'd had the feeling, when I was picking my way through the bush alongside the creek, that someone was following me. I'd felt that prickle along the back of my neck, a cave man sense, that there was a predator around. And I'd ignored it, convinced it was my worrisome nature, my paranoia . . . because everyone always made me feel like I worried for nothing.

'I snuck in through the hole in the fence and watched as you caught up with Michelle.' She comes towards me. There's a menace in her eyes. I take a step back. The wind is blowing harder now and my hair whips around my face, lashing at me. 'I saw Sofia hand her an envelope and then you snuck inside through a window . . .'

What else did she see? It feels like my heart rate has slowed to an impossible pace. Each dull thud sends shockwaves through my veins. Blood rushes in my ears. Or is it the ocean? Can this really be happening?

Does Lily *know* what Sofia did to Mr Quinn? What we all covered up? Could she be behind the messages?

'Everybody knew that Michelle would take money in exchange for homework and assignments. But there is only *one* reason you'd be meeting her to sneak into school after hours.' Overhead, a streak of lightning flashes and I see her anger in all its full-faceted detail. Her eyes seem almost black, the dark brown irises we get from our mother consumed by her pupils. Her jaw is tight, teeth clenched. Her hands are balled by her hips. 'And that's so she could hack into the system to change Sofia's English Lit grade.'

'You followed us inside?' I ask, my throat so dry and tight I can barely get the words out.

'I didn't need to; I knew exactly what you were doing. I saw Sofia go red in the face when Mr Parker handed our assignments back and I heard her ranting to you after school. Funnily enough, the day after you guys snuck in with Michelle she was no longer giving him dagger looks in class. She was sucking up again, sweet as pie. She knew she didn't have to worry anymore.'

So she doesn't know about Mr Quinn. If she didn't follow us inside the school building, then she couldn't have seen what happened. Did she suspect us, after the news came out? Or did she think it was a coincidence?

'It was supposed to be *me*!' she says, jabbing a finger towards her chest. 'I had one chance to be number one in the whole school. One chance and you took it from me! It wasn't enough that you had to win every gold medal whenever we swam, you had to steal my chance to get gold in my arena, too.'

'Not like it stopped you getting plenty of gold after that,' I say bitterly. Her knowledge of us changing Sofia's grade doesn't mean anything now – Sofia never finished university after her father died, because she dropped out to take care of her mum. Ironically, after all we went through, the changed grade meant nothing. 'You've got enough medals to fill the MCG.'

'Yes, I do. I made sure of that.'

I turn to walk away. I can't ask her for anything – not now, not ever. We might be sisters by blood, but DNA is all we're ever going to share. I'll never have with Lily what Sofia had with Daniella. It's time to let it go.

But then her words dawn on me.

'What do you mean?' I look back at her. Something thick and sluggish is running through my veins. It's slowing me down. I swipe the rain from my cheeks with one unsteady hand. 'You made sure of what?'

'Jesus, Rose. You still haven't figured it out?' She rolls her eyes like I'm the biggest idiot on planet earth. '*I* gave you those drugs. The Furosemide. It was me.'

I shake my head and I don't stop. Back and forth, back and forth. I'm glitching.

'No . . .' I'm blinking, my poor brain scrambling to catch up. 'It was a mistake. It got into my system by accident . . .'

'It wasn't a fucking accident, Rose. I got those drugs and I crushed them up and I put them in your food.' There's no guilt on her face. No remorse. 'You needed to learn a lesson.'

It wouldn't have been hard – I hated mornings and was always half out of it during those super early starts before swim practice, almost sleepwalking as I made my porridge. She could have waited until I had my back turned, stirred something into my food and let me eat it, none the wiser.

'Why?' It's all I can get out – my whole body trembling like I've been plunged into an ice bath. My teeth chatter, eyes unable to focus. 'How could you do that to me?'

'I evened the score. You stopped me from being number one in what I wanted, so I stopped you from being number one in what you wanted.' She folds her arms across her chest. 'I didn't expect that you'd *never* come back. I thought you'd take the ban for a few years and then get back in the pool. But I guess you were too weak—'

She doesn't get to finish her sentence because I lunge for her, a deep, bellowing cry ripping out of me as every little hurt I've experienced all coalesces into one brightly burning ball of fury. I grab her by the tops of her arms, shaking her with every bit of strength I have. Strength I didn't even know was still there.

'How could you do that to me? You're my sister. You were supposed to love me, not ruin my life.' The words tumble out of me as I shake her. The ground is slick beneath our feet and I almost fall, but it's my tight grip on her shirt that keeps me upright. I hear a loud rip, the fabric of her shirtsleeve tearing. 'You took everything I had and burned it to the ground.'

'Get off me!' Lily tries to squirm away, but my grip is like welded iron. She yanks backwards and I manage to hang on. We're in a tug of war. 'You're a psycho.'

'No, you're the psycho, Lily. Ever since you were born you were never right – you used to steal my toys and hit me when Mum wasn't looking. You hated me from the beginning.'

'I was *first*,' she almost spits in my face. 'And I wish it had only been me.'

She shoves me so hard I stumble back, this time losing my grip on her, but the force of her movement sets her off balance and she steps backwards. Only there's nothing behind her. We're on the edge – it's nothing but beach below, many metres down.

Lily's arms pinwheel and her eyes go wide. Thunder ripples through the air and there's another white-blue streak overhead that lights up her face – pale with terror. I lunge forward, reaching out to grab her. To save her. But my fingertips only catch the soft cotton of her shirt, the place where it tore moments ago, and she falls backwards. The sound of fabric ripping cuts through the air as she tumbles into the dark night, a scream erupting from somewhere. Me? Her? I can't tell the difference.

Then there's nothing.

The utter silence is suffocating, filling my throat and nose as if with water. It's like plunging into a pool, unprepared. The quiet of drowning.

A shred of green cotton flutters in my hand like a tiny flag, the only proof there were two of us on this edge moments ago.

'Lily?' My mouth is agape and I suck in quick bursts of air, shock settling into my bones as I try to look over the edge. But I'm scared to get too close. 'Lily!'

I back away from the edge and look around. Nobody is there. The Glass House is empty and the main lights have been turned off. I didn't even notice it happen. Inside, I can see a soft glow emanating from the event kitchen, the door partially open, but nobody is watching me.

'Oh my God, oh my God, oh my God.' I scramble around the side of the building and head towards the stairs that lead down to the beach. I have to find her.

I use the torch on my phone to light the way, but the blackness is all-consuming and I can't go as fast as I would like. Growing up near the city, you forget how dark it is out in the country. The ground is wet and I keep one hand out, ready to brace myself if I fall. I have to get to Lily to make sure she's still alive. That fall . . .

I hurry down the steps, almost tripping over my own two feet, and feel the soft, shifting texture of the sand. The granules fill my sandals and I plough forward with the stars and my phone torch as my only guide. I see something on the sand, crumpled. I run towards it.

'Lily, oh my God . . .'

She's on the sand, her legs twisted at impossible angles like a broken doll.

'Rose.' The voice from the ground is strained. 'Call for help.'

Then she goes silent.

I kneel there, on the ground next to her, stomach heaving, the knowledge of tonight swirling in my brain like an ocean rip. My own sister . . . How could she take my life from me like that? How could she drug me and let the whole world call me a cheater and say *nothing* for a decade? Telling people now doesn't do anything – she'll deny it and no one will believe me. The world has already proven as much.

She's unconscious on the ground, probably from the pain. Or maybe she hit her head.

I should call for help. It might take an ambulance a while to come all the way out here, but if I call now she might be okay. I stare at her unmoving form – her face so like my own. If she never woke up it would be so easy to slip into her shoes, take the life that she stole from me.

I struggle to get to my feet, an acrid taste burning my mouth, and dust the sand from my palms as I watch her. The rain is coming harder now, my clothes becoming soaked and sticking to my skin.

I could swap our clothes, say it was me who went over. Assume her life. Her achievements. Her success. Malachi would think I did it on purpose. In the grief, would people even notice our bodies look slightly different? She's not as slim as when she was competing and our hair is the same now. Maybe I could pass her off as me. Malachi would mourn me and move on with Morgan and her perky tits.

But what about Isaac?

My sweet baby boy. I think of him as I stand there, in the rain, being pelted from above. I could have everything I ever wanted if I swapped places with her . . . except him. I'd have to live as his aunt, let him think his mother was dead. Let him grow up without me.

I swallow.

I can't do it. For all the years I wished to swap places with Lily, to have her success and her career and her adoration . . . I can't do it. I drop down by her side and press my fingers to her neck, like they taught us to in our mandatory first-aid classes at the swimming centre. Rain slides down over us, making her skin slick. But I know where to look. There's a faint pulse.

I swipe my thumb across my phone screen and dial triple 0.

Chapter Twenty-Nine

Sofia

Suddenly there's a surge and a buzzing and the sound of electronic products beeping as the power comes back on.

I wish it hadn't.

A pool of red spills across the floor, a violent scarlet nightmare. A body is crumpled at my feet.

'Oh my God . . .'

It's just like the anonymous text message said: *You like vows, Sofia? Here's one for you: I vow to make you pay for what you did.*

I hadn't wanted to believe it was true. That someone was capable of this. That someone knew what really happened that day. But they do. And they're here. There are forty people on the grounds right now – thirty guests and ten staff.

And one of them is after payback.

'Oh, Michelle. No, no, no.'

I crouch down, hands shaking as I panic about what to do next. With the power turned back on, there's no hiding. No slipping away. But at least I can see my phone. It's fallen in the blood and when I pick it up, it slips out of my hand, clattering back to the floor.

'Fuck.' I'm shaking so bad that I can barely think straight, my hand grasps for the phone again. A crack now snakes through the glass screen, but it's working.

I have to get out of here.

Before I can make it to the door, it swings open. I see the gun before I see who's holding it.

'Back up,' a voice says. 'You're not going anywhere.'

Chapter Thirty

Sofia

'Morgan?'

Ellie's assistant stands in front of me, blocking the only exit. If it wasn't for the gun and the gleeful, almost manic look on her face, she could be any other young woman on her way to a party. Red dress, shiny blond ponytail, cherry-tinted gloss, nails shaped into fashionable points and painted in a gleaming pearl colour.

She doesn't *look* like a murderer.

But then, I guess, neither do I.

'What are you doing?' I shake my head, eyes blinking rapidly. 'Why do you have a gun?'

There's a fine sheen on her skin – sweat or rain, I can't tell. She's breathing hard. Did Michelle put up a fight?

'To get revenge for Dad.' She looks at me, eyes piercing blue and it dawns on me. They're vibrant blue, like Mr Quinn's were. 'You know, when I gave Ellie all my details for the employment contract, I kept my real surname on there. Quinn. But she didn't put two and two together. It's a common name. And Morgan is my middle name – that was the one that Dad chose for me, but Mum overruled him. Sarah Morgan Quinn, that's me. I switched to Morgan in his honour after he died.'

That explains why her name never raised a red flag.

We'd all read the articles, knew the name of Mr Quinn's wife and his daughter who suddenly moved away when he died.

She takes a step forward. The office is spacious, for what it is, but with Michelle's body lying on the floor, blood pooling beneath her, it leaves little room to move around. Making a break for it is not an option.

I glance down at Michelle. Could she still be alive? There's so much blood.

'Or, should I say, after you killed him.'

'I didn't—'

'Oh come *on*, Sofia. Don't lie to me. I know it was you.' She waves the gun back and forth, dismissing my attempt to lie. Her free hand slips into a side pocket in her dress and she pulls something out. 'You see, I have this.'

She holds up an item I haven't seen in a *long* time – a Swarovski crystal key chain with my initials on it that Daniella gave me before she died.

The one I misplaced the day I killed Steven Quinn.

My mouth opens and closes like I'm a goldfish blowing bubbles. 'How . . . ?'

'It was in his personal effects. The police put everything to one side after the investigation was over. After they ruled it an *accident*.' Her glee turns bitter as her lip curls back. 'But it wasn't an accident, now was it?'

She's right.

I killed a man. I *murdered* someone. It might not have

been in cold blood. It was, in fact, very hot, grief-stricken, vengeful blood. But I still did it.

I killed Steven Quinn in a rage because I held him responsible for my sister's death.

'Like slipping over and falling would cause *that* much of a head wound. They said it was unlucky, but I knew better.' She shakes the gun again and I hold my breath, hoping to dear God that it doesn't go off. 'You see, the police didn't even think for a second that this shiny piece of crap was evidence, because it had his initials on it. SQ. Steven Quinn.'

And Sofia Quadrini.

'Mum and I had never seen it before but Mum thought he must have bought it as a present for me, because I shared those initials too. After all, it was my birthday, that day.'

Oh God.

'Do you have any idea what it's like waiting for your dad to come home on your thirteenth birthday, with Nanna and Pa waiting and a cake sitting on the table, and he just . . . never shows up?' Her teeth are gritted, the edge of her lip twitching, eyes filling with rage. 'Do you have any idea?'

She's so angry that I don't think she realises that her voice is rising. That's good for me! It will alert someone. The staff have to come back here soon, right? Someone will hear. Help will come.

'It's time we had a little talk.' She smiles, giddy all of a sudden. The drastic swing in her emotion has me on edge. 'And before you think about screaming for help, this room is fully soundproofed. Those pesky computer servers make so much noise, you know. I couldn't have asked for a better place to do this.'

That explains why I never heard her attack Michelle while I was waiting in the kitchen.

'Here I was thinking I'd need to lure you somewhere quiet, or get you close to the cliff edge so I could push you off.'

My head swims, stress making me woozy. Or maybe it's the sight of all that blood. The iron, stomach-curdling smell of it. 'This was all you . . . the text messages, the seagulls—'

'The deepfake video of you and Mitch, the bad reviews for your business. Yep, all me. You were an easy target, Sofia. And I didn't need to do much with Ellie. Just a few photos of her and that Frenchie, which I've kept in my back pocket for *years* hoping they would come in handy. *Waiting* until she could pay a high enough price. The funniest thing is, I'd only planned to get her kicked off the movie by sending them to her director and undermining her professional reputation. Shipping them off to the press was a genius move. I'm a little jealous I didn't come up with it myself.'

I blink. 'What?'

'Oh, her mum did that. Can you imagine?' Morgan chuckles. 'I popped the photos in her letterbox to freak her out, but it seems dear old Mum got there first and saw an easy payday. Didn't even hesitate before she sent them off to the media. What a bitch, right?'

I always knew Ellie's mum was a leech. She's been sucking Ellie dry from the second she got to Hollywood.

'This has been such a long time coming. And I really thought I'd be happy enough to torture you all for the rest of your stupid lives. But I had an epiphany tonight.' She looks thoughtful, contemplative. 'Eventually, I would take away everything there was to take . . . and then it wouldn't be fun anymore. So the only way to *properly* settle this is to take an eye for an eye. What do you think?'

I am royally fucked.

There's no way out of here. Morgan is going to kill me. I can feel it in the air, the blood lust. The need for vengeance.

I know it well.

But I'm not prone to giving up. Or giving in. I survived after Daniella died, I survived after my dad died and I had to quit uni to take care of Mum. I survived the early days of my business when people didn't want their weddings planned by some girl in Kmart shoes who worked out of her mum's crappy dining room off a laptop that died the second you unplugged it. I survived it all.

If I keep her talking, then I can bide my time until she's distracted enough that I can knock the gun out of her hand. It's my only chance.

'What . . . what about Rose?' I stammer.

'I thought about kidnapping her kid,' Morgan says, like she's simply talking about what she might have for dinner tomorrow. There's no remorse in her voice, no sign that she understands how heinous her actions are. 'But I know more than anyone, how painful it is for a child to be separated from a parent. Since Rose fucked up and lost her career all by herself *and* she has a shit relationship with her sister, the only thing left was her marriage. Fucking Malachi was the hardest one of all. He was *not* interested, no matter how hard I tried. So I had to keep sending him pictures and turning up at his house, hoping she would catch us. I'm lucky he was too weak to get a restraining order.'

She looks down at the body at her feet and my gaze follows. Michelle's eyes are closed. She doesn't move.

'I notice you haven't really tried to deny it. Just one weak little protest, Sofia? I expected more.' She looks almost disappointed.

Just keep her talking. Buy as much time as you can.

'How did you know it was us?'

'I got a job at the school, working part-time in the administration office. Said I wanted to feel close to my dad, but really I needed access to the school's records. All the students and faculty who had the initials SQ. There were only three the year he died out of eight-hundred-something students. No teachers with those initials, either. Turns out Q is one of the least common surname initials in the whole alphabet.'

It was one of the reasons I'd chosen to keep my surname after I got married – both to honour my father and because it was unique.

'Shihan Qu moved to China with her family after finishing university, so I had no hope of following her movements. And Samuel Quarterman was a boy in year eight who wore a leg brace and used a cane. No way was he strong enough to kill a grown man. It seemed *far* more likely that a seventeen-year-old girl was involved, especially knowing my dad was a heart-throb.'

'He was a paedophile.' The words spill out of me before I can think about how dangerous they are.

Morgan steps forward, avoiding Michelle's body, and whips me with the pistol. It happens so fast that I stumble back against the desk, my cheek throbbing in agony, and when I bring my hand up, my fingers come away with blood. Above us, there are footsteps. People have returned to the building.

I open my mouth to scream, willing to test Morgan's theory about the soundproofing, but she holds the gun right up to my face. I freeze, no sound coming out.

'At this close range, you *might* get a scream out. But your head will be a burst watermelon all over the desk behind you so it won't do you any good.' Her eyes are glass-like, impenetrable. 'Now, do you want to hear the rest of the story or not?'

'S . . . sure.' I nod, not wanting to do anything else to anger her.

'Knowing you were my main suspect, I did some digging. I studied you, looked at the year books and at your socials as far back as they would go and two names kept popping up – Rose and Ellie. One of those names sounded familiar. There was a police report from a person who lived next to the school saying they saw four girls near the creek that day and he recognised two of them. The Asian girl was an athlete. A swimmer. The mixed-race girl was named Michelle Smith. He knew her because she used to live next door. The other two white girls were an unknown brunette and an unknown, very tall blonde. You were all in the same year, all spotted near the school the day he died and he had *your* keyring on him.'

I wonder how this never came out in the police investigation. The cops never came to us. Never asked questions. Never called on Rose, to my knowledge. Maybe they called on Michelle, but we never heard about it.

'But the police didn't . . .'

'The police were led astray by my idiot mother because she told them Dad had been dizzy lately. Feeling off. The autopsy showed he had a brain tumour. He would have likely died from it, they said, but he must have blacked out, fallen and hit his head really hard.'

The words splash like ice water over me. Mr Quinn would have died anyway if I hadn't killed him. Daniella would have gotten her justice no matter what. The universe would have set things right. I could have walked away that day with a clear conscience . . .

I could have lived my adult life *not* being a murderer. Not having a big painful secret to hide. Not having blood on my hands.

My lip trembles.

'Oh don't say you're sorry now,' Morgan spits.

'I wasn't going to. They're happy tears.' I lift my chin up. 'He was going to die anyway.'

'Nobody knows for sure he would have died! He might have lived. He might have been able to walk me down the aisle one day. You robbed me of that chance.' Morgan rams the gun against my cheek and I wince. 'Now, Sofia . . . I'm going to force this gun into your mouth and make it look like you shot yourself after you killed Michelle. I've got everything set up – there's already an email in your inbox from her, saying she can't take lying anymore. Threatening to go to the cops about what happened to my dad. You went on a rampage and you killed her. Then you killed yourself because you couldn't stand what you'd become. I'll take care of Ellie when I drive her home. We're going to have a little accident. And Rose . . . I might let her live so someone's alive to take the brunt of the fallout. I'll let *her* live with the pain.'

Tears are leaking out of my eyes and running down my cheek. There's no way out. She's going to kill me and let my family believe I'm a killer. Mum will be all alone. I won't see Nonna ever again. I close my eyes, blurry with tears, waiting for it to happen.

But then I feel something move by my feet. Michelle suddenly reaches out and grabs Morgan's ankle, trying to throw her off balance. I duck and the gun goes off, the bullet flying into the wall behind me and showering us with plasterboard, but as Morgan steps back, trying to correct herself, her foot slips in the puddle of blood. She tumbles backwards and cracks her head against the filing cabinet. The sound is sickening. Like a bad special effect in a movie.

Her body slides down to the floor, head lolling back, and the gun skitters out of her grasp.

'Michelle, you're alive.' I crouch down and try to help her up, but it's like lifting a sack of potatoes.

'The gun,' she croaks. 'Grab it.'

I use my foot to kick it out of Morgan's reach to make sure she doesn't get there first. But she doesn't move. I don't want to touch the damn thing with my bare hands, so I grab some tissues from the desk to pick it up. They immediately turn red with blood.

'Come on, it's time to go. Can you stand?' I try to help Michelle up, but she's moving slowly and Morgan is starting to stir. 'Please try.'

I loop one of Michelle's arms around my neck and strain to stand, pulling her up with me. She's woozy, swaying like a tree in an ocean breeze. She must have lost a lot of blood. We stumble forward, skirting Morgan's body as she starts to come to. Barely able to breathe, I try for the door handle. But I've got Michelle in one arm and the gun in my other hand. And I'm slick with blood. I slip, not catching the handle properly and I try again.

I feel something wrap around my ankle. It's Morgan's hand – she's dazed – and she has my pen. She sinks it into my calf and I cry out, buckling from the pain. Michelle slides to the floor and I drop the gun. There's a loud *bang!*

Then everything is silent.

I wait for the pain to come, but I keep breathing. When I look down Morgan is sitting, her hands clutching her stomach as blood oozes through her fingertips. She looks up at me, shock settling into her face, skin pale and clammy. Her eyes are unfocused and a strange, rattling sound comes out from between her lips, followed by a sticky red trail.

This time it really was an accident.

'I'm going to see my dad,' she says, before her eyes flutter shut.

Epilogue

Ellie

Four months later

The house feels quieter these days – not as many people come round. Without Morgan as a shadow by my side when I'm home, I feel a little lost. And there's no Mum, either. There's no one to pick up my mail or spray the bugs in the letterbox or pack my pills or organise my chaotic arse when I'm rushing to get ready. Mum didn't even try to deny selling the photos to the media. When I asked her how she even knew where to send the photos, she said she just googled it.

She never wanted me to get married – it was as much about that as the money. Because she thought I'd forget about her, leave her behind. Abandon her like Dad did to us.

Funnily enough, after all these years of thinking the worst of my dad, he was right. She *is* manipulative. But he was wrong about one thing – she doesn't know how to get what she wants. Because I might not have gotten married after all, but I still ended up leaving her behind. Maybe one day I'll be able to forgive her. But it hasn't been long enough for that, yet.

'Want me to take these over to the table?' Sofia asks. It's been great spending more time with her – she's busy, handing her business over to Tiffani and applying to return to university so she can finally finish her law degree.

'Sure. I'm almost done, here.' I stir the prawns simmering away in a rich cream sauce, almost salivating. Since I don't have any movies scheduled for a while I can afford to indulge. I wade my fingertip in and get some of the sauce, bringing it to my mouth to taste it. Perfect. 'Michelle, can you grab the glasses?'

'On it,' Michelle says.

There's a nasty red scar on her neck from that day. It's a miracle she's alive, really, with how much blood she lost. If it wasn't for Sofia flagging down the ambulance meant for Lily, Michelle might not have made it. I suppose the sight of Sofia, covered in blood, running screaming out of a building was enough to persuade them. Or else she lied and said *she* called the ambulance.

I wouldn't put it past her.

I serve up the creamy prawns onto neatly moulded mounds of rice and add the sides in a visually appealing way – some garlic and chilli green beans, edamame and fresh coriander from the backyard. I've been spending a lot of time out there, lately, while I'm on my sabbatical and working on my screenplay. A lot of people have told me I'm crazy to take this time away from my prime acting years, that if I leave it too long Hollywood will think of me as a has-been. They still think me an adulterer. But that's okay, I'll survive.

Now I can create something of my own. *My* story. It's about a mother who'll go to the ends of the earth to control her daughter. If I can get it green-lit then I'll play myself.

'Oh, that looks great.' Michelle is at my side, having set the glasses on my dining table.

'Don't you pick these up – they might be too heavy,' I say and she shoots me a look.

'I can carry a bowl of rice and prawns. What do you think I do at home on my own?' She smiles, and the edges of her eyes crinkle. Up close, they're the prettiest colour. Light brown with hints of gold and green. 'I mean, when you don't come around.'

I feel warmth in my cheeks and I look away, but can't help a smile tugging at the corner of my lips. Michelle and I have been spending more and more time together lately, too. It's nice, having someone to hang out with. I've told her about my screenplay and she came around one day with a pile of helpful books from the library – *Save the Cat* and *The Writer's Journey* and Stephen King's book on writing. It was so sweet. She is like that. Thoughtful.

I enjoy her company a lot.

'I just want to make sure you don't hurt yourself,' I reply. 'That's all.'

Michelle nods and takes only one bowl away, knowing I'll scold her if she tries to carry two. Sofia comes in and picks up the remaining bowls and I carry the final bits to the table – a bottle of white wine and the salt and pepper shakers all bundled up in my arms.

As we settle at table, the life chatter begins.

'What a shame Rose couldn't come tonight,' Michelle says, taking the spot next to me, across from Sofia.

'She's been doing so well, lately.' I smile. 'I couldn't believe how she was glowing last week when we went to the movies.'

Strangely, since the wedding that wasn't, Rose is like a woman reborn. She's taken up Pilates – we go together once a week – and she's wearing trendy, form-fitting clothing and has this wonderful air of confidence about her that I've never seen before. She even told me recently that she's been helping Lily with her physical rehab. It's great to see her thriving. Mending bridges.

'Where is she tonight?' Michelle asks.

'She and Malachi decided to take a last-minute holiday.' I unscrew the cap on the pinot grigio and pour some into Michelle's glass. Then Sofia's, then mine last. 'They left Isaac with her folks and took off for the week. Somewhere in Europe, I think.'

Sofia raises an eyebrow. 'Good for her, getting out there and living it up. It's about time!'

'So they resolved everything after . . . ?' Michelle spears a prawn. 'Well, you know.'

'Malachi told her Morgan had been harassing him for a while but he was worried about how to handle it. She's young, white,' I say. 'He was worried people wouldn't believe him.'

Michelle nods. Her dark curls are longer now and they tickle the hollows under her cheekbones. After two weeks holidaying in Mexico, she's deeply tanned and it suits her well.

'It took them a while to sort things out,' I add. 'Rose has a hard time trusting.'

'It wasn't like there was a lack of evidence that Morgan was behind it all, though. Thank God.' Sofia gives a little shake of her long, dark hair, as if trying to get the memories out of her head. For a moment, my usually steadfast friend looks misty-eyed. 'I don't know what I would have done if I'd lost Rob and you.'

Morgan had left her laptop in the cottage she was staying in, and it had every bit of evidence required. There was the original video of Sofia and Rob having sex that had been altered after Morgan broke into their house – with the spare key Sofia left at my place in case of emergencies – and planted the camera, as well as the invoice she paid for the VFX artist to doctor it. There were dozens of messages between her and Malachi, him pleading with her to leave him alone. The cops found another weapon in her car, along with the heads of all the seagulls in a garbage bag.

If that isn't a sure sign someone is a psycho, I don't know what is.

It was enough that police didn't explore alternative theories for long. Enough to prove her being shot was an accident. Or at the very least, self-defence. We're still waiting to hear from the police how – *if* – they're going to proceed with any charges, but I doubt it. There's nobody left to advocate for Morgan. Turns out her mum died about six or seven years ago – cancer. It was the final straw that broke Morgan, making her determined to get revenge.

'Oh, it's almost time for the news. Turn it on.' I point to Sofia, because the remote is closest to her.

She pushes the power button so the TV screen comes to life. The theme music of the Channel 9 news plays through the speakers and we all look on, excitedly. The headlines flash up with the presenter's voice over the top.

'Tonight, two injured and one dead in level crossing

accident, blazing Blues crush the Cats on Geelong's home turf, sextortion case goes international, and our home heroes representing Australia for Paris 2024.'

'This is Nine News,' says a disembodied voice.

The presenter's face appears as she sits at the news desk wearing a bright pink suit, an image of Melbourne's skyline, bisected by the Yarra River, behind her.

'This year, eleven thousand people from around the world were selected from over a hundred thousand applicants to take part in the prestigious torch relay taking place for the Paris 2024 Olympics. Reporter Aimee Lang has the story.'

The image cuts to a woman with a microphone standing in front of a beautiful city with cobbled streets, describing the path the torch is taking on its journey from Athens to Paris.

'Do you think this is why Rose decided to go away, last minute?' Michelle asks, reaching for her wine glass. 'Must be hard to sit at home and watch her sister do everything she never got to do.'

'I don't know. I think Rose is happy with her life now,' I reply. 'She's got a family, a little boy. A husband who adores her.'

'It's a lot to be happy for,' Sofia murmurs. 'We should all be thankful.'

For once, she doesn't snark at Rose's life choices. We've all been changed by what happened – we've been twisted up and turned inside out, our flaws exposed. Where Rose has gained confidence, Sofia has softened and me . . . I care a little less what people think. Maybe we'll all go a bit easier on each other now, and hopefully the world will go easier on us.

'True.' Michelle nods. Her eyes slide to me. 'That's all any of us want, isn't it? To have people who love us.'

'And trust us,' I add.

After all, that was the nail in the coffin for Mitch and me. In the moment where I needed him to believe me, he didn't. It was only when the tables were turned that he wanted to make amends. Even though I know now that he and Sofia didn't actually sleep together, the damage was already done. I was hurt he'd thought me a cheater, even if only momentarily, and he thought my life had too much drama. Even though we cancelled the wedding after all the chaos, we'd tried to repair things for the first month. I even went to couples' therapy with him twice. But it wasn't the same. So we went our separate ways.

Part of me is sad, because I could have seen a future with him up until that point. But I'd rather have a relationship where the trust is mutual. And in hindsight, I don't know that Mitch ever loved me like that. And trust is more important than anything. I would know – I've had it broken a lot recently.

Under the table, I feel fingertips brush mine. A spark of excitement races through my belly as I catch Michelle's gaze. We've been inching towards this for weeks now. I open my palm and feel her hand slide into mine. It feels right.

Sofia, oblivious on the other side of the table, suddenly points. 'Look!'

The reporter is still talking, but in the background is a shot of Lily holding the torch and walking gingerly down the street.

'One former Olympian almost didn't make it to the relay. Former gold medallist Lily Henderson-Lee was involved in a shocking accident when she slipped off a cliff at Victoria's Turmoil Bay and broke both her legs. Her miraculous recovery shows the grit and tenacity of all Aussie athletes . . .'

The three of us stare at the screen as it cuts to close-up footage of Lily walking slowly, holding the torch, which bears a modern, sleek and elongated shape in a matte champagne colour.

'The torch's design was inspired by equality, water and peacefulness with perfect symmetry, featuring an equator of gold. The sleek design was fabricated from one hundred per cent scrap steel with a nod to sustainability . . .'

'How is she . . .' I blink, not sure what my eyes are seeing. 'Lily is supposed to be in a wheelchair. Rose said she wasn't walking properly yet.'

The woman on the screen, however, is definitely walking.

Michelle and I exchange a glance and Sofia begins to laugh, shaking her head. 'Now they're finally acting like twins, after all these years.'

The note of respect in her voice feels new.

We return to our meal, unsure where to take the conversation next. So we eat and drink and revel in the quietness of friendship. After months of talking to each other and the police, it sometimes feels like there's not much left to say even though secrets still lurk in our pasts.

'Well, here's to going after what we want in life,' Sofia says raising her glass up to the group. 'To success.'

'And trust,' I say, bringing my glass as well.

'And relationships.' Michelle and I exchange glances as we all clink glasses, and then Sofia finally catches on. She raises her eyebrows, shooting me a surprised look and I simply laugh, shrugging.

My life might have been turned upside down, but I'm finding moments of joy in between the grief of what I've lost. Knowing there is still love in my future helps. Michelle leans in and her eyes meet mine, filled with meaning. I don't hesitate to meet her there, brushing my lips against hers. It's soft, sweet.

Filled with the promise of more.

'Well, if you ever decide to get married again, *don't* ask me to plan the wedding,' Sofia says, taking a long glug of her wine. 'I'm done with vows for good.'

Acknowledgements

Sisterhood is something that has always fascinated me. The strength of female relationships is often laced with complexity and contradiction, and it makes for an endless well of story ideas. Here I wanted to explore the differences in sibling dynamics, and how these women could be pushed to do terrible things with the perfect storm of environmental factors swirling around them. Siblings often see the ugliest, most inner parts of ourselves, beyond any façade that we put up for the world because they have been with us since our earliest moments.

Naturally, I must start by thanking my sister, Sami. She is a far better person than I could ever be, with a huge heart and a capacity for patience that I can only admire. Thank you for always wanting to hear about my stories and for hand-selling my books whenever you spot a stranger browsing in the bookstore. I couldn't imagine my childhood without your enthusiasm and steadfast positivity.

I'm blessed to have three siblings by marriage as well, who've given me the best big family vibes one could ask for. To Albie, for running our awesome D&D game with the best puns ever and for your delightfully infectious laugh (even if it comes with dad jokes). To Brett, for making everything feel like a celebration and, most importantly, for the spirit of the Chi Chi. To Sam, for your sense of adventure and love of getting out into the world, it inspires me to want to see and do more.

Of course, I must thank my husband, Justin. After forty-something books, I never struggle to write your name into the acknowledgements. Thank you for being there for every word, every tear, every triumph, and every up and every down, always unwavering in your belief that I can do anything. You're my orchid.

Thank you to my agent, Jill Marsal, for always lending an ear and offering your guidance and advice, both on my stories and on my career. Thank you to the editors who worked on this story, Sarah Bauer, Emma Grundy Haigh, and Helena Newton, for your clever insights during the editing process and helping me to make this book shine. Thank you to everyone else at HarperCollins UK and Avon who touches these books and helps bring them out into the world.

There are so many other people I could thank and I'd hate to leave anyone out. But I want to say a blanket thank you to all the people who've ever supported my writing in any way, big or small. It truly means the world. This job is not for the faint of heart but I can't think of anything I could possibly love as much as dreaming up stories, and I couldn't do it without readers, reviewers, librarians, booksellers and everyone else who touches the publishing industry. You're all amazing.